She

keep it hot!

Lucinda
Betts

She

LUCINDA BETTS

APHRODISIA
KENSINGTON BOOKS
http://www.kensingtonbooks.com

APHRODISIA BOOKS are published by

Kensington Publishing Corp.
850 Third Avenue
New York, NY 10022

ISBN-13: 978-0-7582-2215-2
ISBN-10: 0-7582-2215-7

First Kensington Trade Paperback Printing: July 2008

10   9   8   7   6   5   4   3   2   1

Printed in the United States of America

Dedication

For WTT, who knows how to catch a unicorn.
For SKK, the best critique partner in the universe.
For HS, who provided much sage advice.

1

_____

The most powerful book in the history of humankind had vanished—on Blaze Williams's watch.

He slammed his palms on his father's cylinder desk, anger chasing fear through his veins. The antique framed photos jumped across the aged mahogany, as did the yellowed files. Blaze had lost the *Canticles Al Farasakh*.

He couldn't believe the wonder he'd let slip through his hands. Murad II made peace with the Karaman Emirate in Anatolia after years of bloody war with the book. Thomas Jefferson helped build a nation with the book's knowledge. Nelson Mandela had read smuggled copies of its pages and used its wisdom to demolish apartheid.

But now it was gone. After two hundred years of care by Blaze's family, it was gone.

With a sigh, Blaze sat back in the heavy chair, and the cushion shifted under his ass. His dad belonged here, not him, and all the frustration in the world wouldn't bring his father back to life, wouldn't change the cold, hard facts—his dad was gone, and so was the book.

Still he opened the bottom drawer, as he'd done at least five times since he'd come back from the funeral. In his mind's eye, he saw the book, the *Canticles Al Farasakh*, just as he'd seen it throughout his entire life—the scarlet, velveteen cover worn thin around the edges resting here in this drawer.

But his mind's eye was wrong. Now he saw only the swirls in the dark-brown wood of the drawer's bottom. He touched the panel just to be sure, but grainy unevenness, not velveteen, met his fingertips. And although he'd already checked several times that day, he squatted down and peered to the back of the drawer.

But the book wasn't there.

Where the hell was it? It'd been here the night his father died. It'd been here after the paramedics left, because Blaze himself had put it in the drawer. The housekeeper wouldn't have touched it, not in a million years. As far as he knew, no one else had been up here. No one else even knew about it.

So where the hell was it?

A braying ring from the yellowed rotary phone gave him a start. Blaze stared at the length of coiled wire connecting the handpiece to the body as the phone rang a second time. Something more antique than the rotary would have suited this office. But nothing in this office had changed in years since they'd left the backwater of Cameron County, Pennsylvania, for Manhattan.

Nothing had changed except the *Canticles Al Farasakh*, which was now missing. No good could come of this.

The phone rang a third time. "Blaze Williams," he said, catching a whiff of his father's scent on the handpiece. The pain of his loss washed through him, leaving him almost breathless with sorrow.

"Blaze," a deep voice said in his ear. "It's Kellogg Brownroot."

"Kellogg."

"I just called to tell you how sorry I am," Kellogg said. "You have my condolences."

"Thank you. And thank you for the flowers. My father would have liked them." Not.

"You're welcome," Kellogg said. "Look, I know this is a terrible time to bring up business but—"

"You're right. This isn't a good time, so—"

"So you know I wouldn't mention this if it weren't important," Kellogg insisted.

"What do you want?"

"I didn't want you to get hit by another nasty surprise," Kellogg said. "I thought I should warn you."

"About what?"

"Your father and I reached an agreement I believe made it into his will."

"What sort of agreement?" Blaze couldn't imagine his father agreeing to anything concerning Kellogg Brownroot.

"Well, maybe your father already told you," Kellogg said, "and this call is needless."

"Told me what?"

"Zachariah was going to sell me the logging rights to your virgin timber in Cameron County. He was going to put in a logging road first to sweeten the deal. He said you'd oversee it."

"What?" Blaze couldn't keep the incredulity from his voice. His father would never have let Kellogg Brownroot log the land.

"Yes," Kellogg insisted. "I'm logging that forest."

"You know that land's been in my mother's family since Europeans first set foot in the New World," Blaze said. "Logging it isn't high on my list of priorities."

"May your mother rest in peace," Kellogg said. "And that's why I'm giving you a heads-up. I didn't figure you'd need another shock at the reading of the will. Just in case Zachariah didn't tell you, that is."

"He didn't tell me," Blaze said. There was no hiding his surprise anyway. "And you're right. I probably didn't need another shock."

"That's what I thought."

Blaze chuckled in response.

"Why're you laughing?" Kellogg asked.

"I'm just surprised."

"Well, that's why I called."

"No," Blaze corrected. "I'm surprised at you."

"At me?"

"Yeah," Blaze said. "I'd have figured with all your fingers in the coal and oil pies, you'd been too busy to dip into timber, too."

Kellogg chuckled, a deep, smooth sound—almost practiced. It reminded Blaze of a late-night deejay's laugh. "It was actually your father's idea. Zachariah said I should try something different. Spread my wings."

"Look," Blaze said, with a patience that surprised him. "The lawyer's reading the will tomorrow. We can talk after that." He hung up the phone before Brownroot could answer, before Blaze said something he regretted.

He drummed his fingers on the antique desk, at a loss. His father would not have agreed to give Brownroot the logging rights. He definitely wouldn't have *suggested* it. But then why did Brownroot sound so certain? And where was the *Canticles Al Farasakh*? He had a strange feeling that the two were related, and he'd learned not to ignore that feeling. God, what he wouldn't give to have one more conversation with his father.

"Dad, I wish you were here right now," he muttered to himself.

"I'm here, son."

"I can't believe how much I miss you," he said without thinking.

"You don't want," the ghost of his father gave a dramatic gasp, "*help*, do you?"

Blaze blinked and looked. Sure enough, Zachariah Williams sat opposite him in the chair Blaze himself usually used.

Zachariah's quirky grin covered his face, and Blaze saw laughter in his eyes. His dad had always enjoyed a good prank, and coming back from the dead was amongst the greatest practical jokes.

"Your pride will be your downfall, son," the ghost said with that crooked smile. "Don't be so afraid to ask for help."

"Dad!" Blaze stepped around the desk to hug his father. The feel of his dad's warm flesh under his ever-present suit and the astringent scent of his cologne made Blaze hug him closer.

"You're squashing me, son," he said. "I can't breathe."

"Of course you can't breathe. You're dead."

"Don't hold it against me."

"Sorry." Blaze pulled him tighter for a minute. "It never occurred to me a ghost would feel so alive." Keeping his hands on his father's shoulders, Blaze stepped back and looked at him. Zachariah's hazel eyes sparkled with life. "I can't see through you or anything."

His dad smiled and squeezed Blaze's arms. "Have a seat," he said, stepping back and indicating the chair behind the mahogany desk.

"But—" Blaze stopped a moment. "That's your chair."

"Not anymore," Zachariah said. "And some ghostly clichés may be wrong—like this transparency thing—but one rumor's true: I don't have much time. And we have big problems."

Blaze sat. "It's Kellogg Brownroot."

"Yes," Zachariah said. And all the warmth and laughter that had been in his gaze was gone, sending a serious chill through Blaze.

"What's that bastard done?" Blaze asked.

"Crossed a threshold."

"What kind of threshold? Is he dead too?"

"We could only wish," Zachariah said. "He'd be less trouble that way."

"So what threshold are you talking about?"

"When Genghis Khan stole the *Canticles Al Farasakh*, he crossed the threshold and conquered the Jin Dynasty, killing hundreds of thousands. Then he invaded the Khwarezmid Empire and the Kara-Khitan Khanate, killing thousands more. He was a uniter among the Mongols—until the *Canticles* made him cross that threshold." His hazel eyes looked pained as he spoke.

"And Brownroot has the book?" Blaze guessed.

"Brownroot *stole* the book."

"And what happens if we can't get the book back?"

"Idi Amin had the *Canticles* for a short time," his father warned. "So did Mussolini."

"But so did Jefferson and Gandhi."

"They weren't innately evil; they didn't cross the threshold. Brownroot is greedy and immoral—and he stole the book."

"That bastard." Blaze ran his finger around the neck of his shirt, trying to loosen the tie, which suddenly felt like a noose.

"It's not good," his father said. "Not at all."

"What do we do?"

"There's only one option: you've got to toss that SOB into the second dimension."

"The second dimension?" Blaze pretended he didn't know what his dad was talking about.

"Use the final spell in the *Canticles*," his father said, flashing him a knowing look that did little to dispel the dark feeling in the room. "The spell I forbade you to memorize."

Blaze looked silently at his father for a moment before he said, "I memorized it anyway. When I was eighteen."

"Ah," his father said. "Nothing like the taste of the forbidden.

I'd hoped you might do that, thought it might stick in your memory better if I told you you couldn't."

Blaze shook his head. His dad had always been able to see him so clearly. But then a darker thought sprang to mind. "Who's helping him?" Blaze asked. "He doesn't have the training to use the book alone."

"You have to find that person, that assistant."

"But who'd work with him?"

"A dragon . . . or if he finds an evil magic user . . ." The ghost of Zachariah Williams ran his thumb over a carved groove in the armrest. "If he's smart enough, he might even figure out some of the spells himself. And no one said he's brainless—just evil."

"Dear God."

"And it gets worse."

"How?"

"It's started already. He's using it. Look." Using a wizard's gesture, Zachariah Williams rolled his palms open with a great flourish, his stubby fingers elegant despite themselves. Blaze felt the ambient magic converge in his father's hands, throbbing and powerful. Then, as his father's fingertips came together in a final gesture, an image appeared, smoky and translucent where his father's ghost self was solid. It shimmered right above his desk.

Among thick palm trees, a unicorn stood, her red and green mane rippling. She seemed to be standing atop a Mexican-looking pyramid, and her nose hung to her knees. At first, Blaze didn't see the cause of her angst. But when he did, he wished he hadn't.

Thick blood poured down her forehead, matting her forelock to her face—and her horn was gone. An oozing stump stood in its place.

"Who took her horn?" Blaze asked, fearing he knew the answer. A heavy rage grew in his heart.

"Brownroot."

"Is this the only unicorn he's attacked?" An image of Ivy's

face flashed before his eyes, and adrenalin raced through his veins. "Is Ivy . . . ?" He couldn't finish the question.

"He's attacked others but not Ivy," his father said. "In fact, Ivy approaches the injured creature as we speak. Whether or not she can save the unfortunate creature's life—or her ability to channel magic—remains to be seen. Much depends upon Ivy herself—her confidence in her own skills, her ability to find the right kind of assistance."

His father closed his hands completely, and the image evaporated like smoke.

"I don't understand," Blaze said, rubbing his forehead. In his eyes, Ivy was the epitome of skill and confidence. "How's Brownroot doing it? Unicorns are damned hard to catch." He should know. He'd tried his best to capture one in particular.

"He's already using the *Canticles Al Farasakh*. He must need unicorn horns to do whatever evil thing he has planned."

"But why? Horns purify. They heal. If he was using a unicorn horn to stop an assassin, maybe I could see him stealing one. But multiple horns? Why?"

"*What* he's doing is not in question. But I don't know why." Zachariah raised a shaggy eyebrow. "That's for you to discover."

"So why'd you get him interested in timber? We don't want him near Cameron County. If he learns about the Heart of the World, we're in big trouble. Add the Heart's power to the *Canticles*—and greed . . ." Blaze shook his head. "He might be unstoppable."

"You don't want him near Ivy," his dad said.

Which was true—but not the point. Blaze asked, "Can't we kill him? Getting this bastard might be worth the bad karma."

Zachariah held up his hand. "We can't kill him. Aside from the moral issue, killing him will just loose whatever evil's inside him on the world. It'll land in someone else. And if a dragon gets his hands on his greedy little soul . . . our work would be prolonged."

Blaze sighed, seeing no other options. "So I need to use the last spell in the *Canticles Al Farasakh* to shove Kellogg Brownroot into the second dimension."

"Yes, and it's a difficult enchantment, requiring more magic than any magic user has ever used."

"Even you? Even when you locked the Dragon Fafnir away with his horde of gold?"

"Your task is similar, and I had the book," Zachariah reminded him. "And even if you memorized the spell with all the zeal of a sneaky adolescent, you need *all* the power you have now—and it'll still be difficult."

His dad opened his palms again, and an image reappeared above the desk. The hornless unicorn was gone, replaced by an image of Blaze himself. He stood tall and strong, his shoulders confidently back as his hands prepared a spell. Thick magic coalesced around him, pulsating in the way only magic can. Suddenly an apparitional dragon flew toward the image of himself, and Blaze watched the face of his ghost self focus in concentration. He dropped the beast with confident ease. The dead dragon's chin rested on Blaze's feet.

"My shoulders aren't that broad, Dad."

"They are, and you're missing the point."

The man in the image looked mighty—not a word Blaze usually associated with himself. But it was a father's prerogative to believe the best of their children, and Blaze said, "I got it. I need all my power."

"Without fail," Zachariah said.

"I get it," he snapped. He read his dad's message loud and clear. He'd been reading it so long it'd become ingrained. He'd never jeopardize his power for some quick lay. "I've kept my virginity this long," he said, hating to use the word *virginity* in reference to himself. "I'm not going to throw it away at this point."

The left side of Zachariah's lips curled high, and he shook his head. "It's not going to be easy for you, going back to Cameron County. Seeing those lovely green eyes, all that blond hair."

The smoky image above his desk shifted. The apparitional Blaze faded, and a woman appeared—a beautiful woman. Hypnotic green eyes laughed behind thick lashes, and a wild mane of golden hair tumbled over her shoulders to her perfectly rounded ass. Her full lips curled in a playful smile, a smile that proffered an irresistible invitation.

Suddenly nervous, Blaze swallowed. Finally he croaked a name. "Ivy."

"In the flesh—flesh you need to resist."

"That image," Blaze pointed to the smoke vision teasing him from the top of his own desk. "That's not real. That's your interpretation of her."

"It's real. No need to deny her beauty," his father said, thumping the arms of the chair again. "No need to deny the attraction."

"Jesus, Dad," Blaze said. That old buzzard had taken a hit in his own power when he'd succumbed to Blaze's mother, but Blaze couldn't see taking that route. And he didn't like discussing it, not even with—no, especially with—the ghost of his father. "Do we have to talk about this?"

"She was beautiful when you knew her, son," Zachariah said. "She's even more stunning now. You know you want her. You always have. But you can't give in to those lustful urges."

"I can control my—"

But the image above the desk shifted again. The ghost Blaze walked up to Ivy. No, he strode up to her. Then he wrapped his hand around the base of her neck and pulled her to him, his fingers twining through her hair. Only she didn't resist—not at all.

Pressing her lithe body against him, her lips opened to his. The image was so powerful, Blaze could almost feel her tongue dancing over his. He could almost feel her soft breasts pressing against his chest, her supple thighs pressing against his cock.

"Jesus, Dad," he said. "Stop it." Just what he needed—a raging hard-on in front of his father's ghost.

"I just want you to see how easy it'll be to give in to her."

"I won't and she won't," Blaze said, knowing his words held an absolute truth.

"Why?" his father said. "Maybe she won't love you now your eyes have changed colors? Maybe she only liked green-eyed boys?"

"That's not what I meant."

"But it doesn't change the fact—you can't bed her. Especially now."

The image above the desk responded to the old wizard's words. The apparition Blaze stepped away from the translucent Ivy, and she kept a civilized distance between them too. In real life, she wouldn't be smiling. She'd be scowling—at him.

"Okay," Blaze said. "I get the point." He trained himself to ignore that need, channeling all his sexual energy into his magic. Why would he throw away all those years of work? Not even for her.

"Good," Zachariah said. "Because you're going to need her help."

"What?" The word came out thick with incredulity.

The image shifted again to another figment of his father's imagination. The apparitional Blaze stood, power pouring from his palms. Ivy stood at his side in unicorn form, channeling ambient magic through her horn. Aimed at a faceless foe, their magic twined together, wrapping around each other for support. In the vision, they looked invincible.

The image was intoxicating.

And impossible.

"I already outrank every other wizard," Blaze said. "She hates me, and I don't need her help."

"She'll forgive you. What lies between you is a small thing."

Blaze just grunted. His father had no idea.

"She'll hate you more when you and Brownroot start that road in her forest." Zachariah sat forward as if uncomfortable in Blaze's chair.

"What road?"

"The road Brownroot wants for his timber—that's why I sold him the rights. It's the bait. You need to lure that bastard right to the Heart where your power will be strongest."

"Putting a road near the Heart of the World will drain its power," Blaze said. "Hard to cast that two-dee spell if the Heart's weakened."

"Of course," his father agreed as the apparitional Ivy and Blaze vanquished an apparitional foe on his desk. They turned toward each other, both wearing satisfied expressions. They walked into the mist, his hand on her withers. "So you need to banish Kellogg before that road does any damage to the Heart of the World, and it helps to have the unicorn on your side—at your side only and not in your pants."

"Right after I get the book back." The comment was wry.

"Yes," his father said with a chuckle. "Right after Ivy helps you get the *Canticles* back. She can help you lure Brownroot to the Heart too."

"So you keep saying."

"I do keep saying." Zachariah closed his palms, and the vision above the desk vanished. Blaze wished his father had left the image so he could look at Ivy a few minutes longer. "And you know I'm right."

"You usually are, you old goat."

Blaze paused, looking out the window. He couldn't ask Ivy to help him. Not after the way he'd left her.

"No," he said. "I can get rid of Brownroot myself—without Ivy." But when his father didn't answer, he turned to see his reaction.

His father was gone. Blaze was alone in the antique office.

Blaze couldn't help himself then. He might not want to ask Ivy for anything, but the visions his father had peppered him with left him aching for her—and he could salve that ache without breaking any rules.

With his mind, he focused the surrounding magic into his own hands. He let it pulse there, gathering strength, and then he opened his palms.

As the smoky image shimmered to life, Blaze caught his breath. He and the dream Ivy lay on the shores of Lake Kinzua, the last place he'd seen her all those years ago. Her hair was slicked back, wet from swimming, and her skin was as slippery as an otter's pelt. They were both completely naked in front of each other for the first and last time in their lives.

The air between them crackled, tight with possibility. Blaze remembered the vibrant energy of the night. He was a man, and she was a woman, and for the first time in his life he was aware of his strength. His thighs were so much larger than hers, his arms so much stronger. He could carry her, protect her . . . hold her.

Rolling in the sand, Ivy nibbled on the back of his ear, and the hairs on his neck rippled. He'd kissed the side of her neck, slowly, as his cock throbbed against her thigh, her soft breasts teasing his chest.

Ivy tilted her head to the side, inviting more kisses, yielding. His palms caressed her bare shoulders, and hands traveled lower to her upper arms. The backs of his fingers brushed the sides of her breasts, almost on accident.

For deliciously long moments, the pair learned the simple pleasure of their bodies—his hands on her breasts, his fingertips on her pearled nipples. Ivy arched her back, pressing her breasts into his palms.

The sensations felt so pure and good. The sand felt soft underneath. They'd had no reason to stop.

The apparitional Ivy shifted around. Not satisfied, she sat back, tracing a finger over his pecs, over his nipple. "You're so damned gorgeous," she'd said, wrapping her long fingers around his cock. "Why'd we wait so long for this?"

Blaze put his fingers under her chin, meeting her eyes. They'd been so green in the light of the full moon he felt like he would melt. "Because it's worth waiting for," he'd said. Then he'd kissed her.

Heat raced into their kiss, and nervous fear fell to the background. She ran her hand through his hair, sending a shiver of delight through him. But that pleasure was nothing compared to what he felt when she pressed her breasts into his chest, shifting to maximize the friction. She rolled her head back like she was savoring the sensation, savoring him.

And, oh, how he'd loved her then.

He kissed her nipple, hardly believing she was letting him, hardly believing she wanted him as much as he wanted her. He buried his face there, licking and teasing and biting.

Ivy laid back in the warm sand, inviting him with her eyes, tugging with her hands.

And Blaze hadn't stopped. He hadn't known his wizard's heritage yet, hadn't known he was doomed to a life of celibacy.

She stretched her hands high above her head and arched her back as he straddled her, his cock so hard it ached. Blaze ran his palms over the planes of her stomach, drinking in her beauty. His hands memorized every detail of her waist and hips, the softness just under her belly button.

"Please don't stop," Ivy whispered between kisses.

Having a woman—no, having Ivy—spread naked before him, his for the taking, went right to his brain, to his cock.

"No stopping," he promised, his voice barely a whisper.

Ivy had sighed and parted her thighs.

His hard, swollen cock pressed against her sex, but Ivy didn't flinch. Blaze had started to thrust into her and—

Disgusted with himself, Blaze stopped the image with a wave of his fingers. This was no way to behave. It was self-defeating. He replaced the scalding image with something different, something more likely to help him keep his cock in his pants.

Ignoring the pain of his throbbing cock, he watched the new image. In it, he held Ivy's hands and looked into her intelligent eyes. He explained what he needed from her. In the image, her expression was dismayed.

In reality, which would shock her more? The complete change of his eye color, or the fact that he needed her help to save the world?

2

No one hurt unicorns. Not on her watch. She was the Guardian of the Forest, and she had never let any magical creature come to harm—not since she'd reached her full powers.

But someone had harmed. Someone hunted a creature in her care. Ivy burst into the clearing where the Chacchoben pyramid stood, following the odor of blood—unicorn blood.

Then the wind shifted, bringing the scent of something more sinister. Needing to concentrate, Ivy slid to a stop, her hooves skidding in the sand. She sniffed, inhaling deeply, and she knew— the hunter was still here, a vague odor of . . . something . . . swirling around him.

She madly galloped up the steep, narrow steps, her hooves clattering. The power pulsing from Chacchoben had a dark, brooding taste, different from the cool, clear flavor exuding from the Heart of the World. Had the unicorn blood or the hunter caused this?

But the answer lay just before her.

For a heartbeat, horror paralyzed Ivy.

In unicorn shape, Ivy's cousin lay at her feet, tortured and dying. She'd been skinned alive, her snow-colored coat stripped from her to reveal the muscle and flesh beneath. Her cousin's dark eyes looked at Ivy, not through her white face but through a crimson one. Blood puddled in her dilated nostrils and along the line of her lips. Blood puddled in her ears.

You . . . can't . . . help me, Tchili said. *My horn . . . it's gone.*

I can help. But Ivy knew she didn't have much time. Tchili's lifeforce was draining away with the trickling blood.

Ivy stepped toward her cousin, preparing to heal her, but a figure caught her eye. It raced in the shadow of the pyramid, hugging the stone sides. She caught an impression of masculine shoulders, dark hair, but the figure moved so quickly, Ivy barely saw it, barely smelled its odd scent. Still she knew—he was her foe.

The need to hunt the hunter warred with the need to heal her cousin—but only for a heartbeat. Hunting could wait. Her cousin could not.

Standing as still as the massive structure beneath them, Ivy concentrated on her root chakra, imagining its sexual power. When she was open to the flow of energy swirling around her, she focused, drawing from the distant Heart of the World. The nerves in her horn and chakras were so attuned to the Heart she could feel the energy leave Pennsylvania and flow toward the Yucatán.

The first taste of the power made her weak with desire, filling her root chakra, then spreading throughout her being. Her thighs ached; her nipples hardened. The length of her neck craved a lover's hot kisses. Her knees actually shook with the lust rushing her veins. If a man—any man—had been standing there, she would have wanted to curl around him, fill herself with him.

But she wouldn't have. She was the Guardian. She protected and healed. She put the need to chase the hunter firmly from her mind, and she took the overwhelming sexual energy, neatly twisting it into healing energy. The moment she began working the power, the lust subsided, freeing her mind and allowing her to work.

Finally her horn radiated healing power.

Glinting with healing green, golden loops spun around the base of her sharp-edged horn, slowly gathering speed and texture as they swirled wider and wider.

She dipped her head toward her cousin, letting the radiant rings drip down. She embraced the flavor of Tchili's soul, the texture of what made her unique. Emeralds and rubies glinted through Ivy's mind; the flavor of ferns and Mexican green chilies danced over Ivy's tongue as she gently rested her horn on her cousin's skinless shoulder.

Tchili's recovery didn't take long. Skin erupted over the raw muscle, covering sinew and tendon. Milky white fuzz spread over the skin, then grew in full and thick. The bloody stump of Tchili's tail regained a lawn of emerald hair, then the hair grew long and flowing, like pampas grass. Her mane grew back too, as green as the moss beneath them. Streaks of sumac red shot through her mane and tail, giving her almost the appearance of normality. Almost.

Tchili's forehead remained stubbornly shorn, the bloody stump the only indication of Tchili's true nature.

My horn, Tchili moaned in faint mindspeak.

Oh, honey. I haven't even tried to heal that yet, but don't worry—you won't die. Not from this.

As she prepared to heal Tchili's horn, the wind shifted, bringing the smell of the hunter. He was running, slinking into the surrounding jungle. Ivy would leave him until she was finished here. He couldn't go far. She pulled power from the Heart.

But as she started to weave its energy, the wind shifted again. It brought his true odor, raw and unmasked now. And his smell scared her.

He bore the irresistible fragrance of a virgin.

With a cry of anguish, Ivy tore herself away from her cousin. Ivy was as much a slave to her biology as any unicorn, even if she was the Guardian. She had no choice—she had to follow the virgin's scent. She stepped toward the edge of the pyramid, forgetting her cousin, forgetting herself.

Ivy! Tchili called, still too weak to walk. *Don't leave me.*

I can't let him go, Ivy said as she trotted down Chacchoben's stairs. *He might attack someone else.*

Like you. He'll do the same to you!

I'll be right back.

Ivy!

But the virginal perfume had its claws in Ivy. She chased the aroma around a dune, ready to lay her life at the feet of the owner of this smell. She'd die, but she could accept that if her virgin required it of her. She'd die at his feet, adored.

But by the time Ivy entered the dappled green of the jungle, all trace of his fragrance was gone. His compelling spell was gone.

Ivy shook her head as she slowed to a walk, hating this weakness of her flesh. How could she fall prey so easily? Was this how a moth felt when it found a flame? But with her rational mind once again in charge, she still wanted to find the Mutilator. She needed to find him and kill him—and she'd need to be careful and quick. She'd have to skewer him before her biology betrayed her again.

No one hurt her friends.

Glancing through the tangle of palm trees and fig vines, she saw nothing. Her horn detected no pulse of magic. Listening, she heard no rustle of leaves. No birds, either.

But then she spied a trail of unicorn blood, no doubt left from Tchili's leaking skin, her dripping horn, as the Mutilator escaped with his prize. With Ivy's rage barely contained, she followed the trail for ten steps, then twenty. She'd kill the bastard who'd done this. She'd run him through with her horn, stick him to a tree like a bug on a pin.

Except the trail had vanished. Ivy looked among the dead palm branches and forest detritus, sure she must just be missing the blood. But no, all signs of the blood had vanished. The Mutilator had evaporated like water in the desert.

Ivy stood for a minute, puzzled. When she'd first scented the Mutilator, he'd smelled strange. Odd. Not like a human virgin, but like . . . someone masking as one? Could a wizard do such a thing? Could a dragon?

A sudden thought hit Ivy like a blow. It was a crazy thought—she would have felt the beast's presence, after all—but dragons were unicorns' only predator. Had Lord Uroboros done this?

Ivy had locked the dragon away a few years ago, but the wizard who'd helped her had been weak. Lord Uroboros could have escaped. But, no. She would have sensed it if he'd broken free of her magic. Besides, sneaking wasn't the dragon's style. He'd swoop down and attack, not slink amongst the shadows.

Ivy shook her head. Perhaps she'd only imagined it. Perhaps the Mutilator was just a virgin. With his shoulders and dark hair, he'd looked human enough. In fact, something about him seemed familiar. . . .

Shoving away her jumbled thoughts until she could make more sense of them, Ivy turned back toward Tchili. She still had to heal her horn.

Tchili, Ivy called in mindspeak, *are you safe?*

I am. Are you?

Yes. Ivy leaped up the narrow steps again, clattering over the top of the pyramid. *I'll finish what I started here.*

Thank you. Tchili stood, her nose to her knees. She looked naked without her horn. *This is no life, Ivy. I don't want to be a horse for the rest of my days.*

Without her horn, how did Tchili have any magic to draw upon? How was Tchili speaking mindspeak? *You don't mean that*, Ivy said.

I do! Kill me if that's my fate. Please. I can't live without magic.

I can heal you, Ivy said with sympathy. Without her horn, Tchili couldn't protect her friends, couldn't heal. What kind of life was that? *I'm going to repair your horn,* Ivy told her cousin. *I can do this.*

After a moment of weaving the Heart's power, fat coils of healing strength slithered through Ivy's horn. But she needed more power for this task, more power than she'd ever used for anything.

Ignoring the burning Yucatán sun, Ivy stepped toward her cousin's head, repressing a shudder of revulsion as the reality of the injury became clear. The stump of her horn was caked with dark blood, but the hardening scab pulsed with Tchili's heartbeat.

I'm losing my magic now, Tchili said in a fading voice. *Help me! Please.*

I'll help you. Vowing to do everything in her power, Ivy refocused her efforts. The golden loops spinning around the base of her horn grew fatter than she'd ever seen them, gathering crazy speed, swirling tornado fast. Her power practically crackled. Green sparks of healing flew from the coils.

She let the coils loop around her cousin's stump; then she envisioned the missing horn with such clarity she could almost touch it, could feel the warm strength and power of its razor-sharp edge.

And the magic began to work. The jeweled reds and greens of Tchili's horn danced right before Ivy's eyes, reforming in the center of the healing loops.

But was it solid yet? Was it reattached? Ivy couldn't tell. For good measure, she kept the healing coils over her cousin for long minutes. Sweat dripped down her face, obscuring her vision, and foamy lather covered her chest and flanks.

Still, Ivy kept channeling, spinning the power from the Heart. Not until her knees began to buckle from exhaustion did Ivy recoil her loops with methodical slowness. She stepped back and looked.

And she'd succeeded.

For a moment, Tchili's horn glimmered in the light, sun glinting off the edge, sending diamond sparks glinting over the ancient gray masonry.

But only for a moment.

Ivy blinked, and Tchili's forehead was bare again, save the pulsating stump. Then her cousin fainted, her body collapsing in a heap on top of the pyramid like some offering to an ancient, bloodthirsty god.

Ivy looked over the pyramid's edge and suppressed a moan. She'd failed to catch the Mutilator. She'd failed to heal her cousin. And she was the Guardian.

In her rational mind, she knew this injury, terrible as it was, lay within her power to heal. She'd come so close. She looked at her unconscious cousin—knew it was her cousin—but saw her little sister Chicory, dead for years now. She'd failed then, too.

Looking at Tchili now, hornless and suffering, panic filled Ivy. Her mind screamed. She wasn't good enough. She wasn't strong enough.

But her rational mind took over, bolstered by the echoes of her surviving sister's voice. "You can do this," Crystal would say. "Think!"

And those stern words brought Ivy back to reality, her calm confidence returned. Ivy realized something important: Tchili's horn had been back for a heartbeat, and that meant something. That meant something good.

She put her muzzle on her cousin's shoulder and nudged her. At her feet, Tchili groaned. *Ivy?* she said in mindspeak.

We almost did it, Ivy answered. *There's hope. If we get your physical horn back from whomever took it, we can reattach it.*

You think you could put it back on? Tchili's voice sounded so weak. *Maybe with a wizard's help. . . .*

A wizard? An image of Blaze Williams danced through Ivy's mind, his broad shoulders and dark hair, the muscles of his arms. Forget reattaching a horn: if he'd been a wizard, he'd have been mighty enough to help her take on Dragon Uroboros himself. If he'd been a wizard *and* if he hadn't fled Cameron County, leaving her behind without a glance back.

Ivy shoved that thought to the back of her mind. Finding a wizard might be impossible, but it might be the only way to accomplish this task. *We'll reattach it.*

But how? Tchili almost howled with dismay, her mindvoice fading and cracking. *If you think—* But Tchili's words broke off, and she looked at Ivy with growing panic in her eyes.

Quickly Ivy shifted to human form, pulling her hair out of her face as the wind blew. "Is your magic gone?" Ivy asked, laying a comforting hand on Tchili's withers.

The mare nodded her head, her nostrils dilated in fear.

"Don't worry," Ivy said, the wind whipping her human voice around the pyramid. "We'll find your horn and reattach it. I'll heal you. I promise."

Ivy needed the strength of a virgin warrior. She was on the prowl.

Flicking a lighter over the candle's wick, Ivy sent a mental welcome to the night. The comfort of her bed called as starshine poured through the window, reminding her of the jewel-bedecked ether she was about to enter. The anticipation of the hunt filled her veins.

On one hand, she wished finding Tchili's horn would be easy. Tchili would be back to normal that way. But on the other hand, a threat menaced her land, and she looked forward to the challenge that lay before her. The man who'd skinned and de-horned her cousin—the Mutilator—must be found and stopped at any cost.

If the Mutilator had hurt one unicorn, it wouldn't be long before he'd strike another.

Only one fly marred her ointment. To have any possibility of success at this quest to recover Tchili's magic, she needed the strength of a virgin warrior, and such men were hard to come by. A wizard virgin warrior would be even better, but Ivy didn't even hope for one of those.

The oldest male virgins she'd found on previous quests were in high school, and they didn't have enough power to serve her. They lacked the rugged strength necessary to match her heart-song. Not even the lacrosse players could muster that kind of might.

In her most positive experience, the virgin warrior she'd found had a peculiar fetish with feet that made most women uncomfortable. She'd worked with him to quell the Dragon Uroboros, but the result hadn't been particularly solid. She hadn't been able to bury him in time as Dragon Fafnir had been buried.

She'd need to rebuild her enchantment around the Uroboros soon. If she'd had a virile and mighty virgin warrior, humans and magic folk would be safe from this particular dragon for millennia, but she didn't need to worry about him tonight.

Something about the night's starshine pulsed with promise, and Ivy realized her heart was filled with hope.

As she lay in her lavish bed, Ivy took a minute to appreciate the Italian-made linens. The way their sateen smoothness slid over her naked hips pleased her in a sexual way, charging her root chakra with lustful energy. She knew the Heart's power was strong.

A cool breeze blew in from the window, making her nipples harden and her skin ripple with gooseflesh. Needing to keep her chakras open to the flow of magic and energy, she fought the urge to wrap her arms around her breasts. Instead, she breathed deeply, opening her heart to the wonder surrounding her, embracing the strange sense of wonder surging through the night air.

"I can warm you, unicorn." Seal's voice was barely louder than a hummingbird's hum.

Hating the interruption in the night's promise, Ivy tried to focus on her friend flittering around her face. No bigger than a monarch butterfly, his skin was as dark as loamy soil, and his wings flashed the silver of moonbeams. "Your help isn't the kind I need, thank you."

"Oh, so formal," Seal said, and she heard the moue in his tiny voice. "You shouldn't say such definitive things. You might need my help someday." He fluttered madly toward her, dive-bombing her naked midriff. "Besides, we could have a lot of fun together."

"You're too small, Seal," she said, shooing him away while trying to keep that rich promise wrapped in her mind.

"I'm not too small," he insisted. "I'm big in lots of ways."

"Maybe for the fairy women," she said, looking at him. Without a doubt his miniscule features were beautiful: a chiseled chin, deep-set eyes the same color as his silvery wings, full lips. The muscles of his thighs and chest would please anyone—of his own size.

"Fairy women and others too," he said, buzzing her ear to give it a suggestive caress.

His touch echoed the energy flowing to her from the Heart of the World. A wave of desire rippled through her, softening her core and tightening her breasts. "You make me sorry I'm not a fairy," she said. "But I'm not."

"If only I were the same size as you," he said in that sulky tone.

"If only," Ivy agreed. Even as she argued with Seal, she focused the earth's energy through her body. She didn't want the strange sense of wonder to slip away.

"I heard about a magic book once," Seal said, still buzzing around her face. "It had a spell to make fairy folk bigger so humans and fairies could . . . play."

"Sounds like wizard's magic—maybe the *Canticles Al Farasakh*, which you know I don't have." Was it a coincidence that he was mentioning wizard's magic on the night she sought the same? In her experience, coincidence was its own kind of magic.

"But you're so beautiful, unicorn," the fairy man said, redoubling his awkward efforts to seduce her. "You won't be sorry for my help. I'm really quite good at what I do." He flicked his hot tongue over her nipple, sending the Heart's energy crashing through her.

"Seal!" she said, laughing. "I'm very flattered, but I'm just too big for you. Now, please, let me find Tchili's horn." She caught him in her hands and tossed him toward the window.

"Hmph," he said, leaving the cabin with an angry buzz. "You don't know what you're missing."

Seal was probably right, but Ivy didn't care. Light from the rising moon filled her room, bringing with it that sense of impending promise. Seal hadn't ruined it.

Controlling her breathing, she relaxed her body into the feathery mattress and closed her eyes. Her mind quieted, her brainwaves slowed, and she knew she'd found the alpha level required for her magic to work.

With the Heart's energy pouring into her root chakra and evenly humming through each of her other chakras, lust filled her every breath. For this quest, lust would help. She embraced the desire coursing through her, only barely resisting the need to bury her fingers between her thighs.

Ivy focused on the image of Tchili's horn, the lovely, spiraling curves. Within heartbeats, her soul disconnected itself from her body and swam in the ether, jewel-colored souls pulsing around her.

She luxuriated for a moment, savoring the sea of delicious colors. But she didn't wait too long. Lust burned through her, and she wanted a neck to bite, a cock to fill her more than she'd ever wanted a man. Knowing the moment was near, she reminded herself of the need to find Tchili's horn. Her power twined around that of the Heart like a climbing rose creeping up a cottage trellis.

Ivy allowed the Song of the Unicorn to imbue her. Learned from her mother, who'd learned it from her mother before her, who'd learned it from her mother, the beauty of the rhapsody filled Ivy's mind, her very cells. As endless as time, heart-aching loneliness thrummed in conjunction with soul-filling desire. Her soul thrummed with a desire worthy of John Coltrane.

The song reached out to all the virgin dreamers in the world.

Ivy let the song build in her, savoring its purity and truth. When even the mitochondria of her cells danced in lust, she loosed the song in the ether, letting it float over the pulsing, jeweled souls. The unicorn song drifted through the dreams of virgins, awakening their innocence, unburying their magic.

The song woke intense feelings of longings in the world's virgins, those who were asleep at the moment, and Ivy tweaked the melody so it would appeal mostly to men. The ether twinkled around her as the jewel-toned souls of inappropriate dreamers faded to the background. The sleepers' jewels intensified in the ether, throbbing in rhythm with her melody. Their dreams would be hotter for her touch. For some, they'd have the most scorching dreams of their lives.

Now. Now she could sift through the ether, looking and seeking.

Jade and onyx glimmerings of a virgin pulsed to her left. But was it her warrior virgin? With lust thrumming through her, Ivy skimmed his dreams. He was eyeing the blue bloomers of his high school sweetheart, a cheerleader intent on staying a virgin until married.

The boy dreamed of flipping up the blue and white mini-skirt and caressing the girl's milky thighs with his hands. He wanted to run his tongue over her until she fell prey to his heat. He dreamed of running his thumb under the elastic band encircling the girl's thigh and touching what he envisioned as heaven. His fingers thought they'd know just how slippery and smooth that creamy spot would be.

The intensity of the boy's desire made Ivy groan with a desire of her own. The girl must be crazy not to delight in her guy's lusty devotion. Ivy barely resisted the urge to make herself come, but she couldn't lose her connection with the night.

His intensity made her think that maybe he was strong enough to serve her purposes.

Following the glow from the boy-man's jade and onyx amalgam, Ivy wrapped her song around the energy from the Heart and spiraled down toward the sleeping almost-man. In spiritform, Ivy appeared at his window. Bringing her whole body to his room would be too dangerous. Unicorns were beholden to virgins, even weak, sleeping ones.

The dreamer was alone in his single bed, someplace in Kentucky, Ivy thought, from the texture of the air and the smell of the grass.

Her spirit resting easily at the window, Ivy looked in at her potential assistant. Baseball pennants decorated his walls, and a simple oak bureau stood adjacent to his closet. He lay sprawled atop what looked like a handsewn quilt embroidered with cowboys and horses. Ivy sighed. This was not the room of a man.

Still, she'd come this far, and he was now dreaming of sliding his finger deep inside the cheerleader. He'd be a good lover—even in his dreams he gently rubbed the girl's clit as he plumbed her depths.

Ivy let her unicorn song reach a crescendo in his dreams. She sensed his visions intensify in response; the cheerleader eagerly writhed over him, rubbing her breasts over his chest. She removed his fingers and sheathed his cock between her thighs.

The dreamer's erection throbbed, and this was the moment of truth. If he sang her song back to Ivy . . .

She held her melody strong and true, letting it reverberate its message of love and longing through the dreamer's heart. No song he'd ever heard on the radio, no concert he'd ever attended matched the ethereal beauty bombarding his brain and his soul.

But what would he do with it?

Sing! Ivy found herself urging with her rhapsody. *Sing!*

In the sleeper's dream, his lovely cheerleader slid herself up and down his cock, pushing him deep with each thrust. The bounce of her nubile breasts as she fucked him silly was the most erotic image the boy-man had ever seen.

Sing, Ivy urged again.

The cheerleader pounded over him, her breasts bouncing crazily, her head thrown back in pleasure so her long, silky hair tickled his thighs. And as the dreamer reached to her ass and ran the pad of his thumb over her most private spot—he sang.

Ivy listened with disbelief. He sang like fetid water gurgling down a rusty pipe. He didn't sing from his abdomen or his heart—he sang from his nose, and the song ran out of him like snot. He had no depth, no heart, no strength.

Stubbornly Ivy tried to wrap her voice around his, to augment it and lend it power. But nothing helped. Her power couldn't hide his lack. He was too young and too weak, and the only magic that could help him was time.

She should've trusted her instincts. Ivy needed someone older, someone stronger. She left this boy-man to his cheerleader and retreated to the ether.

Discouragement never helped, but the raunchy innocence of the boy's dream left her too hot to feel disheartened. Burning with a need of her own, she cast her melodic net, seeking a virgin who rippled with might.

A malachite and rose quartz glow of one particular dreamer struck Ivy as promising. Unlike many of the others that flickered and sputtered, this one pulsed steadily. Weaving her song toward him, she checked out his unicorn-enhanced dream.

In his dreams, he worshipped *Playboy's* Miss July. He loved her heavy tits and the oval shape of her areolae. The raspberry purple of them made his mouth water, and the way they'd shaved most of her pubic hair drove him crazy. He wanted to lick her and see how smooth the shave really was.

Seeing potential in this dream, Ivy wrapped a bit more of the Heart's power around her song. In the jewel-filled ether, the Heart's power crackled around this dreamer's soul and carried her spirit to his doorway.

The man was older, perhaps thirty, which was promising. He lived not with his parents but in a studio apartment. Led Zeppelin posters covered his wall. His well-muscled form sprawled over a king-size bed that filled most of the room. He must work out because his arm muscles were huge. Ivy wondered why the man was still a virgin, but his obvious potential pushed her question aside.

With high expectations, Ivy boldly poured her song into his dream and watched what happened. He dreamed about running his cheek along Miss July's sleek side, down the curve of her waist and around the slope of her hip. Miss July turned to him and said in a voice as sultry as a Southern summer night, "Oh, Phillip, I love it when you do that."

And without any further stimulation from his dreamgirl, Phillip came all over his sheets.

Damn. Ivy sank herself back into the ether to regroup. Phillip would be no use to her now.

She allowed the ether to embrace her, letting her gaze soften and her frustration wash away. Jewels sparkled all around her. Surely one of them amongst the millions would be an appropriate assistant for the task at hand.

But then a tigereye glow grabbed her attention. She didn't simply see the tigereye and wonder—the honey-brown soul blasted its glow right into eyes, into her heart.

Ivy paused for a moment. Something about its beauty gnawed at that ache in her heart, reminding her how lonely she was. In the handful of times in which she'd tried to harness the power of a virgin, she'd never seen such power in the ether. The tigereye sunk its claws into her, making it impossible to simply consider using it. She *had* to use this virgin's dreams. She was compelled to use it.

Or maybe the dreamer used her. She couldn't tell.

Pulling power from the Heart of the World, Ivy wrapped her song around the virgin's dream. It was easier than anything she'd ever done in the ether. She didn't need to skim his fantasy to see if his sexual energy was up to the task. She didn't need to urge him to sing. His song already filled the ether.

As her melody drifted over his dream, his bursting song filled her heart, a perfect counterpoint to her unicorn rhapsody. He was Monk to her Coltrane, and their music would have brought down New York's Five Spot Cafe. Her heart beat to his tune; her clit and breasts throbbed.

But where her song exploded with purity and unicorn innocence, his added the tension of dark desire. His song smudged her soul with earthy browns and honey golds, darkening her light.

His song began to ooze the sensuality of a samba then a tango; she was helpless to do anything but join him. Their notes rolled over each other, twisting and roiling, and her heart ached with longing, with desire for fulfillment. Back in her cabin, an ache filled her core so that she couldn't help but touch herself.

She slid her fingers lightly over her swollen clit. She danced her fingers lightly over her nipples. For a heartbeat, her own touch alleviated the lust thrumming through her veins in beat to his song, but then it began to flame the burning desire.

She redoubled her effort to focus on him. She wasn't a young teenager who couldn't control herself. She could concentrate her magic, her thoughts.

But focus didn't help. Even as his rhapsody promised to cherish and adore, she couldn't detect the object of the dreamer's physical attention, which struck her as strange. He seemed to be dreaming of someone with abundant gold hair, with disheveled hair; he wanted to bury his nose in that mane. He wanted to hear her laugh and hold her hand.

His desire to make love to her until the sun rose was secondary to his genuine attraction to her. Who was this man? Was he thinking of her? It seemed that way, but that had never happened before—and it wasn't like she knew a lot of men, living as she did in the backwaters of Pennsylvania.

Again his soul's voice wiped away her questions, her confusion.

She didn't care.

For the first time since Blaze had left Cameron County—and her—she felt whole. She could heal her cousin with the help of this tigereye soul.

She needed to transform lust into power. She twined her desire into rope, weaving in the power coming from the singer. Then, gathering her inner strength, she focused on Tchili. The Heart of the World helped her touch her cousin's equine mind, and with her cousin's help, she envisioned every detail of her horn. The curve of it, the emerald and ruby color of it, the citrus scent of it—Ivy held these details in her mind. Then she coaxed the minutiae into the dream of her virgin warrior.

Together they would find the missing horn.

Their combined power was so strong and so perfect that the wait was no more than a heartbeat. All the longing in the unicorn song directed her power and the dreamer's, and the power from the Heart of the World. All that longing, the beauty of the melody—these called to the magical cells of Tchili's horn, beckoned it, pleaded with it to join them.

And the horn's cells sang back!

Ivy leaned on the dreamer's strength and the power from the Heart to follow the wisp of magic singing from Tchili's horn. Like a fat braid, her song, the Heart's and the virgin's supported her. From the ether, Ivy slid her soul into her human body; she dressed, then she followed the rope of power toward the horn's location. She planned to grab the horn in her physical, human hand and pull it through the ether to her home in Cameron County.

Her booted feet hit the ground with precision, and she hoped no one saw. Ivy wasn't too worried about being detected. Most humans simply refused to believe their eyes when real magic exploded right in front of them.

Given the surrounding field of thick grass, the scent of car exhaust and the sound of heavy traffic surprised her as she re-appeared. But then she looked around her and saw she stood on a sidewalk bathed in lamplight. A black limo made its stately way down a wide street maybe a hundred feet ahead of her.

Only then did she realize she was in Central Park facing Fifth Avenue.

Ivy blinked. Was Tchili's horn in the middle of Central Park? What kind of sense did that make?

She shook her head. Nothing made sense, and she'd lost her hold on Tchili's horn while dressing and pulling her physical body through the ether. Placing the image of Tchili's horn wholly in her mind, she closed her eyes, searching for the power of the Heart of the World and the dreamer's song. Tentatively she sent a fragment of the unicorn melody toward the ether, trusting the strength of her warrior virgin to find it and bind to it.

There it was. The song pulsated through her, and she breathed a sigh of relief. The tigereye soul throbbed with pure strength, embracing the image of Tchili's horn. She and the dreamer were back in synch, and together they invited the cells of the lost unicorn horn to sing with them, to add its rich voice to their chorus.

And there it was—the horn's song, as achingly beautiful as a Montana sky. But its melody was muffled—no, something muffled its song. If a bird were singing in a closed room it would sound like this. Ivy didn't understand, not at first.

But then a cold finger of dread wrapped itself around her heart and squeezed. The horn had been corralled behind an enchantment, and few dragons had the magic to ensnare a unicorn horn. Only a human magic user could build such a wall, and the human had to be a virgin warrior. Maybe the Dragon Uroboros could do it.

Sure as hell, Uroboros wasn't here. Limos wouldn't be moving at stately speeds if a dragon had attacked Manhattan. Ivy could come to only one conclusion: a very powerful magic user resided in Manhattan.

The cocky assurance that had filled her earlier evaporated instantly. Wizards' power was on par with hers, and it came from the same source—the Heart of the World. A wizard who mutilated unicorns was bad news indeed.

As though sensing her concern, her dreamer increased the intensity of his song so that it exploded through Ivy with renewed vigor. His honey browns and golds throbbed through her pinks and yellows. Maybe they could burst through the wall of magic.

But the dark enchantment held, even as Ivy became increasingly aware of a different sensation. Her dreamer, like Tchili's horn, lay in close proximity.

Ivy panicked. She wasn't singing in tandem anymore. She wasn't singing a duet. His song sank its claws into her and pulled in. Maybe he wasn't helping her find Tchili's horn—maybe he was hunting her. Ivy needed to—

Suddenly the horn's song was cut off. A black pall hung where it had been.

Her dreamer's song took on a forlorn note. Were they different? Ivy wasn't certain. She struggled to make sense of what she heard and what she felt, but acrid panic blocked her chakras.

What if . . . No, the idea struck her as too terrible. But she had to face it. What if the dreamer—whose power she raided while he slept—what if her dreamer was the same man who'd built the enchanted barrier around the lost unicorn horn? What if her virgin warrior dreamer had mutilated Tchili?

It might be true. She had to see.

Ivy knew she should take her body back through the ether to the safety of her bed, but her feet already walked the streets of Manhattan, and a sense of urgency filled her.

With trepidation, Ivy poured her unicorn rhapsody back into the ether, drawing on the Heart. Then she found the rope of her dreamer's song and followed, working hard to keep her melody pure. She didn't want to warn the sleeper she was tracing him.

A unicorn should never hunt a virgin, she knew. Her mother had pounded that message into her brain, using tale after tale to make her point. Many of her European kin had fallen to such trickery.

In any form, a unicorn struggled to maintain her free will in the presence of a virgin. The battle was easier in human form but only slightly. So Ivy didn't want to find her dreamer, not in a hands-on sort of way. This far from the Heart of the World, she'd be more subject to his whim than she would in her own forest.

Would that be so bad? a naughty part of her mind whispered. *Wouldn't it be nice to lay your hands on that warrior virgin?*

But that was an absurd idea. He'd lose his power, and she'd lose her assistant. She just wanted to peek into her dreamer's room, preferably through a closed window while she held her breath.

But what if she found Tchili's horn in the dreamer's bedroom?

Ivy kept her song steady, drawing the Heart of the World's power around her like a cloak. Following the dreamer's song was easy—as it would be if the magic user slept unguarded by any warning spells, as it would be if the wizard had placed the song as bait to trap her.

Ivy looked down Fifth Avenue as she crossed.

Focused on the hypnotic call, Ivy walked past several high-end condominiums. The song grew clearer in her mind, and she knew she was closer to the singer.

She inhaled deeply, alert for danger. She smelled exhaust and dried urine and cigarette breath and cut grass. The scent of sexual excitement hung between a couple who walked past her, playful eyes locked on each other. But the Manhattan air didn't carry the scent of a virgin warrior, and Ivy relaxed.

But then she heard the words.

"They're for Zachariah Williams," a man said.

Hearing the name of Blaze Williams's father stopped her in her tracks. She peered, but a huge bouquet of funeral flowers covered the speaker's face.

"It's too late at night. I'll take them up later," the doorman told the florist, reaching for the bouquet. "The son left a message not to be disturbed by anyone. He's taking the death hard."

"Fine," the florist said, handing over the dark red blooms. "You mind signing this?"

Ivy's brain worked slowly, as if lubricated by molasses. Was Zachariah Williams dead? *A* Zachariah Williams was dead, that much she understood. Standing on the Fifth Avenue sidewalk surrounded by summer heat and a throng of people, Ivy found she couldn't breathe. She'd heard that Zachariah and Blaze had moved to the city, to Fifth Avenue. The dead Zachariah must be Blaze's Zachariah.

Her head reeled with information overload. Her pent-up anger at Blaze seemed petty in the face of his loss. Moving away from your high school sweetheart and never once calling, never once sending a letter, seemed like a huge offense—until she saw what real loss looked like. Sympathy for Blaze's loss pushed out other emotions.

Inhaling almost against her will, Ivy turned toward the blue-coated doorman. She didn't care if Blaze wasn't seeing anyone. He'd see her, even now in the middle of the night. As she stepped in the doorman's direction, the dreaming song of her warrior virgin burst to the foreground of her consciousness. He was here!

And then Ivy realized: *Blaze did this. Blaze stole Tchili's horn and skinned her alive.*

No, the rational part of her brain told her. *That can't be true.*

But was any other explanation possible? The horn, the dreamer, and Blaze were all here, in Manhattan, probably in this building. But Blaze couldn't possibly be a virgin—

Ivy! She heard frantic worry in the tiny mind voice.

Seal, she said as she walked toward the doorman. The little fairy always found the most annoying times to try to get into her pants. *What is it?* Just to be safe, she'd knock on Blaze's door and offer condolences—while she searched for the horn.

It's a tractor, Seal shouted through the ether.

Tractor? What are you talking about?

Then a sudden vacuum in power knocked the breath right from her lungs. She fell to the ground, gasping like a fish in a boat.

"Ma'am!" the doorman shouted as she crumpled to the floor. "Ma'am, are you all right?"

But Ivy couldn't answer, couldn't reassure the man and the other people gathering around her. She couldn't answer because she couldn't speak.

Something had cut into the power pouring into her from the Heart of the World.

And tree choppers, Seal cried in her mind. *They're cutting a—*

A further dip in power from the Heart silenced her fairy friend's voice. Ivy was alone.

Riding in Kellogg's oversized Hummer on Township Road T-343 through Cameron County, Blaze thought he'd have sensed the evil in Brownroot even if his father hadn't warned him. The vast space of the vehicle pulsed with a dark intensity. He wondered if the *Canticles Al Farasakh* was in the truck with them.

"So what changed your mind?" Kellogg asked Blaze, resting his elbow on the black jockey box. The astringent smell of his cologne filled the space. "About the logging road, I mean."

"Well," Blaze said, looking out the window. The forest reminded him of . . . something. Then he remembered. He'd had the strangest dream last night . . . something about the most fantastic music and . . . Ivy's hair. He'd been saving the world somehow. No, that wasn't right. He'd been helping Ivy save the world.

"Well, what?"

"My father's will," Blaze said, reeling in his mind. "He wanted us to work together on this." No need to mention the information provided by the ghost of Zachariah Williams.

"But still," the coal and oil magnate said, stepping on the gas as they rounded a corner. Blaze noted with disgust that the man's hair was cut to look like a rock star's. "Zachariah's will wasn't binding in this regard. Your father only suggested you work for me."

"My father wanted it." Blaze hoped the simple explanation would satisfy.

"Good," Kellogg said. "Good."

Blaze sat in silence, wondering if he could grab the man's throat and squeeze until Kellogg gave him the *Canticles*. Then he'd tie him and bodily drag him to the Heart of the World. He'd effortlessly cast the spell, and Kellogg Brownroot would vanish forever into the second dimension.

Of course, if he used violence first, he'd be breaking the moral code of all wizards. Strength could be used only in defense.

"You know . . ." Kellogg said, lingering until Blaze looked at him.

"What?"

"Until your father and I began our conversation about the timber industry," Kellogg said, "I'd almost forgotten." The sly look in the man's eyes made Blaze believe he'd forgotten nothing.

"That you'd forgotten what?" Blaze asked, running the tip of his finger over the tip of the button that opened the window.

"That you're from this godforsaken empty country." Kellogg gestured to the ubiquitous trees.

"I was born here, lived here until high school," Blaze said, knowing Kellogg Brownroot must know this.

"Yes." Kellogg took his eyes from the road and turned toward Blaze. "And maybe you've heard about a big rock around here someplace."

A quick anger laced through Blaze. Why would Kellogg take the conversation in this direction? "There're a lot of big rocks in this woods." He remembered climbing them as a kid, usually following Ivy.

"So I see," said Kellogg as they passed a hulking outcrop of moss-covered granite. "But there's supposed to be a particular big rock around here. A special one."

Blaze had a bad feeling Kellogg was asking about the Heart of the World.

"I've heard this rock makes your compass stop working," Kellogg added.

"Sounds like iron ore. That'll mess with a compass." Then he shrugged. "But mining's supposed to be your bag. If there were iron deposits around here, you'd know better than I."

"Not iron," Kellogg said. "This rock affects electronics— GPSs and things."

"I don't know. I never walked through this forest with a GPS." It seemed Blaze had always known where he was when he'd lived here.

"But you've heard rumors."

He had a feeling Kellogg Brownroot had set up his entire logging thing to ask him this question, to find this boulder. And that feeling concerned him. If Kellogg had the *Canticles Al Farasakh*, and if he knew about the Heart of the World... Blaze had to act now.

But what could he do by himself? Nothing—not without making matters worse. His father had always been after him for refusing help. Well, he'd ask for help. This once. Maybe the magic creatures of the forest could do something, help him protect the Heart of the World.

"Yes," Blaze answered finally, opening the window. The clean air washed over him, welcomed and hot. Then he turned his head, as though sniffing the fragrant air. "I've heard rumors," he said out the window, "about the so-called magic rock."

"I thought you might have," Kellogg said with satisfaction.

The incoming wind whipped out the scent of the man's expensive cologne and replaced it with the pine. "I've started the road right by the rock—well, by what I think is the rock. I want you to confirm it."

The Hummer began to cross the Castle Garden Bridge, and Blaze remembered when it used to be the old Tom Mix Bridge, a rusty structure that discouraged the timber industry.

"Confirm what?" asked Blaze loudly, pretending he couldn't hear over the wind rushing into the Hummer.

"Close the damned window!" Kellogg shouted as though he'd just realized the danger. "They might hear you."

"Who might hear me?" Blaze asked, closing the window halfway. "The trees?"

"Never mind," Kellogg said, clearly angry. "I've started the road by the boulder. I want you to tell me if it's the right one."

"You want me to take you to the special rock?" Blaze asked, projecting his voice out the window. If he could get the word out to the centaurs and fairies . . . If Ivy knew what danger he was bringing to her doorstep, she could help.

"Yes, I do."

"I can take you there, but why do you want to see it?"

"See it?" Kellogg scoffed. "I don't want to see it. I want to blow it to hell."

"What?" Blaze couldn't contain his disbelief. What kind of sense did that make? "You mean, like, with dynamite or something?"

"Yep." Kellogg pointed toward the back of the Hummer, which was loaded with huge boxes. "That's what's back there— dynamite."

Jesus, Blaze thought. *Ivy really needs to know this.* Could he try his mindvoice to warn her?

Suddenly a flurry of blue, iridescent wings bombarded the windshield. Blaze caught a glimpse of a tiny face set in deathly determination. He'd seen photos of Japanese Zero pilots locked in the grips of a suicide attack. The fairy's face reminded him of that as she hit the windshield with enough force to create a spider-web of cracks.

"Christ almighty," exclaimed Kellogg, slamming on the breaks. A red smear dripped down the shattered glass. Tires squealed as he manhandled the hulking vehicle to a stop, inches shy of the cement wall of the bridge. "You see that?" he demanded. "What the hell was it?" Kellogg whipped off his seatbelt and opened the door before Blaze could answer.

"It looked like a hummingbird," Blaze called out the door. He unhooked his own belt and stepped out onto the pavement. After the chill of the air conditioner, the humid summer day seemed amazingly hot.

"That wasn't a hummingbird," Kellogg said, scanning the black asphalt, hands on his hips.

"It was some sort of bird. What else would it be?"

But Kellogg ignored him, getting on his hands and knees to peer under the Hummer. "Maybe I ran over it."

"What're you doing?" Blaze asked, examining the windshield wipers for a little corpse.

"I'm looking for it."

"Looking for what?" If Kellogg could see magical creatures, Blaze knew he was in trouble, bigger trouble than even his father had anticipated.

"I'm looking for the fairy."

Blaze's stomach tightened. He had to get rid of this madman now—or convince him he'd lost his marbles. "Have you lost your mind?" The black road heated the summer sun to a broil, making Blaze's head swim. But then he saw it, the dead fairy, her blue wings crumpled and torn. She was stuck in the windshield-wiper well. Quickly he scooped her up and put her in his shirt pocket. "What the hell are you talking about?"

Kellogg stood, wiping the black tar from his hands with a white handkerchief. "That fairy hit my windshield when I said I was going to blow the hell out of the damn rock."

Blaze squinted at Kellogg, at a complete loss for words. What the hell was he going to do?

"I'm going to make sure that little fucker is dead," Kellogg said. He looked oddly reptilian in this light. His skin had a scaly texture, or maybe it was the light. "Before it warns whatever else lives in this forest, I've got to kill it."

For a moment, Blaze considered lunging for Kellogg, throttling him until he was blue in the face. He could not let this monster stay around Ivy. He could not let this monster live in her forest.

And then Blaze saw the dead hummingbird, no doubt magicked into existence by the creature he'd thought dead in his pocket.

"Jesus, Kellogg. I don't know what to make of you." Blaze reached for the bird sitting right where the fairy had been. "Here's the hummingbird." He held up the thing like it was a dead fish. Its head flopped convincingly, but it didn't feel at all like a real bird—it felt like a glob of leaves.

"Let me see that," Kellogg said, grabbing at it.

But Blaze had already chucked it over the bridge's low wall into the Sinnemahoning Creek. A convincing ripple ensued as the alleged corpse floated downstream.

Brownroot's eyes narrowed as he examined Blaze. "Whose side are you on, anyway?"

Blaze looked at Kellogg, considering. He kept his face as impassive as if he were playing high-stakes poker with his buddies. "I wish I could say I knew what you were talking about."

"That fairy viciously attacked my truck." Kellogg's voice was cold and measured.

The creature in Blaze's pocket began fluttering, and Blaze turned so Kellogg couldn't see the movement in his pocket.

Blaze could have squashed the thing himself, he was so irritated with the stupid creature. But he reminded himself to be patient—fairies were not known for their rational choices.

"You saw the face just before it hit," Kellogg said, his deejay voice cracking, becoming almost gravely. "You know you did."

"Kellogg, it's hot. A bird just smashed in your windshield, and I think the nine-hour drive has gotten to you." Blaze said this as if he were speaking to a deranged man. "Why don't you give me the keys, and I'll drive to the diner? It's just up the road. We'll call someone there to fix your windshield, okay? And then we'll check in to the cabins."

For the first time that day, Kellogg Brownroot appeared embarrassed, perhaps unsure. The reptilian look evaporated, and his skin looked smooth, human. "Um," he said. "Here." Kellogg gave Blaze his key ring, and Blaze breathed a sigh of relief.

He stepped toward the driver's door, but Kellogg put out his hand and stopped him. The oil magnate's hand was inches from the fairy in his pocket, and even the heat of the man's hand on his arm felt malicious to Blaze.

"It's just that—" Kellogg started.

"What?"

"I thought—you know—since your father was a magic user—"

"Magic user? Let's get you cold water and some lunch."

"But I thought you could help me."

"I'll help you, Kellogg," Blaze said. "Here, let me get that door."

From the fluttering in his pocket, he knew someone was laughing about this whole ordeal. Blaze just hoped the stupid fairy had been smart enough to pass on the fact that the Heart of the World was in danger before it had dive-bombed Kellogg Brownroot's Hummer.

"Would you like some water, miss?" the doorman asked, concern etched on his wrinkled features.

"Yes, please." Sitting on the lobby sofa, Ivy accepted the cool bottle from the doorman, still hoping she'd somehow slipped into a nightmare from which she'd awaken. Blaze hadn't really gone over to the dark side, had he?

Of course, maybe she was wrong about the whole thing. Maybe Blaze didn't even live here.

"You know," Ivy said after taking a long drink of water, "I was here to give Blaze Williams my condolences for the loss of his father, but I think I'd better go home. I'm not feeling too well."

The kindly doorman looked at her. "You look real pale, miss. You should go home." Then he looked at the elevator as the door opened and said, "Besides, Blaze was real clear he didn't want to see anyone for a while. I'll tell him you stopped by, and you can leave a note if you want."

"No, thank you," she said, feeling her jaw tighten. Blaze did live here—there was no doubt. There weren't too many Blazes and Zachariahs in the world, not even in Manhattan. "I'll call him myself when I get home."

"Okay, miss. Who should I tell him stopped by?"

"Please," she said, touching the doorman's arm, "don't worry him on my account." She would have used a touch of magic to reinforce the plea, but she still felt only a faint thrum of power from the Heart of the World. She needed to conserve that energy.

"Can I call you a cab, then?" he asked.

Ivy hesitated. When she'd pulled herself through the ether, she hadn't thought about bringing a purse. She had nothing—no money in her pocket, no wallet, and not enough magic to draw her home. Worse, she had to get back home—now. Something had scared Seal out of his mind, something was interfering with the Heart's power, and she needed to stop it before she could solve the mystery around Tchili's horn.

"A cab would be nice," she said finally, hoping she wouldn't need to skip out on the fare. She had no idea when she'd have time to atone for that kind of bad karma.

"Just a minute then," the man said, bustling out the door.

Through the glass windows of the apartment lobby, Ivy watched him raise his arm commandingly while filling the night air with a shrill whistle. Two cabs passed right by him.

She picked a gold thread from the sofa on which she sat. It seemed so strange that Blaze must walk past this seat daily, that the elevator door could open and he could walk out of it. Blaze himself could've touched the thread she now held in her fingertips. All the sexual energy she'd had from channeling the Heart and singing with that tigereye soul was gone, but her heart still pounded when she thought of Blaze—and that embarrassed her.

But seriously, since Blaze lived here, did that mean he was the warrior virgin, the tigereye soul? He couldn't possibly be a virgin. He couldn't. Years ago she and he had been so close to crossing that line. If it hadn't rained acorns . . . if he hadn't left Cameron County the very next day . . .

Finally a scuffed, yellow cab halted for the doorman, and he gestured toward her.

Steadily Ivy left the lobby, but as her feet connected with the sidewalk, the Heart's power surged through the ground, nearly knocking her to her knees.

The doorman came running and grabbed her arm, but the thrumming power beneath her steadied. She found her footing.

"Thank you," she said to the doorman in a voice that surprised her in its strength. "You've been very kind."

"Should I tell the cabbie to take you to the hospital?" he asked.

"No, thank you." Ivy shook her head, using the power of the Heart to fill the doorman with an understanding of truth. She was fine. Now that the Heart thrummed beneath her, she was fine.

"You be careful then, miss."

She slid into the cab, grateful she wouldn't have to hitchhike home. She could pull some cash through the ether from her cabin.

"Where to?" the cabbie asked over his shoulder as the doorman closed the car door.

"Um," Ivy said. She needed a minute to think. If Blaze wasn't a virgin, perhaps the song of Tchili's horn had led her to him. But that would mean he was the Mutilator, wouldn't it? Was that any easier to believe? Ivy rubbed her eyes in frustration. She was so confused.

"I said, where to?" the cabbie barked with typical New York brusqueness.

Taking a deep breath, Ivy focused. She could zip back through the ether and leave the cab empty. But she wanted to talk to Seal first, find out what had happened before she rushed headlong into whatever danger had invaded her forest. "Could you drive toward the Natural History Museum, please?"

"Sure thing," the cabbie said, easing into the traffic. "But you know it's closed now."

"That's okay." The drive would buy her some time. Shoving her worries about Blaze to the back of her mind, she sought her friend.

Hey, Seal, Ivy called.

You're back, Seal said, his voice uncharacteristically free of its sulk.

What's happening over there? First, no power from the Heart, now it's back to normal.

There're a lot of tractors here, Ivy. Loggers snuck them in when it got dark.

Who was it?

Ivy could feel Seal pause. Then he said, *Well, it's some big oil magnate newly come to lumber.*

Lumber!

They're saying the C word here.

Clearcut. The word hung in the ether between them.

Damn, Ivy said.

Yeah, and it gets worse.

How could it possibly get worse?

They've got plans to log Blaze Williams's forest. . . .

And? Ivy prompted, fear lacing through her at Seal's unusual reticence. Blaze owned sections and sections of forest.

And the fairies heard Blaze is helping the loggers. He sold them the rights. He's helping them build a road day after to-morrow.

Jesus, Ivy said, mostly to herself. The development made it seem much more likely that Blaze was the Mutilator and not the tigereye virgin. *What the hell are we going to do?*

We have to stop Williams. We have to stop all of them, Ivy, Seal said. *If they log the forest around the Heart of the World . . . we'll all vanish.*

Leave it to a fairy to state the obvious.

I'll be home in a few minutes.

Ivy stared out the cab window, suddenly aware of Central Park's trees. She saw so many different species, including some she didn't recognize. They were probably from Asia and Europe, like the starlings taking flight above the Natural History Museum.

Even Central Park's hills and lakes seemed contrived. She bet they were all manmade. And the layout of the trees seemed unnatural compared to her thick forest. Gardeners had probably planted them decades ago.

Central Park wasn't without its charms, though. Thick stands of rare American elms filled the landscape, which was cool. Dutch Elm Disease had killed elms across the globe, although she'd saved the few that lived in her forest.

Ivy wondered what kind of trees had filled this area when the Lenape Indians had sold Manhattan to New Netherland.

Not this mishmashed collection of eclectic trees, Ivy was certain. Had the original inhabitants cried when they saw all the native trees fall under the ax to make way for forts and sprawling buildings? Had anyone tried to stop the deforestation, or had the potential environmentalists slinked off to the surrounding wilderness of the 1600s?

What she needed to stop the impending logging was a group of rabid environmentalists. Ivy sat up, electrified with her realization. She didn't need magic. Not in this case. After all, she wasn't the only one in the world who protected trees.

"Excuse me," she said, leaning into the cab's window.

"Yeah?"

"Do you know where the Greenpeace office is?"

"Yeah, but it'll be closed."

"Could you take me there anyway?" Ivy asked. She had that strange feeling of hope again, and she knew someone would be in the office.

Blaze Williams, stand back. She was bringing in the big guns.

4
———————

"I need the unicorn!" the smashed fairy squeaked at Blaze when they finally entered the privacy of his cabin. He pulled her out of his pocket and carefully set her on the table, but she didn't thank him. Instead she brushed off her arms as if he'd contaminated her. "My wings are ruined."

He examined all two inches of her, amazed at her tiny perfection. He'd left Cameron County before he'd come into his powers, before he'd even known about them—he'd never seen a fairy before now. Apparently they didn't like living in the city. As he looked at her, the reality of fairies became something more than theoretical.

"Maybe you should've considered the possibility of bodily harm before you attacked the Hummer," he said finally.

"I couldn't let that creep blow up the Heart of the World," the fairy insisted, marching across the table crossly.

"Maybe you should've flown off and told your friends before you tried to slay the mighty steel dragon." He tried to keep his tone neutral, but she distracted him. Her green skirt made of leaves flounced as she walked, highlighting the perfect proportions of her calves. And her naked breasts shimmied.

"Who's to say I didn't?"

"Did you?"

"No."

Blaze couldn't help himself. He laughed.

But his new companion didn't join him. She crossed her arms over her tiny, flawless breasts and said, "I thought that's why you were shouting out the window." Blaze could hear the frustration in her voice. "I thought you needed help."

Was this his fault? He'd finally asked for help, and this crazy creature had flattened herself on a windshield? She might have killed herself.

He should've kept his mouth shut.

"Look, I think you need to stay on the floor," Blaze said. "What if Kellogg Brownroot walks by that window?" A big bay offered a panoramic view of the Sinnemahoning Creek.

"He'll think I'm a butterfly," she said with a pout of her raspberry-colored lips.

"A butterfly? Clomping across the kitchen table?" Blaze shook his head. "I wouldn't take the chance, if I were you. He already saw you once." Her topaz skin shimmered as she stomped through a sunbeam.

"He *thought* he saw me," the fairy said. But she jumped nimbly to the floor and walked closer to the wall. Blaze saw supreme unhappiness on her tiny face.

"I'm sorry about your wings." She'd been brave—at his request—and he shouldn't bait her. Her gossamer, blue wings were tattered, and blood was caked around the base of them. "Does it hurt? Can I get you anything?"

"Yes, it hurts," she snapped. "And you can get me to Ivy."

He ran his hand through his hair, at a loss. "You're free to leave. I'd go through the back, though, and stay away from Brownroot."

"What am I supposed to do?" she demanded in her little voice. "Walk halfway across the forest? On my feet?"

Blaze shrugged. He had no idea.

"Fairies don't walk. You have to take me to Ivy."

"I can't do anything that'll make Kellogg Brownroot suspicious—more suspicious," he said. "And neither can you. That includes me leaving here to deliver a fairy to a unicorn."

"My wings need to be healed!"

"I'm sure we'll catch up with her sooner or later." Blaze tried to placate her. "And then she'll fix your wings."

At those words, the fairy stopped and stared at him. "You're right," she said, snapping her miniscule fingers. Her little nails were the color of ripe peaches. "We can meet up with her tonight when she chains herself to the tree choppers."

"What?" Alarm raced through Blaze. Had Ivy lost her mind? Did she know the danger she was in? Brownroot wasn't just any logger.

"Yes," the fairy said gleefully, perhaps seeing that she'd struck a nerve. "Ivy brought in Greenpeace activists from the New York office. They've just come back from a virgin timber site in Ottawa, and they're chaining themselves to the trailers tonight so you can't start the road tomorrow."

Fighting a growing anger, Blaze looked at the tiny fairy.

She danced a little pirouette and laughed. "Ivy's chaining herself to the tractors too. She's a hero."

"But it's just a sham," Blaze said. "I'm not really putting in a road. If I'm busy battling Greenpeace, how the hell am I going to lure Brownroot to the Heart of the World?"

"Yes, well, I suppose the protector of the forest doesn't know your scheme."

"It's not a scheme. It's a plan."

The fairy turned toward him and put a mocking expression on her tiny face. Perfectly mimicking the tone he'd used on her, she said, "Maybe you ought to have thought to inform her of your plans then, before you carried them out."

Blaze plopped himself back in the dusty orange sofa and laughed, shaking his head. "You've got to be the snottiest creature I've ever met. What's your name?"

"Vinca."

"Like the plant?"

"Yes, it grows everywhere."

"Mmmm," Blaze said.

"And I'll grow on you."

Blaze shook his head again, chuckling.

"When you smile like that," Vinca said, "I can see what Ivy sees in you. That dimple is yummy, and your chest muscles are delicious."

Sees? Blaze thought to himself. *Saw* would be more appropriate. But he refused to let the fairy bait him in that direction. "Vinca," he said. "Let me introduce myself."

"Blaze Williams." Vinca put her hands on her little hips, making her topaz hair slither across her breasts. "I know who you are. I knew who you were before you did."

"You did?"

She smiled, something both playful and devilish. "And I knew your father . . . well."

Blaze blinked but then realized the fairy's sharp wit was something his father would've appreciated. No doubt her perky breasts wouldn't have been lost on his dad either.

"I'm charmed to meet you, Vinca," he said with a courtly bow. "And I'm sorry I didn't make your acquaintance before my father and I moved to Manhattan."

"I'm pleased to finally speak with you, Blaze, but everyone around here knows who you are. And everyone—except me—thinks you're here to put in that hateful road. They think you've sold out. Ivy is pissed as hell at you."

He raised his eyebrows at her. "So my only friend in this whole damned world is a fairy?"

"Yes," she said. "A fairy with broken wings, which makes me cross. So you'd better be nice to me."

"Oh, I'll be nice, all right," he said, snapping open his cell phone.

"What are you doing?" she asked, but he turned away, hoping she'd get the hint. The last thing he wanted Kellogg to hear was her chattering. "What're you doing?" she asked again, but the phone was ringing, and he waved a hand at her to shut her up.

"Brownroot here," the deep voice said.

"Kellogg, we've got a problem."

"What's that?"

"Greenpeace guerillas are chaining themselves to our trucks tonight."

"The fuck," Brownroot said. "You sure?"

"Yeah, I'm sure." Blaze looked at the fairy sitting below the window in the faded shag carpeting. The rich topaz of her skin made the orange carpet seem nicer than it was. "I've got it from an impeccable source."

"Damn," Brownroot said. "Good job getting that piece of information. I knew you'd be perfect for this job."

"Yeah," Blaze said, less than pleased with the compliment. But he needed to control this situation perfectly, so he kept his tone dispassionate. "I'm thinking we should leave the cops out of this one."

"My man," Kellogg chuckled in his ear, "I like the way you think. We'll drive up to the site in the middle of the night."

"You drive," Blaze said. There was no way he could let this man get to Ivy first. "I'll walk."

"Why?"

Why, indeed? When Ivy caught ahold of his smell . . . Jesus, she would not be thanking him.

"Why you walking?" Kellogg asked again.

"If the ecoterrorists," Blaze tried not to scoff at the word, "try to run off into the forest. I'll be right there. I know this place, and you can't follow in the rental car."

"Good plan," Kellogg said. "So I'll catch up with you at what? Three in the morning?"

"Sounds great," Blaze said, snapping the phone closed.

"What are you doing?" Vinca asked. Her fox-colored eyebrows were almost to her hairline. "Why're you tattling on Ivy?"

Blaze heard alarm in her voice, but he shushed her with a wave of his hand. He opened his phone again and dialed directory assistance. "Can you connect me with *The New York Times*? I need the news department."

If Ivy was bringing in the big guns, he would too.

Breathing in the hot night air, Ivy crept across the lonely Castle Garden Bridge, trying not to let the long chains she carried clank. Not that anyone could hear her—even loggers slept at this hour.

But still. A girl carrying chains through the Pennsylvania forest in the middle of the night might provoke a call to the sheriff—and a girl with a fairy fluttering around her face might be particularly suspicious. The Cameron County cops were the last thing she needed at this point.

"Ass," she growled under her breath as she power marched over the long stretch of bridge. "What'd I ever see in him?"

"Who?" Seal asked, fluttering just right of her face. The starlight caught the white of his wings and made them sparkle, but his dark skin was lost in the black of the night.

"Blaze Williams, of course."

"He's got a hot ass," Seal said unhelpfully. "Or he did the last time I saw him, anyway. And that hair—so thick and rich. Like

chocolate. I could just eat him up. He was yummy. You think
he still has that dimple?"

"Not that fairies are known for their discriminating tastes,
but he's an ordinary mortal. That's slumming it, even for you."

"Mortal, yes," Seal agreed. "But ordinary?"

Ivy snorted.

"I'm serious, unicorn," Seal insisted in his little voice. "He
had an untapped power back then—just like you did, before
you knew your full heritage."

"You're *not* suggesting Williams is a unicorn," Ivy said.

"No. . . ." Seal's voice trailed as he buzzed a few loops, a
habit that indicated he was thinking. "He's not a unicorn. He's
just not ordinary."

"That's right, he's not ordinary. He's logging the forest he
grew up in." And maybe he was mutilating unicorns.

"True," Seal agreed. "But I bet he's hotter than ever. Evil
does that to a guy."

"Bastard," Ivy muttered to herself in the dark. She shouldn't
be saving the Heart of the World from an ex-boyfriend. No,
she should be walking the streets of Manhattan, homing in on
the song from Tchili's horn. She should be reveling in the strength
of the tigereye soul. She should be doing any number of things
besides undoing Blaze Williams's damned road. "Bastard," she
repeated.

"My parentage has never been questioned, unicorn," Seal
said with his ever-present pout.

"Not you," Ivy explained needlessly. "Him."

"I know." Seal landed on her shoulder with a flourish of his
tiny wings. "I'm trying to distract you." His little fingers stroked
the soft part behind her ear.

"You're distracting," Ivy reassured him. "And you're going
to have to get lost pretty soon. I don't want the humans to see
you."

"Hmph," Seal said in a dismissive tone. "They won't see me. They'll see a firefly or something."

"Or a bat."

"Now that's not very nice." He licked her ear suggestively, sending a shiver of lust through her veins. "What bat would do that?"

"A dead—" she began, but an aroma stopped her in her tracks. The fragrance was compelling, like the smell of baking bread when she was hungry, only more so, more intense. She couldn't ignore it.

"What?" the fairy asked.

"Do you smell that?"

"Smell what?" Because he was sitting on her shoulder, Ivy heard the tiny fairy sniff the air. "I don't smell anything."

She wiped her damp palms over her khaki-clad thighs and realized her breasts ached to be touched. Maybe it was because of Seal's tongue, but she doubted it. There was something in the air. . . . Ivy sniffed again.

"I still don't smell anything, unicorn," the fairy said. "You're hallucinating—or whatever you call it when you imagine a smell."

"Shhh!" She had to smell it again.

The gurgle of Sinnemahoning Creek mingled with the trilling whir of a nightjar, which was as it should be. Frogs were croaking, and that was normal. But that scent. What *was* it? Ivy sniffed again.

"There it is," she said, locking on to it. "Surely you can smell it."

Sharp and musky, and as alluring as a spring moon, she'd never smelled anything like it. A vision came to mind—young warriors swimming in a lake, cool water sluicing down the planes of their chests, across their stomachs. Oblivious of their strength, they radiated masculine virginity, delicious and—

"Ivy—" Seal began, but she shushed him with a hiss.

Her nose quivered as she turned, seeking the strange perfume that had shifted in the breeze. She turned again, but it was gone, leaving her knees quivering, her lips tingling.

"Damn," she said finally. "It's gone."

"What was it?"

"I don't know. I've never smelled anything like it."

Thank God, the scent was gone, she thought. If her human nose found that scent so enthralling, what would happen if she smelled it in animal form?

"You were pretty captivated for a minute there," Seal noted.

"Mmmm," she said noncommittally. *Captivated* seemed like a strong word.

But maybe it wasn't. Maybe the last thing Tchili had smelled before she'd been skinned was this spring-moon scent.

That thought chilled Ivy's heart. If she were right, someone was hunting her right now—in her home forest.

Suddenly a subtle vibration snagged Ivy's attention. It started in her feet and worked its way to her knees. Then the concrete beneath her feet began to quiver, and she froze. She heard it—the deep grumble of a semi engine coming from the forest.

"A truck's coming, Seal. Better get lost." They were in the middle of the bridge. The last thing they needed were headlights spotlighting the fairy.

"Outta here," he said, zipping away.

At a distance, he looked just like a gnat, but Ivy would never tell him that. "Careful," she called to him.

"You be careful, unicorn," he cried as he flew out of sight. "You might look like a girl, but they get into trouble too—especially standing on the road in the middle of the night carrying chains."

He was right. Ivy heard the truck's whine drop a pitch, shifting gears. And she understood the driver must carry a huge load of dead trees—from her forest, where the Heart of the World beat. Under her protection.

If Blaze's road went through, the Heart would be razed. The Heart of the World needed trees, a lot of trees. They buffered the power from humankind.

She looked at the bridge sprawling behind her. In human form, she couldn't sprint back before the truck arrived; the distance was too great. And she was too far from the other end of the bridge. *Damn.*

Quickly she slung the steel chains around her neck. She'd hidden her identity far too long to be undone by random chance.

Sweating with effort, Ivy climbed the short, concrete wall separating the road from the creek, and she leaped over the side just as the truck's headlights arced over the pavement.

Headlights came within inches of her human leg as power from deep within the forest surged through her. She hardly had time to register the sexual strength from the Heart as she twined the lust into transformational power. Forgoing her human form, she landed thirty feet below, all four hooves solidly in the river.

As the cool water of the Sinnemahoning rushed over her thighs, Ivy looked up, the weight of her silvery mane caressing her neck. The dark world brightened to near daylight with her animal vision, and as the truck rumbled past, she recognized mud flecks on the truck's door, splattering the Emperium Hardwoods logo.

The scent of burned diesel and tree sap filled her nostrils, and the iridescent glow of depleted magic swirled behind the receding semi, momentarily dazzling the dark road even as the Heart's power bled into the night from the dead trees.

Just as the truck left the bridge, the loud growl of the engine and the bright flood of its lights startled a doe. In her panic, the deer leaped in front of the truck, crashing head-on into the radiator grill. Ivy cringed as the crunch of smashing bones and ruined flesh filled the quiet night. But without slowing, the truck continued down the road, its roar fading away.

Ivy galloped toward the fallen creature, drawing on the Heart's power to gain speed, but when she arrived, the doe stared blindly at the cloud-chased sky. Ivy could see she was in shock and near death. The scent of milk wafted around her, and Ivy knew a fawn lurked in the shadows, waiting for its mother.

Ivy didn't have much time. Standing still as the massive rocks in the riverbed, she concentrated, working lust into her magic without a thought. In a heartbeat, healing coils spun from her horn.

Ivy dipped her head toward the doe, letting the golden loops drip down. She rested her horn on the deer's skull where bone and brain glistened sickly in the scant moonlight.

The recovery didn't take long. Bone knit together, legs straightened, and the doe's barrel uncrumpled as Ivy's magic took force. Finally, animation once again gleamed in the animal's eyes. She jumped up and bolted toward her woods, toward her fawn.

Standing alone in the middle of the road, Ivy breathed a sigh of relief, letting the adrenaline drain from her jangled nerves. Oh, how she wished she'd been able to do that for her sister. How had she become so tangled in lust she couldn't see her way out?

"Because you were eleven, you nitwit," Ivy's surviving sister Crystal would tell her. "Get over yourself and concentrate."

Ivy looked around the night forest for a moment. Blaze's road would bring more roadkill—and worse. As trees were cut, the Heart lost its power, and Ivy would gradually lose her ability to heal, to channel magic.

But that wouldn't happen, because she wouldn't let it. Ivy drew upon the Heart's power again to shift to human form, complete with soaked khakis and sopping boots. She didn't care about the wet clothing—the deer hadn't died, and the driver hadn't seen her . . . this time. With squishing footsteps, Ivy walked back across the bridge and into the woods.

Ancient hemlocks surrounded her in a familial embrace, their fragrant boughs gently waving above her head. Then, turning at a stand of beech trees, their papery leaves whispering in the breeze, she entered the property of Blaze Williams—knowingly and without invitation. She let her feet crunch loudly underfoot.

"That you, Ivy?" a feminine voice whispered from behind one of the massive tree-shearer tractors. The pristine machines would cut through trees like scissors through paper, but, as yet, they remained untainted by the scent of hemlock sap.

"Yeah, Ann, it's me," Ivy whispered. "I'm so glad you're here." And she was. Greenpeace generally fought its war against the timber industry in Canada, and Ivy had worked hard to convince them of this Pennsylvanian threat.

"Me, too," Ann said. "Glad we could come."

"You bring the locks?" Ivy asked her.

"I've got them," Clay answered. "You remember the chains?"

"All ten feet of them, and, Jesus, they're heavy." Ivy set them carefully in the dirt at her feet.

"That trucker see you?" he asked. "You must've been on the bridge when he drove by."

"He didn't see me."

"How's that possible?"

"He didn't see me," Ivy repeated.

The ecoguerrillas had come to Cameron County at her request, but she sensed they doubted her motivation.

"How'd you get here without a flashlight?" Ann whispered.

"I know this place," Ivy whispered back, the receding adrenaline leaving her nerves jagged and her temper raw. These people didn't need to know she had the senses of an animal despite her perfectly human appearance. "You ready to do this?"

"Yeah," Clay said. "Are you? Not having second thoughts, are you?"

Ivy opened her mouth to retort, but Ann beat her to it.

"Fuck off, Clay," Ann said. The words were affectionate. "Of course she isn't having second thoughts—she brought us here." In the humid darkness, Ivy watched Ann turn her face toward where she thought Ivy was and say, "He thinks anyone not trained by Greenpeace is a poser."

"Fine, Ivy," Clay finally said. "Join us. Be an honorary member of the anti-Kleenex brigade tonight. But just so you know, after the media descends on us like flies, your name'll be mud in this town. Everyone'll hate you for jeopardizing their jobs." He paused, then said, "Leave now and no one'll know you brought us in. We'll take the flack. It's our job."

The offer was tempting. The families of all the kids she'd gone to school with were lumberjacks or foremen or mechanics. They were all grateful to have work close to home. But first and foremost, Ivy was protector of this forest. She had to stay and help, no matter what methods were employed.

"This forest has been here ten thousand years," Ivy said. "Pristine. I can't sit by and let Williams turn these trees into toilet paper."

"Fine," Clay said with a sigh. "Hand me the chains then."

Without difficulty, Ivy scooped the lengths off the black earth in the black night, seeing what the mortal humans could not. "Here," she said as Clay groped blindly for it. She placed them directly in his hand.

"Thanks. Let's chain you to the last trailer. It's probably the safest."

When the workmen came in the morning, they'd be unable to remove the tree-shearer tractors without squashing the tree huggers or cutting the chains free—and the reinforced steel links were as thick as Ivy's wrists.

Clay stumbled behind Ivy as she walked to the trailer. He started to lock her to the machinery, and she breathed in, catching his scent.

It was masculine, yes—he smelled like old cigarettes and

spearmint gum. He had his own personal tang, too, but the ecoguerrilla smelled nothing like that fragrance she'd caught earlier.

He certainly wasn't a warrior virgin. *He* couldn't have captured and skinned Tchili. He couldn't hurt her.

Of course, she thought, as he snapped the padlock closed and tossed the key into the forest, she had never scented a warrior virgin. Her mother had said she'd know one when she smelled one, but that hadn't happened yet.

The touch of Clay's hand on her hip brought a sudden memory, powerful as a summer squall. In the soft grass around Lake Kinzua, she'd lain on top of Blaze Williams, their lips drinking each other greedily, exploring the new pleasures unfurling before them. His warm hands had crept under her shirt, finally daring to slide under her bra strap to caress the expanse of her back.

That innocent bravery had left her breathless with desire, as wet between her thighs as the deep lake lapping at their feet. And if they'd made out even one more time, she might've let Williams go all the way.

If she'd known he'd turn into a greedy slaughterer of trees, if she'd known he'd lay down a road right next to the Heart of the World, she would never have so much as kissed him. She would've had her mother trap him in some enchantment or another. He could be a frog hopping around this very forest.

"Let me chain your wrists now," Clay said, his scent wafting around Ivy's nose.

"Fine." Ivy held her arms to accommodate him, remembering. The last time she'd smelled Williams, he'd been on the cusp of manhood, the scent of warrior virgin beginning to coalesce around him. His scent made her follow him through the high school halls, stalk him to football games.

Not that he'd objected to her. Far from it. But he'd left

Cameron County for Manhattan before he'd grown up all the way, and she'd smelled nothing like him since.

Which was a good thing—warrior virgins were too dangerous to her kind. Just ask Tchili.

"There," Clay said, pulling on her chain. "You're secure." He turned away from her.

Funny, she didn't feel secure. Since Tchili's call for help, since the rumor of the road going right to the Heart of the World, her universe had been threatened on all fronts.

But she couldn't tell that to the ecoguerrilla. "Thanks," she said.

"No problem." He touched her shoulder in acknowledgement. Then he hesitated for a moment, and Ivy caught his concern.

"I'll be all right," she reassured him. "Really."

He nodded in response. "Ann," he called in a whisper. "Where are you?" Thick clouds had obscured the faint moonlight penetrating the hemlocks, and darkness enveloped them.

"Over here," Ann whispered. "I've got a flashlight if you need it."

"No. Let's not take the chance."

The ecoguerrilla found his colleague. He wrapped the chain around Ann's waist and wrists. But unlike the brisk efficiency he'd shown with Ivy, his touch slid over Ann as if luxuriating in the silky texture of her skin. And, like a cat, she arched into his palms, telling him without words how she longed for him.

For a moment, Ivy was shocked at their brazen desire. But then she remembered—they thought absolute darkness shrouded them. And they had no conception of her animal abilities, of the way the scent of their blatant sexuality filled the forest.

Clay chained Ann's hands behind her to a bar just above her ass. The moon broke from behind the clouds for a heartbeat, and Ivy caught the silhouette. It was delicious. The chains pulled

Ann's arms down behind her, and the bar curved her back so her breasts were offered to the night. The graceful curves of the woman's thrust breasts made Ivy think of war goddesses carved into prows of Viking ships. Ann seemed strong enough to live up to the image.

Clay's hands rested easily on Ann's waist despite the fact he was finished chaining her. He rested his cheek against hers. Ann struggled against the chains, trying to get closer to Clay, but a teasing grin lit his face as he moved away from her, just barely.

"Is that all you're going to do?" Ann asked in her husky whisper.

"You want something more?" His lips were so close to Ann's now that Ivy knew they could feel the heat from each other's bodies, even on this sultry summer night.

"You know I do," she said.

"What do you want?"

"You know." Ann shifted so her breasts nearly touched Clay's. Her lips were a hair's breadth from his.

"Ask," he teased.

"Kiss me," she said so softly Ivy wouldn't have been able to hear it if she weren't magical.

"You want me to kiss you?"

Ann paused, her eyes locked on his. "Yes. Kiss me."

"Say please."

Ivy held her breath, wondering if Ann would play this game. She thought she might not.

"Please, Clay," Ann breathed. "Kiss me."

He let his lips caress Ann's. His tongue stayed inside his mouth, but the lingering touch made Ivy's heart race as she watched.

"Is that all you want?" Clay asked Ann.

"You know it's not," Ann said.

"Then ask for more."

Ann said nothing for a long moment, although her nipples were hard. A wave of desire washed over Ivy, the voyeur. Unbidden, the memory of that delicious perfume danced through her mind.

Finally the tree hugger whispered, "Clay, I want more. I want your mouth. I want your cock. I want it hard, and I want it deep."

Without a word, Clay descended on her, inhaling Ann's lips in his own. Ivy could too easily imagine the way their tongues darted and explored. She could imagine the pleasure of one mouth sucking the other.

Clay's hands climbed from Ann's waist to her breasts, and she pushed toward him, only to be pulled back by the chain. With a pleased grin, Clay broke away from her. "You're at my mercy," he whispered to her.

Ann shifted so her erect nipples brushed over Clay's arm, and Ivy pretended not to hear the stifled groan from him.

"You're at *my* mercy, Clay. Not all chains are made of steel." Ann arched her back, offering.

Clay accepted, nipping Ann's flesh through the fabric of her T-shirt. His hands held her heavy breasts as if he held a gift from the gods. He worshipped her—even Ivy could see.

And Ann was right, Ivy thought. Clay looked like Ann's slave. Despite the chains, Ann ruled him.

"Touch me," Ann said.

"Here?" Clay's hand rested on her thigh just below the hem of her shorts.

"That's nice," Ann said. "Higher would be okay too."

Clay's hand slid to the top of her thigh. Over her clingy shorts, his hand pressed against her mound, and Ann pressed right back.

"Can I . . . ?" he asked.

Ann didn't answer. Instead, she shifted, opening her thighs to his hand. Ivy imagined the heat Clay's hand felt as he caressed the thin cotton covering between her thighs. She watched his thumb slip under the shorts.

"Not yet, big boy," Ann said. "Don't move so fast."

"But, Ivy," he whispered. "She might hear us."

"She can't see us, and we'll be quiet," Ann assured him. "Besides," Ivy could hear the evil grin in the girl's voice, "she might like it."

And Ann was right. Ivy found she was incredibly turned on—and a little frustrated. Where was Seal when she needed him? Probably laughing at her from a branch above her head.

Clay pushed up Ann's shirt. "I want a taste of these," he said. "Your nipples are sweeter than honey." Lifting a breast, he licked a nipple as if it were sacred, as if it could save him.

With another scarcely restrained groan, Ann leaned against the truck bed. "My shorts," she whispered. "They've got to go."

"Gone," he said, pulling them down.

As Clay's fingers slid over Ann, the scent of her desire curled around Ivy, awakening something in her.

Ivy watched his fingers disappear deep in her, and Ann pushed hard against him, biting her lips. Then she whispered to him, "Fuck me. Now."

The words held an unmistakable tension Clay didn't ignore. In a smooth movement, he unzipped his khaki shorts and buried himself in her. She watched pleasure build with every thrust, and the power of their lust reminded her of a summer thunderstorm, dazzling and mighty.

Perched on the trailer, Ann wrapped her legs tightly around Clay, pulling him deeper inside, forbidding him to leave. Their bodies connected, as did their mouths and hands. Together, their breathing became shallow, quick. As the spasm of pleasure grabbed Ann, Clay's following close behind hers, Ivy realized she'd rarely seen anything so wild and wanton. Not among humans.

Clay rested for a moment, collapsed against Ann, and she laid her face on his shoulder, apparently unmindful of the chains binding her. His broad hand stroked the dark length of her hair, and she seemed blessed.

"I love you," she heard Ann whisper to Clay.

"Be brave when they come in a few hours."

"Williams has been in the city so long," Ann whispered hopefully to Clay. "Maybe he'll drop the whole logging idea once he sees how beautiful this place is."

"Maybe," Clay said, and Ivy didn't hear much conviction.

Hands chained behind her, Ann leaned into her man. "This'll force him to see."

And Ivy held back a scoff. Williams might have been born in Cameron County, but he wasn't *from* Cameron County. After he'd left, he'd never looked back—not at Ivy, not at the beauty here. Apparently the forest's sacred aura paled in comparison to the glittering bauble of Manhattan, to what the timber industry would add to Blaze's bank account.

But maybe he's here for something more. . . . The thought chilled Ivy.

She hated him for that, for both desertions. And for mutilating unicorns.

"You make this place beautiful," Clay said to Ann, and Ivy rolled her eyes. But Clay's hand ran behind Ann's neck, and he comforted her with the press of his body. Ivy had to admit: humans were beautiful in their dedication to each other. Like swans or mourning doves.

Ivy didn't mind the way these two had assumed she was too blind to see or hear or smell what happened just feet away from where she stood. What she minded was the loneliness. Ivy realized she wanted what Ann and Clay had.

In fact, she ached for it.

5

Blaze had been living in Manhattan for so long he expected the woods to feel foreign. As a child his feet had always known where to go, and he'd attributed that knowledge to the fact he'd pinned his heart to Ivy—and she was always right in front of him.

But sneaking through the night forest as an adult—an adult with intense magic user's training—he realized his feet actually did know where to go. And he didn't believe the fact he was searching for Ivy was the cause of it.

"Amazing," he whispered to Vinca. "I can feel the power from the Heart of the World pounding through my feet." In fact, the power seemed to pour right into his cock.

From his pocket, Vinca ran her little palm over his pect and said, "I'm thinking of a different pounding altogether."

"Jesus," Blaze said in a hushed voice as Vinca tweaked his nipple. An image of Ivy raced through his brain, but he managed to thwart the impending erection. He needed complete control. "Stop that."

"You're no fun," the fairy said. "And of course you can feel the power. All magical creatures can."

"It's like a built-in compass."

"Always pointing south," Vinca added running her hand toward his navel.

"I'm going to take you out of that pocket and make you walk if you can't behave." She had no idea what her teasing did to him—or maybe she did. But he couldn't risk it.

"Fine," Vinca said sulkily. "I'll stop."

"You have a job here," Blaze reminded her.

"Job?" she asked. "As in, blowjob?"

"Are all fairies this focused on sex?"

"Just the lucky ones."

"Seriously, Vinca," Blaze said. "Can you help me find her?"

"Ivy, Ivy," the fairy chanted. "It's always about Ivy."

"You're the one with the squashed wings."

"It's a tragedy." The fairy sighed. "But you're right." Blaze felt her pull herself partially out of his pocket, and he assumed she was looking around. Finally she said, "I think Kellogg's just driven up this road. Can't you smell the exhaust? The quickest way for us to get to the tractors is via the deer path."

If Brownroot were gone, Blaze could rifle his cabin for the *Canticles*. Would he get another chance like this? But, no, Blaze couldn't leave Ivy alone with the unicorn killer. And what if the car exhaust belonged to someone else?

"Will this path get us to the unicorn before him?"

"No, but it'll get us behind her. The bad guy'll be driving right to the front of the glade, but we'll sneak up from behind."

"Can't we get both behind her and ahead of Kellogg?"

"You worry too much, wizard," Vinca said, patting his chest. "Ivy's a strong creature. She doesn't need a knight in shining armor."

Something about that image—him rushing to Ivy's rescue—

caught at his heart. Didn't heroes get at least a kiss? "Don't underestimate how evil Kellogg Brownroot is, Vinca," Blaze said. "He's stealing unicorn horns, sawing them off living, breathing creatures."

"That's terrible," Vinca said with a shiver Blaze felt through his shirt. "But it won't happen to Ivy."

As Blaze tripped over a log on the deer path, he wished he could share Vinca's assurance. For his own peace of mind, he wanted to get Ivy out of these woods before he banished Brownroot to the second dimension. He didn't need to be worrying about the safety of his high school sweetheart while battling evil.

"We're here," Vinca said as Blaze pushed some vines out of his face. "The trailers with the tree choppers are in that clearing there."

Blaze looked, but clouds filled the sky, making it too dark to see well. "I don't see her," he said.

"Try looking with your heart, wizard," Vinca said. "Didn't your dad teach you anything?"

A distant rumble interrupted Ivy's pang of loneliness, and it wasn't the sound of tires on the pavement of the bridge; this was the softer sound of tires on dirt.

"Someone's coming," Ivy hissed to Ann and Clay.

"I don't hear any—" Ann whispered.

"It's probably Emperium," Ivy said. "Maybe it's the foreman checking on the equipment."

"Damn it," Clay said as the headlights weaving down the dirt path became visible. Ivy watched him adjust his khakis and lock himself to the third trailer. "Someone did see you, Ivy. Now we won't get any press coverage."

But the truck's driver hadn't spotted her, she knew. This was something different, a random check, maybe. She hoped.

Regardless, having the foreman here ruined their plans. He

would raise the alarm, get the cops before the press got here. But how could she get rid of him?

Suddenly Seal was fluttering around her face. Ivy realized he must've been keeping an eye on her since they'd parted company on the bridge.

Be careful, unicorn, he said in mindspeak. *That guy driving here isn't the watchman. Get him out of here.*

Ivy wished her friend would buzz off, but she couldn't even whisper without raising the attention of the Greenpeacers. She waved an angry hand at him in the way she would've swished her tail at a fly.

Get him out of here.

But what was she supposed to do? Get her fairy godmother here and wish him away?

Do something! Seal insisted.

Then Ivy realized she had an option. A dangerous option, yes, but what choice did she have? The road must be stopped. The Heart must be saved—at any cost.

Trying to see with his heart, Blaze took a moment to center himself, to exist in the moment. In his mind, he pictured Ivy's face as he'd last seen it. Her fine blond hair, always a little disheveled, tumbling down to her ass. Her pink lips parted, her breath sweet. Her heavy-lidded green eyes filled with a knowing laugh.

And—like magic—he could see her in the glade. Her snug white T-shirt glowed slightly in the faint light, and her khakis hugged her slim hips. The huge tree shearers hulked above her, resting on the flatbeds of the trailer. She had chained her arms to the piping behind her, but even in the erratic moonlight, he could see the silhouette of her breasts.

The erection that'd been dogging him since Vinca had tweaked his nipple threatened to return. Not good. "Mmmm," Vinca hummed in his ear. "She looks good, doesn't she?"

Blaze sensed rather than saw the approaching rental car. "Kellogg's coming," Blaze said, walking faster into the glade. "We still have time to get to her first."

"But stop!" Vinca cried from his pocket. Blaze might've ignored her, but the power beneath his feet suddenly flared, shocking him as lust burned his veins. Had that come from Ivy? He stopped.

"What is it?" His voice was husky, as if he were speaking to a lover.

"Just watch," Vinca said. "But don't interrupt."

"Interrupt what?"

"Shhh!"

With her eyes locked on the truck, Ivy knew she had to wait until just the right moment, just the right heartbeat. The eco-guerrillas' attention was on the dark sedan vibrating over the rutted path, but she needed more.

Look at me, she willed, watching the driver's face through the windshield. *Turn your eyes toward me.*

And as though he'd heard her, he looked. But it wasn't the gentle old foreman she saw. Across the distance and through the thick hemlock trees, she saw a strong jaw and hair cool enough to make Bon Jovi jealous. But his eyes locked on her, and his gaze was as cold as February. Cold and evil. Almost crocodilian.

Now, she told herself, and she shifted form. Her legs and neck lengthened. Her hair grew so it fell to her knees in a silken cascade. Her chains changed to accommodate her new form, but her clothing simply vanished. Animal eyes caught the silvery glint of her mane as her hands turned to hooves, and her forehead ached as the horn burst from the bone.

With satisfaction, Ivy watched incredulity freeze the driver's broad face. She didn't recognize him—and she wouldn't have forgotten this hottie—but she knew his emotions. Blood drained, and eyes grew wide. His mouth stood open.

"Good job, Ivy," Seal cheered in her ear, and a flash of pleasure rushed through her. Her plan had worked. Whoever was driving that sedan thought he was losing his mind. Good, let him take his imagined insanity back to wherever it originated.

Then her animal nose locked on the scent too diffuse to have attracted her human form—the scent of a warrior virgin.

Can you smell that? Ivy asked Seal in mindspeak.

I have no idea what you keep talking about. I don't smell anything.

The shock of the fragrance assaulted her again, her equine form so much more susceptible to the scent of virginity than her human one.

Come on, Ivy, Seal cajoled, fluttering right inside her equine ear. *You need to change back to girl form.*

But her need to immerse herself in the delight of the fragrance, to fill her nose and mouth with that exotic perfume, flooded her veins. She had no choice. Ivy forgot her burning quest to save the Heart. She bunched her powerful legs beneath her and leaped toward the source. She needed it, couldn't live without it.

Ivy, don't!

His words didn't stop her, but Clay's chains jerked her back to the trailer, the steel links stronger than even her brute force. The sound of scraping metal filled the meadow, followed by the sound of the links hitting the steel trailer. The chain scraped up the front of her shins, and she could feel blood welling to the surface.

She blinked in pain while the sedan barreling toward them swerved off the dirt path. It slammed into an ancient beech tree, and the sound exploded into the quiet night. Papery bark from the beech showered the crumpled hood like confetti as the sweet odor of antifreeze filled the air.

Change, unicorn, Seal demanded, fluttering annoyingly in her face. *Now. You're in danger!*

A heavy link swung back into her just-scraped shin. Jolted to her senses by the pain, Ivy shifted back to human form, the Heart's power coursing through her, flaming the mad lust crackling in her veins.

Good girl, Seal said and then landed on the tip of her ear. This time, she didn't try to shoo him away. *That smell does something crazy to you.*

"What the fuck just happened?" Clay asked, his attention riveted to the hissing, crumpled car.

Realizing how close she'd come to exposing her true nature, Ivy wondered the same thing. She threw a panicked look over her shoulder, examining the forest. Her nose had told her something important, something astounding. But she wouldn't believe—couldn't believe—until her eyes confirmed it.

"Did you see that?" Ann asked, laughing in amazement. "He drove right off the fucking road!"

"He jerked the car like he saw a ghost or something." Clay threw a blind look over his shoulder toward Ivy's direction, but she could tell he couldn't see her in the dark. "Why'd he do that?"

"I don't know—" Ivy started, but just then a warm hand slid over her stomach, and a deep voice, reverberating with melodic strength, whispered in her ear so only she could hear.

"I know what you are, Ivy."

The chilling words might have stopped her in her tracks, but it was his scent that immobilized her, tantalized her, made her knees weak with desire. She'd willingly follow this man to the ends of the earth.

He was a virgin, a warrior virgin.

"I know who you are." He slid his hands over her chained arms, raising the small hairs on her neck. "And you have to listen to me."

He was right. She must obey him. She had no choice. Sirens lured ancient sailors to rocky deaths in the way his scent lured her. And the effects would be as devastating. Marshalling her strength, she pulled away from him, only to be jerked back by the steel links.

"Don't run." His voice echoed with strength and power. "Not from me."

Even through the haze of desire, she recognized his voice, although she hadn't heard it in years. "Williams," she said. "Blaze Williams."

"In the flesh."

"Flesh," Ivy repeated, breathing deeply. He enthralled her; his scent did.

And then a little voice chirped from someplace in Blaze's shirt. "Why didn't you tell me you're a virgin?" The tiny bells of feminine fairy laughter filled the space between them. "Dear God," the fairy girl guffawed. "He's a virgin!"

Seal fluttered off her ear and flew around the newcomer. "His ass is still hot, though," Seal announced in a voice no louder than a hummingbird's wings in flight. "And he isn't bald or fat."

"Unicorn," the fairy woman said in her bitty voice. "You are in so much trouble."

But Blaze thought he might be the one in trouble.

Moonbeams caught golden glints in Ivy's hair as it rippled down her back to her waist. A tendril curled around her T-shirted breast, and a chunky lock fell coyly in her face.

The thing that grabbed his heart and refused to let go was the fierce defiance shining in her eyes. Nothing was coming between this woman and her cause.

Blaze was smitten.

His father's teasing words rushed back at him. He needed more than Ivy's help, but God Almighty, he'd rather chew off his foot than ask her. How the hell could he work with this beautiful woman?

But he couldn't broach that topic, not right this minute. "You shouldn't have let that man see you in unicorn form," Blaze said to her. "He's killing unicorns across the globe."

Ivy didn't believe him for an instant. A virgin had mutilated Tchili, and a virgin stood right in front of her, hot ass or no.

Adrenaline rushed through her blood. His chest was so broad.

Ivy watched Williams's eyes darken, and the merest scent of his sexual interest mingled with his spring-moon scent. From his desire, she knew her beauty tugged at him.

Good. She would use any tool she had. He would never know the power he held over her. Not if she could help it.

"Williams," she said, letting the word fall quietly from her mouth. She didn't want to bring herself to the attention of Ann and Clay. "There'll be no road."

But despite her bold words, her lips longed for his touch, for the feel of his virginal flesh as it slid over hers—regardless of what logic told her.

"Ivy, don't fight this." His voice slid over her like molten chocolate, like single-malt whiskey. Quivering, she wanted to melt into his arms. "I'm on your side."

"It's true, unicorn," Vinca said. "Kellogg Brownroot stole Blaze's book of spells." Vinca leaped out of Blaze's pocket and onto Ivy's shoulder, her tattered wings flapping uselessly.

"Who's Kellogg Brownroot?" Ivy asked, buying time; her guard stayed up. Blaze was dangerous, his scent too compelling. She drew power from the Heart, changing the lust it generated directly into energy—and the padlock fell to the ground with a small *thunk*. She was free.

And all hell broke loose.

"Ivy L'Engle," a man called from the sedan as the smashed door creaked open. "Stop right there."

Even as she wondered how he knew her name, the cultured

authority of his voice made Ivy think him better suited to a boardroom. But his shaggy blond hair made her think he should be leading some rock band.

"That's Kellogg Brownroot," Blaze said quietly in her ear, his cheek pressed against her face. "He's planning on logging my land."

"He's hot too," Seal said. "His ass is almost as good as yours, Blaze."

Brownroot shone a flashlight over the ecoguerrillas. Despite his *Rolling Stone* looks, something about him reminded Ivy of reptiles. "You're trespassing on private property, and I've already called the sheriff." Cold menace laced his deep voice. "This road will go through."

"We'll see about that!" Ann called back. "We've stopped bigger projects than this."

"I doubt it," Brownroot said. "And where's Ivy L'Engle? She's the ringleader."

"The only ivy around here is the poison kind," Ann said. "And you're probably standing in it."

"What the fuck?" Kellogg said, losing his crocodilian appearance as he shone his flashlight haphazardly around his feet. Clay laughed, making Kellogg curse again.

Sending Ann a private *thank you,* Ivy used the distraction to bolt.

Williams grabbed for her shoulder, but she was gone, his scent curling around her human form. As she raced toward the road, a new set of headlights rushed up the path.

Ann shouted, jerking against her chains, "Maybe they're here, Clay! The press. Maybe they came early."

"Fuck," Ivy heard Brownroot mutter.

"Maybe it's the cops," Clay said, jerking his chains.

"No," Ann said. "It's not."

"How'd you know? Can you see?" Clay asked Ann, who stood at a different angle than he did.

"It's the *Corry Journal*." Ann couldn't contain herself. "Or maybe even the Erie paper."

But as Ivy fled past the second car, her feet unerringly missing fallen branches and other detritus, her peripheral vision caught the blue emblem for *USA Today* on the side of a camera. A truck behind bore a CNN insignia.

They'd called in the big guns? Amazing. Relief flooded Ivy. A savvy reporter from a real news agency might stop the logging. Greenpeace and Reuters could do her job for her.

Blaze called in the big newspapers, Vinca said, reminding Ivy of her presence. *He's a good guy.*

He's tricked you, fairy, Ivy answered, fleeing down the deer path. *He's building that road, and I think he's mutilating unicorns. There's nothing good about that man.*

He's got to stop that book-stealing, unicorn-mutilating Brownroot. You're tricking yourself, Ivy.

But Ivy ignored Vinca, the taste of danger still bitter on her tongue.

Blaze Williams isn't your problem, Vinca said. *That Kellogg Brownroot man is.*

Whatever you say, Ivy told the fairy in a humoring tone. *Be quiet until we're away from here.*

Not daring to shift to unicorn form in the presence of a virgin, she ran in earnest under the racing clouds. She ran until her muscles ached with fatigue and blood pounded behind her eyes. She paused for a moment and listened, but she could still hear ecoguerrillas shouting at Kellogg Brownroot. She saw what looked like lightning flashes and assumed the reporters were taking pictures.

She bolted again.

Finally even her enhanced hearing and vision couldn't detect the chaos at the road site. Ivy couldn't smell Williams's enthralling scent either.

Only then did she stop and lean against a tree, panting. She'd escaped.

Or had she?

Will you heal me now, unicorn? the fairy asked from her shoulder. *You're a rough ride when you're a human. Although I doubt Blaze would agree.*

An image of Blaze's naked body pumping into Ivy danced through her mind at the fairy's words, but she quickly squashed it. *Vinca, be quiet a minute, will you? I don't want to change into unicorn form with a virgin in the forest.*

But you can trust him, the little fairy insisted. *He's a wizard.*

Those words shocked Ivy out of mindspeak. "A wizard? How's that possible?" Alarm raced through Ivy. "He's just a mortal boy."

Vinca laughed in a knowing way. "Some boy, unicorn. I rode in his pocket, and I can tell you he's all man."

"Wizard."

"Whatever."

"Why should I trust a wizard?" A wizard—a virgin wizard—could certainly have captured and mutilated Tchili. But what if he were the tigereye soul? Would that explain the strength of his song?

"His father was a magic user, too," Vinca said. "One of the best. And I have a feeling the son will surpass the father in this respect." She giggled. "And perhaps in others as well."

"All these years you've been hanging out with me and you never thought to tell me Zachariah Williams was a wizard?"

"Well, you never asked."

Ivy didn't know what to make of this. She needed a second opinion. *Seal?* Ivy asked. *Where are you?* But her little friend wasn't around. Probably waylaid by some busty dryad. Or maybe he was checking out Williams himself. Seal wasn't known for strict heterosexual preferences.

"If you knew Blaze was a wizard, anyone could have known," Ivy said. "How come nobody told me? Why didn't Seal tell me?"

Vinca shrugged, her breasts warmly inviting in the shadowy light. "Maybe he didn't know."

"Well, how did *you* know?"

A quick grin flashed across the fairy's face. "Like I said, I knew his father."

"But why's he still a virgin?" Blaze Williams's wide shoulders and thick, black hair didn't suggest a man who'd have a hard time finding a mate. Ivy remembered the way his gaze had changed when she'd tossed her hair. The way his dark eyes had burned into hers didn't suggest a man who lacked interest or a man who'd changed his interest in her.

Vinca sighed in Ivy's ear. "Can't you just heal me?" she asked. "I'm tired of not having wings."

"But a man like Blaze doesn't stay a virgin by choice," Ivy insisted. "He should've lost his at sixteen in the backseat of some car, and he should've slept with dozens of women since then."

And he should've lost it at sixteen with her.

"And it should've been you," Vinca said. "I hear what you're thinking."

"That's not it," Ivy lied. "If he's not a virgin for lack of opportunity or desire, why is he?"

"You have to ask him."

Ivy just laughed at that idea.

Vinca shrugged. "I think wizards lose some power when they lose their virginity."

Ivy shook her head. "Is that the kind of crap he's telling you? That's the first I've heard of any such nonsense." She put her hands on her hips and said, "But I hope it's true. Because if he thinks he can come back to town, put in that road, and get me in bed . . ." She snorted a very horselike sound from her human nose. "He's wrong."

"You've got it wrong," Vinca said. "Please fix my wings."

Ivy stood for a minute, remembering the way Blaze's hands had slid over her stomach. He didn't seem like a man interested in keeping his virginity. He hadn't smelled like one either.

She sniffed the air now. Nothing. She didn't hear or see anything suspicious either. "I can fix you," Ivy said, drawing on the Heart to change her form. *Why don't you jump to the ground?*

Vinca left Ivy's shoulder as feet became hooves, and Ivy inhaled deeply, feeling the thick rush of air pouring through her equine nostrils.

Her animal nose caught the faintest whiff of that perfume. Ivy stood, the small hairs of her mane prickling. With an instinctual certainty, she knew.

Williams wasn't a social misfit who couldn't get laid. *Not with those green eyes*, the voice in the back of her mind agreed. He wasn't a priest or some other religious celibate.

Williams was a unicorn hunter.

That thought killed the lust in her from his scent, from the Heart. Swallowing her fear, Ivy stepped away from the ancient oak. More than the Heart of the World was in danger. If a unicorn hunter had tracked her to her home, her very life was at stake.

"Ivy?" Vinca asked.

And then the summer breeze rippled through the forest, bathing her fully in the spring-moon scent. Ignoring the danger, ignoring the fairy, Ivy closed her eyes and inhaled.

The visions returned. Dark-eyed virgins practicing swordplay under an achingly blue sky, pects and chest muscles gleaming in the sun. Steel glinted hard as drops of flying sweat caught sunlight and then were blinked from existence.

She'd kneel in the service of such a virgin. She'd lay her horn in his lap. She'd beg him to take her, make her his and his alone. And how would it feel to give herself to such a man?

For a moment, she imagined Blaze behind a sword, battling dark and evil forces with his brawny might. The vision left her mad with desire, balmy with it. Only yielding to Blaze would satisfy her.

But he'd walked away from her before, without a glance back. And now he was dangerous.

Ivy? Vinca asked. *My wings? Anytime tonight would be fine. We need to hurry. I can still smell him.*

I'm all for hurrying, Vinca said.

Ivy dipped down her head, letting that sexual power coalesce in her horn. Vinca nimbly leaped to a small stump and stood, arms outstretched, allowing the healing coils to pulse over her.

Oh, that's so much better, Vinca said, dancing in a tiny circle, fluttering her wings.

Hold still, Ivy said, trying to keep her horn right above the fluttering creature.

They work! Vinca cried, launching herself into the air. In a flurry of topaz and blue, Vinca flew spirals around Ivy's face. *Thank you! Thank you!*

Ignoring the lust in her veins, Ivy changed back to girl form. She knew her desire was insane, a weakness of her magical flesh. In her human form, logic had a stronger hold on her mind, and her human mind drew an obvious conclusion: someone had been systematically slaughtering unicorns, and Blaze Williams seemed a likely suspect. He'd sell the Heart of the World to the highest bidder and erase that last vestige of magic in this cold world for a profit.

"You're welcome, Vinca. And now you can pay me back."

"What are you talking about?"

"I don't think either of those stupid men—Blaze Williams

or Kellogg Brownroot—should have the *Canticles Al Farasakh.*
So you and I are going to get it—right now."

"Okay," Vinca said. "That sounds fun. How are we going to
do it?"

Wiping her sweating palms on her khakis, Ivy considered.
Unless someone had the wherewithal to use a virgin as bait,
catching a unicorn wasn't easy. Blaze's virginity gave him power
over her, but it was blunted while she was human. He couldn't
ensnare her. He could tempt and beguile, but he couldn't make
her behave against her own best interest.

So while Williams was around, she was trapped in human
form. That was just fine with her.

"Let's go to Brownroot's cabin."

6

"Which is Brownroot's?" Ivy asked Vinca as they walked up the path that passed for a driveway to the hunting cabins.

"That one," Vinca said, pointing east as she fluttered near Ivy's face.

"You going to keep lookout for me?"

"Sure," Vinca said, clapping her hands together. "I love an adventure."

"Don't get bored and flutter away, fairy," Ivy warned. "I don't want to be trapped in here if Brownroot comes back."

"Oh, that couldn't happen," Vinca said. "You'd hear the car."

That was probably true, but still . . . now that Kellogg Brownroot's cabin sat right in front of her, breaking into it seemed . . . daunting.

Ivy rolled back her shoulders and walked right up to the door like she owned the place. She twisted the knob, cool brass in the heat of summer night, and the door opened.

"It's not here," Ivy announced, stopping dead in her tracks. "We should go."

"Just like that? How do you know it's not here?"

"If you had a stolen magic book hidden in here, would you leave the door unlocked?"

"Maybe that's what Brownroot thinks someone would think," Vinca said. "Or maybe the book's so well hidden that locking the door is irrelevant. Or maybe he used a spell that makes you want to turn around and leave if you opened the door without invitation. Or maybe—"

"Shhh, fairy," Ivy said. "I get the point." She stepped carefully into the cabin, unsure why she was taking such care. "Forget guard duty; can you help me look for the book?"

"Sure," Vinca said in her tiny voice. "I even know what it looks like."

"Really? You've seen it?"

"Not recently," Vinca answered. "But like I said, I knew Blaze's father."

She'd said that several times throughout the night, but its meaning finally sank into Ivy's head. "He showed you the *Canticles Al Farasakh*?" she asked. That struck Ivy as pretty intimate, even for a fairy and a wizard.

"Yeah," Vinca answered, and Ivy could hear her smile. "He had a great spell of enlargement. . . ."

"Enlargement?" Ivy asked. "Was he unfortunately endowed?"

"No," Vinca laughed her jingle-bell laugh. "The spell wasn't for him. It was for me."

"I'm so confused."

Vinca landed on her shoulder and whispered, "He made me into human size, and sometimes . . ." She giggled again. "Sometimes he made himself into fairy size."

"Oh." Ivy thought about Seal's wish for size. He'd certainly love to get ahold of that spell. God, how pesky would he be if he were actually human size?

"You see?" Vinca asked. "It'd be fun, wouldn't it?"

Ivy laughed quietly. "Yes, fairy. It'd be fun, but what'd the book look like?" Her eyes had adjusted to the dark cabin, and her enhanced vision let her see the layout—which was good because she didn't want to turn on the lights.

"Red," Vinca said. "The color of . . ." She paused for a moment, thinking. "Hibiscus. And it's made of the softest crushed velvet."

A suitcase lay on the bed, and Ivy walked over to it. She opened it, knowing her quest couldn't be as easy as this. The ancient book of spells wouldn't be sitting in this bag in an unlocked cabin.

"How big was it?"

"I don't know, unicorn. Everything's big compared to me."

Ivy lifted a couple of shirts, relieved that the *Canticles Al Farasakh* was bigger than the fairy. Finding a tiny book might be more difficult.

"Could it fit in a man's pocket?" Ivy asked.

"No, too big."

Ivy closed the suitcase, which held nothing but clothing, and walked toward the bathroom.

"Go look around," Ivy urged her friend. "If Kellogg Brownroot really has the *Canticles*, then it's in here or in his car."

"That's probably true," Vinca said, fluttering toward the bookshelf.

Ivy looked under the mattresses, and Vinca looked in the freezer. As Ivy looked between the sofa cushions, finding nothing but dust and crumbs, she heard Vinca exclaim, "Look at this!"

"Did you find it?"

"I don't know."

Vinca was tugging at a huge flagstone in the hearth of the fireplace.

"What are you doing?"

"It's hollow," the fairy said. "Listen." She tapped the big, flat flagstone next to the one she was tugging at, and a solid sound filled the cabin. But when she tapped the stone at which she was tugging, a more resonant sound filled the air.

"You're right," Ivy said. With a pounding heart she walked over and tried to lift the flagstone. It wasn't easy, but she knew—she knew—the *Canticles Al Farasakh* would be hidden here.

Bruising her fingertips, she lifted the rock. "Is it in there?" she asked Vinca, who fluttered into the opening while Ivy struggled with the weight.

"Um," the fairy said. "No."

"Damn," Ivy said, putting the huge rock down with a grunt. "I was so sure."

"Funny thing, I was too."

Ivy sat in the kitchen chair and rested her head in her hand. "Now what?" she asked the fairy who sat next to her elbow.

"Can you use your magic to find it?" Vinca asked.

"No," Ivy shook her head. "I can find living things. Or magic things. But the *Canticles Al Farasakh* isn't alive or magic in and of itself."

"Maybe it's in his car," Vinca said.

"Maybe he doesn't have it."

"Blaze thought he had it," Vinca said doubtfully.

That idea made Ivy sit up. "Williams *said* he thought Brownroot had it," she corrected.

"What do you mean?"

"Let's go check Blaze's cabin," Ivy said, standing. "In fact, let's go see if there's a loose flagstone in Blaze's fireplace."

"It's not there," Vinca said.

"We can check though, can't we?"

"I guess," the fairy said, and Ivy heard nothing but reluctance.

Blaze walked back toward his cabin, at a loss. He couldn't believe she'd gotten away from him. She'd literally slipped through his hands like an eel. Jesus, and he had no idea where Kellogg Brownroot was. What if he had her?

He'd warned her. He had. He'd told her Kellogg Brownroot was killing unicorns across the globe, stealing their skins and horns. The problem was, he didn't think she believed him.

In fact, it looked like she thought *he* was the mutilator of unicorns.

"There you are." Brownroot strode toward him, looking as calm as could be.

"Kellogg," Blaze said with relief; he hoped it sounded like enthusiasm. "You alone?"

Kellogg looked behind him and laughed. "I sure as hell hope so."

"What happened with the ecoguerrillas?" Blaze asked, too relieved to see Kellogg without Ivy.

Falling into stride next to Blaze, Kellogg huffed an exasperated sound. "I left them to the cops and reporters."

"Reporters?" Blaze feigned surprise.

"Yeah," Kellogg said. "I don't know who the fuck called them, but Christ Almighty, what a fiasco. CNN and *USA Today* were there. *New York Times,* too."

"You're kidding," Blaze answered, hoping he wasn't laying it on too thick.

"You see that blond ecoterrorist?" Kellogg asked in that used-car-salesman voice. "She's the only one from here. Ivy L'Engle. You know her?"

"I went to school with her," Blaze said, careful to keep his voice even. "Why?"

"Do you notice anything..." Kellogg paused, perhaps searching for a word, "*unusual* about her?"

Blaze could think of a whole bunch of unusual things regarding Ivy, but the bewitching shine of her eyes and the ferocious way she protected those she loved wasn't information he wanted to share with Brownroot. "Unusual?"

"I saw her ... change shape," Kellogg said. "You see that?"

"Kellogg," Blaze said. "I was right behind her, and I never

saw her do anything the others didn't do." Blaze stopped walking and put his hand on Kellogg's shoulder. "You didn't hit
your head when you smashed the car, did you? Maybe you
ought to let me drive from now on."

"Get your hand off me, Williams," Kellogg snarled. "I saw
it. That girl changed into a unicorn."

Blaze let doubt creep into his voice. "Fairies at lunchtime and
now unicorns? You need some sleep, buddy. Look, the cabins
are right here."

"Don't patronize me. Where'd she go if she didn't change
shape? How'd she escape?"

Blaze started walking again toward the cabins. "I have no
idea where she went. I chased after her when you smashed the
car, but I lost her in the forest—I chased a *woman* with long
blond hair through the trees. Not surprising I lost her. She
knows it better than I do."

"But how'd she get loose?"

"Maybe she wasn't locked. Look," Blaze said, opening the
door to Kellogg's cabin, "why don't you go to bed? We've had
a long day."

Kellogg turned toward Blaze, his jaw stubborn. "We're not
going to bed. We're going to that rock, and we're going to blow
it up."

"Right now?" Blaze asked. "At four in the morning?" He
shook his head. There was no way in hell he'd let Brownroot
talk him into this, not until he had the *Canticles Al Farasakh*
and Ivy safely under control. "I'm going to bed and we can talk
about this in the morning."

Kellogg grabbed Blaze's arm. "We're going tonight. Right
this very minute."

Blaze shook his head, treading carefully. "Kellogg, man,
what's wrong with you? The rock's not going anywhere, and all
your stuff is in the trunk of that smashed rental. How are you
going to get the explosives there?"

"It's not a problem money won't solve," Kellogg said.

"Hell," Blaze said. "I've been gone from Cameron County for more than a decade, and you want me to find one particular boulder amongst all of them in this forest in the middle of the night?"

Kellogg eyed him, probably wondering if Blaze were lying. Finally Kellogg shook his head and said, "Wait here."

Blaze stood alone on the doorstep, wondering what Brownroot would come up with next.

"Here," Brownroot said, returning and handing him a piece of equipment. "You know what it is?"

Blaze looked at it. "Yeah, it's a GPS."

"Right," Brownroot said. "You go to the rock before ten A.M. and call me with the coordinates."

Blaze looked at the man who'd just given him a command like they were Special Forces in some military operation. "What did you just say?"

"I said," Kellogg said, stepping too close into Blaze's space, "call me from the rock, or I start bulldozing the forest."

The threat hung in the air between them, but Blaze kept hold of the game. "Kellogg, man," he said. "We're *here* to bulldoze the forest." Blaze shook his head as if puzzled. "You need sleep."

Blaze watched something in Kellogg's shoulders soften. From that, Blaze thought he'd won the hand.

Kellogg growled, "Call me with those coordinates by ten."

"Didn't you say GPSs don't work next to the rock?" Blaze asked.

"Move a little away from it and get a reading, then." He turned away from Blaze, closing the door between them.

"Sleep well," Blaze muttered at the closed door, which then flew open.

"One more thing," Kellogg said.

"What's that?"

"Bring me that unicorn and I'll make you half a million bucks richer."

"Kellogg," Blaze said, running his hand through his hair, "there was no unicorn. There was no fairy."

"I'll give you a quarter million for the fairy."

"And two million for the dragon?" Blaze shook his head in fatigue. "Good night, Kellogg."

"Good night," Kellogg said. "And take that GPS with you in the morning. I'll expect that call."

Without answering, Blaze turned and left. Breathing in a deep breath of the clean night air, he stepped toward his own cabin.

Vinca fluttered into Blaze's cabin, which was also unlocked. As Ivy caught up with her, Vinca was tapping the flagstones.

"Is there a hiding spot here too?" Ivy asked.

"Yep. Listen."

But Ivy didn't need to listen. This stone pulled up a whole lot easier than the last one. "Is it in there?" Ivy asked as Vinca dive-bombed the hole.

"Something is," Vinca said. "But it's too dark. I can't see what it is."

"Just a minute," Ivy grunted, setting the stone to the side. "This thing weighs a ton."

Both women gasped when they looked in the hole. "Jesus," Ivy said in a hushed whisper.

"I can't believe it," Vinca said, her little voice tinier than usual. "I just can't believe it."

Ivy squatted down to pick up the *Canticles*, its velveteen soft under her fingers. "Well, believe it, baby, because the book's here, and you yourself said this is Williams's cabin."

"It *is* Blaze's cabin," Vinca insisted. "But he didn't put the book here, I swear it. I was with him the whole time."

Ivy stood, hypnotized by the texture of the *Canticles Al*

Farasakh beneath her fingers. "Maybe he cast some sort of spell on you while he hid it."

"Listen to me, unicorn," Vinca said. "You would've felt the pull from the Heart if someone had worked magic. You know you would've."

Ivy had to concede that was true. No one but she had worked magic around here in forever. "Okay."

"Kellogg Brownroot hid it here," Vinca insisted. "He—"

But just then a shadow fell through the living room. Someone was walking past the huge bay window.

Shit! Ivy said, slipping into mindspeak. *There's no back door.*

It's Blaze! Vinca said. *Ask him about the book!*

But Ivy wasn't doing anything of the sort. The man was a virgin, a danger with whom she could not afford to tangle. *Shhh*, she commanded the fairy, who lit obediently on Ivy's shoulder as Ivy sank into the dark corner.

I am so screwed, Ivy said as the front door swung open. She clutched the *Canticles* tightly against her chest. The second Blaze turned on the lights, he'd see her. And she couldn't even turn into equine form and barrel her way past him. His smell would lasso her more surely than Wonder Woman's magic rope. *Damn.*

And then the door was opening.

Don't panic, Vinca whispered in her ear. *I can distract him.*

And before Ivy could stop her, the fairy was fluttering madly toward Blaze with tiny shrieks of laughter. "Blaze!" Ivy heard the fairy shout. "I've missed you. And look, I've got my wings back! Aren't they great?"

As Blaze batted at the fairy like a bug, Ivy stifled a laugh. "I don't know how they look," Blaze said in his husky voice. "Where's the light switch in this place?"

Damn, Ivy thought.

"No lightbulbs," Vinca said, fluttering right in Blaze's face. "My wings are supposed to be admired in moonlight."

"Moonlight?" Blaze asked. "What about daylight? Why don't you show me in the morning? I'm exhausted."

"Too exhausted to admire my wings?" Vinca asked, pouting, a sound with which Ivy was all too familiar. "But they're so beautiful." Vinca clucked dismissively. "A man like you can't be too exhausted for anything. You look like you could do it at least eight times a—"

"Okay!" Blaze chuckled, sending an unfamiliar warmth through Ivy's chest. "Let's see your wings in the moonlight."

Vinca led Blaze away from the cabin and into the woods, and Ivy breathed a sigh of relief. Even in human form, having a virgin this close to her was too . . . disturbing.

Using her animal agility, she padded out the door as quietly as a lynx. But as she headed into her woods, she heard Vinca say to Blaze, "Did I mention your dad once used that *Canticles Al Farasakh* to turn me into a full-size woman?"

Blaze muttered some reply Ivy was too shocked to catch. *That Vinca.*

But the fairy wasn't finished with Blaze. "You work that same magic, handsome, and we'd have a lot of fun!"

The adrenaline rush of jealousy that laced through Ivy's veins shocked her. Why should she care at all if Blaze romped with Vinca? *Because you want him for your own,* she thought.

But she knew that wasn't true. Her desire for him came from his spring-moon fragrance, and the Heart of the World's affinity for root chakras didn't help. That was all it was. Lust.

Clutching the *Canticles Al Farasakh*, Ivy hardened her heart and headed into the fading darkness toward her cabin. She needed to get home and regroup. Maybe she'd convene a unicorn council to discuss the merits. Surely her mother, now in Giza, would know more about Blaze's family.

Still, Ivy didn't run; she walked deliberately to her car. She'd drive to Erie and hide herself away from Williams's scent.

If she didn't stop the road, the Heart would fail, taking her and all magic creatures with it. It'd be a slower and more painful dehorning than Tchili had suffered. Ivy would lose all her powers, all her abilities. And every magic creature within her forest would endure the same wretched fate.

Not acceptable.

As she stepped over a fallen log, she made a mental list. First, a unicorn council. After that, she'd call the governor's house and write an op-ed, maybe for *The New York Times*. She could follow up on whatever the *USA Today* reporter came up with and—

And she spied her cabin, neat and safe on its hilltop. The sight of safety so close within her reach left her breathless for a moment. Her hybrid car, the perfect symbol of freedom from this mess, sat in the drive.

But she stopped in her tracks, aware of her sweating palms soaking the ancient velveteen. If someone were hunting her, this would be the perfect place to lay in wait. She shouldn't use her own car. She should turn around and go to town, borrow one from any of her friends.

But her own car was mere steps away from her. Her human friends' cars were in town.

She stopped and sniffed, searching for anything out of the ordinary. But the air held only the fragrant scent of hemlocks and summer. The earliest birds were beginning their dawn songs. Scanning the trees, she sniffed again. Nothing.

Reassured, she pointed the blue pad on her key chain at the hybrid and pushed the OPEN TRUNK button. Across the field she heard the trunk click its release mechanism.

Nothing happened. No one busted out of the tree. No one filled the field with floodlights. *Of course, you've just told everyone who's watching that you've arrived,* the cynical part of her mind said.

Batting aside the paranoia, Ivy padded toward the car as quietly as a fox. Reaching the trunk, she slid in the *Canticles Al*

Farasakh. Just putting the book in the trunk made her feel safer. The Heart of the World would be safer with the spells safely out of the hands of the Mutilator. She shut the trunk as quietly as she could.

Feeling more confident, Ivy opened the driver's door—and froze. His fragrance wafted over her like a cool breeze. She was enveloped in the scent. His scent.

Williams took advantage of her shock. He whipped the back door open and leaped out of the car toward her.

"Stop it!" Vinca cried at him. "Just talk to her!"

But even as Ivy stepped away from the danger, his hand clamped her shoulder with an iron grip, and he jerked her toward him.

"Ivy, listen," Vinca cried. "You need to stop Kellogg Brownroot, not fight Blaze!"

But Ivy's breast pressed against Williams's chest, sending a lightning shock of desire coursing through her blood. Her nipples hardened as a finger of desire wrapped around her belly, and lower.

"Ivy—" Blaze began, but she'd regained her senses. Quick as a snake, she kneed his groin and simultaneously sent a warrior's fist into his kidneys.

Groaning in pain, he released her and sank to the ground. "You don't understand," he said, but she wasn't listening.

Ivy opened her driver's door and leaped in. She hit the LOCK button as she slammed the door closed, thankful it blocked out most of his smell. Where were her keys? Frantically she looked on the floor and then felt under her ass. Was she sitting on them?

"Ivy!" he shouted. "Calm down." His hand appeared in her window. The purple crystal on her key chain winked in the dawn's light. He had her keys. "You can't go anywhere."

Ivy looked wildly around her. Could she barricade herself in her cabin? She doubted she could outrun him in the light of day, but she could call for help. She opened her glove box and reached for her cell phone, but it wasn't there. Damn. He had that, too.

Williams hit the UNLOCK button on her keypad, but she hit the LOCK button before he could open the door. Obviously frustrated, he growled, and then his fist slammed through the driver's window, peppering her with tiny shards of glass.

"We have to talk," he said, his voice nearly a growl. "We're on the same side, and I need your help now."

"It's true, Ivy," Vinca cried, her hands fluttering as madly as her wings. "Oh, Blaze," she said. "You shouldn't have smashed her window."

Ivy agreed with the little flying Judas about the window but about nothing else. She lurched for the passenger door, but the cup holder slowed her, and Williams grabbed her shoulder through the hole where the window used to be. He was singing something under his breath, and Ivy could barely hear it, but it didn't sound like English.

She held her breath, not wanting to inhale his enchanting perfume as she tried to yank his hand off her. The steering wheel had never seemed so big, and a man's hand had never seemed so menacing.

But a familiar tingling sensation flooded her thighs and breasts—power from the Heart. The sensation momentarily filled her with fear—she wasn't drawing the Heart's power herself: someone was pouring it into her.

Against her will, she began to change into equine form. In the car.

Suddenly Ivy understood what she was hearing, what Williams was singing in that strange subvocal language. The reality hit her: Blaze Williams really was a magic user, a wizard, no less. That subvocal singing was a spell.

His words coalesced magic around them and forced her transmutation. Once in horse form, she'd be his slave.

"No!" she shouted, but her human mouth morphed into unicorn, and she could no longer scream recognizable words.

"Blaze!" Vinca shouted at him, fluttering around his face as though her proximity might talk some sense into him. "What're you doing to her? What's happening?"

Ivy knew, but she couldn't speak. She fought the change with all her might, trying to draw strength and more strength from the Heart of the World. Her call was blocked by his incredible strength.

"Blaze!" Vinca cried again. "Blaze!"

"Stop it," he said, trying to shoo her away. "It looks worse than it is."

"*You* stop it!" the fairy cried. "This isn't right! I believed you! I thought you were a good guy!"

Blaze ignored the fairy and turned toward Ivy. "Don't fight it. Just change form and then we'll talk."

Ivy had no choice—she did not want to be in equine form in the presence of a virgin. Look what had happened to Tchili.

But his magic was stronger, unbelievably strong. Inexorably she took on her unicorn form, hooves cramming against the car's firewall and dashboard.

"Just relax," Williams said, touching her with his hand. The heat of his palm burned her changing flesh.

And she knew her flesh was changing because his voice actually soothed her. She was becoming his creature, tied to him with links of magic and chemistry much stronger than links of steel.

"Oh, Ivy!" Vinca said, flying toward her. "I'm so sorry! I had no idea he'd do this to you!"

But Ivy couldn't debate the merits of her friend's choice to deliver her to Williams. One of her unicorn legs was tangled in the steering wheel, and she had to concentrate on extricating herself. She jerked her hooves tightly against her chest and rolled out of the car, clumsy as a hedgehog in winter.

"Change her back," Vinca demanded, slapping Williams's nose with her tiny hands.

But he ignored the fairy, waiting for Ivy while armed with the tools of his trade. The rope he held was electric blue, and it crackled with magic energy.

What's that rope? Vinca frantically asked Ivy in mindspeak.

It doesn't matter, Ivy said. *I'm doomed.*

But what is it?

Williams easily looped the slipknot over her horn as she regained her footing, and she knew he'd captured her well and good. Ivy was at the mercy of the unicorn hunter.

It prevents shape-shifters from shifting. I can't turn back into girl form while the rope's around my horn. Ivy hung her head.

Vinca zoomed in toward Ivy's horn and began frantically tugging at the rope with her miniscule hands.

"I know you won't believe me—not yet, at any rate," Williams said, turning his back to Ivy and walking her like a dog. He seemed unconcerned about Vinca's efforts to free her. "But I'm sorry for this."

Ivy wasn't sorry as she inhaled his delicious fragrance and rolled it over her tongue. She wasn't sorry at all.

"We have to be at the Heart of the World before ten this morning," he said. "Otherwise I would've asked you to accompany me using more traditional methods."

"Like a phone!" Vinca said.

"Yes."

The way his ass filled his faded Levi's would have caught the eye of a normal woman, but a normal woman would've stopped herself from grabbing it. Ivy could not.

She closed the distance between them and rubbed her horn on his thigh, then his hip. The nerves in her horn luxuriated in the play of his muscle beneath his skin. She wanted to bury her nose in his chest, feel the slide of velvet skin against velvet, but he pushed her away.

"Please," he said, leading her toward the dawn-lit path. "Don't touch me."

And his words made her heart ache because she craved him like winter craves snow.

He must have sensed her disappointment because he said, "I don't want a slave or a minion."

But I have no choice, she cried toward him, not knowing if he had the ability to use mindspeak. *You're a virgin and I'm a unicorn. It's my nature to be your slave.*

And the rope on her horn keeps her that way, Vinca added. *Get it off her.*

Ah, but you're wrong, Ivy, he said in her mind with perfect clarity. *And Vinca, quit trying to free her. She can free herself at anytime.*

What do you mean? Ivy and Vinca asked at the same time.

The rope doesn't keep you from changing shapes, Blaze said to Ivy. *That's not its function at all.*

But I can't change shape—I keep trying, and I can't.

Your mind and your heart are conflicted about me, and the rope lets your heart win the battle.

What're you talking about? Ivy asked.

I don't have time to explain, he said. *But if your heart and brain both agreed I was unworthy, you'd have been able to change into human form and run away.*

She wouldn't run away, Vinca said indignantly.

Then she would've been able to skewer me with that vicious horn of hers like a shish kebab, and you could've eaten me for dinner.

Vinca paused a moment and then said, *Yummy.*

Ivy snorted in frustration. Her intellect knew: with the right spell, Williams could eradicate the few remaining magical creatures—the unicorns and dragons, the wood sprites and fairies. The magic exuded by the Heart of the World could be all his. And with his knowledge of magic, he could rule the world.

But her heart . . . it kept hearing the song of the tigereye soul.

I still can't change form, Ivy said after trying one more time to shift into girl form.

Once you figure out if your heart or your mind is right, all the Heart's power will be accessible, Blaze said, leading them deeper into the woods.

But even knowing he might hurt her—just as Tchili had been hurt—Ivy couldn't save herself. She couldn't jerk the rope from his hands and run. She couldn't turn her horn to his heart and slay him.

The rising sun bathed him in a pink glow that dappled his dark hair, and she wanted to run her human hands through it, drink in the silky weight of it. She wanted to bury her face in his chest and luxuriate in his scent, in his strength.

Oblivious to her, he glanced at his watch. "Damn," he said in his physical voice. "We're running out of time, and I find I need to apologize again."

With those words he leaped on her back, keeping a firm hold on the electric-blue rope. His thighs gripped her sides, and he leaned forward, urging her to a gallop with his weight and his calves.

"Run," he whispered in her ears. "Like your life depends on it. Run to the Heart of the World!"

7

Ivy couldn't have bucked Williams from her back even if she'd wanted to. Twisting and snorting, she'd thrown a Canada lynx once that didn't cling as tenaciously as this man. Williams held only the enchanted tether to her horn, but his balance above her withers was perfect, even at her breakneck gallop.

But his skill didn't matter. Her heart would overrule her head, at least for the moment, and do his bidding. She cantered through the hemlocks and oaks, bypassing trees with low-hanging branches so her warrior virgin didn't knock his head. She galloped past the tractors and the tree choppers.

You're carrying the enemy right to the source of all magic, unicorn, Vinca cried in her mind, purposefully excluding Blaze from the conversation. *Stop yourself.*

But you were all "Blaze this" and "Blaze that" a minute ago, Vinca, Ivy said back to her. *What's up with that?*

He made you change, Vinca said indignantly. *Against your will.*

Ivy had no reply to that. He *had* forced a change. He might be the Mutilator. . . .

But then again, she might have surfed the threads of his dream song. He might be the tigereye soul.

Then Vinca added, *Although...*

The ground shook under Ivy's hooves as she ran through the morning-soaked forest. *Although what?* she asked the fairy.

Although, Vinca said with relish, *the first time Zachariah changed me to human size, he didn't ask permission first.* She giggled. *And I don't remember being particularly upset about it.*

Knowing the Heart by feel alone, Ivy slid to a stop just shy of a huge boulder. Thick, grassy moss covered its craggy sides. Great power reverberated through her feet and horn, and the small hairs in her mane stood on end.

This close to the Heart, huge spells could be cast. The power exuded by the Heart begged to be used, practically pouring itself into the palms of any magic user. In the right hands, enchantments as big as the sky could echo around the earth.

But Ivy wasn't afraid. As the Guardian, her main job was to protect this phenomenon, and she knew: normal people would walk right past the massive outcrop without a second thought.

"This is it," Williams said. Wonder laced his voice. "The source of all magic."

Sounds like you don't remember your roots, wizard. Vinca taunted him using her mindvoice. Because mindspeech was the only form of dialogue open to Ivy while in equine form, she appreciated Vinca's support.

"It's just that..." Williams paused. Ivy thought he was probably searching for the right words. *I've been drawing magic from this place for almost a decade, but I've never really seen it, not as a wizard. I saw it only in my memory.*

She appreciated his accommodation of her form. *We used to come here a lot,* she said.

We did, Blaze agreed slowly. *But I had no idea this place was so magical then. Did you?*

Not with my mind, Ivy answered. *But my heart felt right*

when we were here. Sitting in that moss, the world felt rich with potential.

Like anything was possible. Remember when we used to play pirates? We could always smell the sea.

And sometimes we could even see it.

Remember the time the cannon shot actual sparks when we blew up the English ship? Blaze asked, pointing at a huge dead tree that had doubled as the enemy. Amazement filled his voice.

Yeah, Ivy said, laughing. *It wasn't sparks—it was an entire cannonball. And my mother told us it was our imagination.*

I thought we'd lost our minds.

But she must have known the truth, Ivy said, thinking about her mother so far away these days that even mindspeech was difficult.

Of course she did. She must have known.

I wonder if the sharks we saw could've eaten us.

I'm glad the bad guys always had terrible aim, Blaze said.

Ivy, look! Vinca whispered in her mind alone. *The rope looks like it's changing. Maybe your heart is winning over your head!*

Sure enough, the blue rope was flickering like a fluorescent light. If she could bring herself to trust Blaze Williams just a touch more, she could run for it.

But his spring-moon scent curled around her nose, binding her heart to him with ties stronger than steel.

Irritation shot through her like one of those imaginary cannonballs. Ivy hadn't chosen these bonds for herself. She was a unicorn, and he was a virgin. That fact alone linked them, and every unicorn knew the dangers of virginity.

Forget the Heart and Tchili and her horn—Ivy wished Williams would ride her to the ends of the earth, across vast deserts and into the crashing waves of the sea. The unhealthy strength of that desire made Ivy resist with all her might.

Damn, Ivy, stop it. Vinca said. *Look at the rope now.*

Ivy looked. The rope had solidified to the point where it no longer glowed. It looked as solid as any horse's lead rope.

Williams didn't seem to notice as he slid from her back. Keeping the spell-cast rope in hand, he walked in front of her, pulling a cell phone from his pocket. Already she missed the heat of his body on hers, pathetic creature that she was.

Seeing him start to make a call, a tendril of relief wrapped around Ivy's heart. Williams had forgotten his roots, had forgotten something obvious. Electronics wouldn't work this close to the source of all magic. He wouldn't be able to call whoever he was calling.

"Damn," Williams said, looking at the readout. "I forgot about the reception."

He stood very still and began singing another spell in the subvocal language. The lacy fingers of fear caressed Ivy's heart. What was he doing now? She wished she could stop him or control him—or even understand him.

She looked at the rope, willing it to be gone. She couldn't give him free rein over her fate, over the fate of her world and the creatures in her care.

But the rope remained as solid as the ground beneath her feet.

Williams's singing stopped, and an iridescent bubble appeared, golden green in the early morning sunlight. The surface of the bubble caught the reflection of the leaves and boughs above, and it reflected them back in greens. White diamonds sparkled off the topmost curve. The bubble was a thing of beauty.

Until Ivy felt its core.

What's he doing, Ivy? Vinca asked. *What is that thing?*

Where the sphere existed, emptiness reverberated. But it wasn't the lack of sound or air. Birdsong filled the early morning, unbothered by this strange magic. A fat, green beetle flew within the sphere.

But another silence filled the bubble's inner area—the silence of the mundane, the absence of magic.

Trepidation coiled in Ivy's belly. She realized exactly what Williams had done. The Heart's sexual power throbbed outside the bubble's skin, but inside no magic existed at all.

That bubble blocks out all enchantments, Ivy said to Vinca. *It's not possible for any magic to exist within it.*

I've never heard of such a spell.

Neither have I, Ivy said, standing as still as the rock by her side. But no matter how she examined the situation, the reality of it was obvious. *It's true nonetheless.*

Blaze called that bubble into existence as easily as you healed my wings, the fairy noted. *He's going to be more powerful than his father, just you see. Maybe he already is.*

Ivy agreed silently. *But is that a good thing or not?*

Williams didn't give her time to wonder. Careful to keep his enchanted rope away from the effervescent sphere, he dipped his cell into the bubble and dialed.

"Brownroot here," Ivy heard as clearly as if the oil magnate stood next to her.

"I found it," Blaze replied. "I'm here now."

"Fast work. Where do I find you?"

"Not too far."

"Can you get coordinate readings?"

"Yeah," Williams said. "Hang on." Holding his phone awkwardly, he pulled a device from his belt and stuck it in the bubble. Ivy understood he didn't want to release the rope; he didn't want to let her go. After a moment, the device beeped.

"You got it?" Brownroot's baritone said over the phone.

"Yeah. Feed these northings and eastings into your GPS," Williams directed.

"Hang on." Brownroot paused a moment and then said, "Ready."

Williams started to read off a long string of numbers while Ivy's heart raced. A slave to her biology, she embraced whatever her virgin warrior desired, but Kellogg Brownroot was a different matter altogether—especially if Williams's accusations were right and Brownroot was the Mutilator.

To have Brownroot near the Heart of the World while being held captive . . . She tossed her head and snorted in dismay. Williams's hand jerked as she shook her head, making him lose his place among the long list of numbers he was reading.

"Stop," Williams commanded her, breaking away from the phone. He readjusted the rope. "Sorry," he said to Brownroot. "I have to start over." Then he began to repeat the first number over the phone.

Ivy stilled her head. Obedience was her only choice, but frustration still squirmed inside her. Aggravation sank to her hooved feet, and she began to prance in place, dancing like a Lipizzaner. The rope holding her captive to Williams began to oscillate through the space between them.

And Ivy saw a door open for her, one that freed her physically—and mentally. She wouldn't need to let her heart override her mind to earn her escape.

She increased the speed of her piaffe until she trotted in place with the elegance of an Olympic dressage horse. Her center of gravity shifted toward her hind end, and her hindquarters lowered with the deep bending of her hocks as she lifted her knees almost to her chin—gaze locked on the blue rope.

What are you doing? Vinca said for Ivy's mind only while Williams rattled off numbers into the phone. *Trying out for the circus?*

Shhh! Ivy said. *Or help me.*

The rope's oscillations increased, slithering closer and closer to the glittering green sphere. It wasn't quite touching the bubble despite Ivy's antics.

Oh! Vinca said. *I get it.*

Vinca flew toward the bubble with all the care of a person trying to catch a rattlesnake, and as the rope slithered in the air, she pushed it toward the bubble, careful not to touch the sphere herself.

And the spelled rope dipped into the large bubble. Ivy froze, though her heart raced.

Keep up that crazy trotting! Vinca said. *You want him to notice?*

Ivy resumed her piaffe, and like the changing colors of a summer sunset, a subtle variation slithered through the lead rope. The electric pressure within her horn evaporated, and Ivy understood—the magic sphere had released the rope's spell on her.

She could change to human form without deciding between her heart and her mind.

But did she want to unbind herself from him?

"Yeah," Williams said into the phone, his voice deep and melodic. "I'll stay until you get here. Should take you five minutes max."

Realizing the telephone held his whole attention, Ivy dared to breathe. Which might have been a mistake because just like the last full moon of spring calls to night birds and frogs, his fragrance called to her. She couldn't leave him.

You hear him yet? Williams said to her, snapping the phone shut. *He's on a motorbike.*

She pricked her ears forward and listened. The faraway whine of a dirtbike buzzed, and she pawed the earth in disturbed assent. *He's coming,* she said in mindspeak.

This business with Brownroot'll be done in a minute, he said, making the sphere vanish with a hum. But whether he was soothing himself or her, she couldn't tell. And it didn't really matter.

What're you doing here? Ivy heard Vinca ask him. *If he's killing unicorns and stealing magic books, why are you—*

But the acrid smell of unburned gasoline and the whine of a two-stroke engine filled the air. Williams had no time to answer.

Go hide in the trees, fairy, Ivy said. *We don't need him to see you.*

I'm not going far, unicorn. Vinca slipped away, but Ivy could sense her nearby. As Brownroot rolled right to them with an easy grace, the dirtbike straddled between his thighs, Ivy was glad the fairy wasn't here. This man exuded sexual danger—not something easy to resist.

"Good," Williams said to him as he cut the engine. "You found it."

"The coordinates worked perfectly."

"Yes," Williams said. "I knew they would." He waved a hand toward Ivy and said, "I found the other thing you were looking for too."

Brownroot's eyes widened when he spied the animal in Williams's possession, and then cool satisfaction settled in his icy blue gaze. Ivy had seen more emotion in a snake. "Two for one," Brownroot said, indicating the captured mare.

"Thought that'd make you happy."

Brownroot grinned. "Very." He swung a rucksack from his back and took something from it. "And the paycheck'll make you happy too."

"Mmmm-hmmm," Williams said. Ivy thought the noncommittal sound could have been mistaken for agreement.

"Half a million dollars' worth of happy," Kellogg said. "You bring me the fairy, or wasn't a quarter million additional bucks enough incentive?"

Is Blaze really selling us out for cash? Vinca asked in Ivy's head, but Ivy didn't know. She didn't know at all.

"There're no fairies," Williams said.

"Fuck, no," Kellogg snorted. "And no unicorns either. You sonofabitch, you thought I was crazy, didn't you?" Brownroot asked.

I still might, Ivy heard Williams say for her mind only. The words for Brownroot's ears were, "Turns out you were right about the unicorn."

"A unicorn in this forest," Brownroot said as though at least a little surprised. "Well, I said I saw one, and I did—I saw *this* one." He waved a hand at Ivy.

For some reason he didn't think he'd find a unicorn in this forest, Williams said in her mind. *But he's been capturing and mutilating unicorns in other places.*

Maybe he's bipolar or psycho, Vinca added.

Has he been doing the mutilating alone? Ivy asked. *Or was it both of you together, virgin?*

He's been doing it, Williams said, annoyance heavy in his tone. *Ivy, I heard it from my father.*

But your father's dead!

"Williams," Ivy heard Brownroot say. "Williams!"

"What?"

"Are you going to stare at that damned animal all morning, or are you going to help me?"

"What do you want me to do?"

"Earn your money, of course."

"I brought you the unicorn and verified the rock," Williams said. "What else do you want?"

"First things first," Brownroot said, nodding at the Heart standing maybe one hundred feet behind them. "Let's blow this rock straight to hell where it belongs." He paused and looked at Williams. "You sure this is it, man? Doesn't look like anything special."

"It's the Heart of the World."

"The source of all magic?"

"I don't know," Williams said, shaking his head. Ivy knew he was lying. "But it matches your description."

What are you doing, Williams? Ivy shouted in his mind. *You can't—*

You have to help me, Ivy, Williams said. *And Vinca, too.*

"Well, let's blow it up," Brownroot said, grabbing Williams's arm. "If we're wrong, we can always blow up another one."

We have to help you blow up the Heart? Ivy asked him. *You know we can't.*

If her equine eyes could weep, Ivy knew she'd cry. Did she need to slay Williams? Should she skewer him just to be safe? She'd kebab Brownroot if she thought she could get away with it.

Williams brushed Brownroot's hand off his arm and stepped away from him. "It's the right boulder."

"Well, if it's not," Brownroot said, connecting wires to the red candlesticks, "I won't pay you."

Williams made a noncommittal sound, and Ivy realized the scarlet sticks weren't candles—they were sticks of dynamite.

Trust me, Ivy, Blaze said. *Like you used to.*

Before you left her without so much as a good-bye? Vinca said.

"Let's get rid of the rock first," Brownroot said. He used electrical pliers to strip the wire tips. "Then getting the horn off the horse'll be a lot easier. She won't have any magic to save herself."

No! Ivy shouted as dread roiled through her.

"Her horn?" Williams asked as easily as if he were commenting on the weather. "What do you want that for?"

"Just like the legends say, my man." Kellogg paused from his task to look at Blaze. "Unicorn horns purify toxins out of liquids when used as drinking cups."

"Someone trying to poison you, Brownroot? Maybe with polonium?"

"I'm poisoning myself and everybody else." Brownroot laughed. "The whole goddamned world." He clipped the wires to a large, rectangular battery and said, "My coal plants in Indiana make buckets of money while dumping shitloads of mercury into the air. The winds carry it to New York and the ocean—and it's making me incredibly rich."

"Nice," Williams said.

"By the time my kids have kids, everything'll be toxic. Every fish, every crab. Everything that eats a fish or a crab. Every pure mountain stream will be dirty."

"Real nice."

"Not for most people," Brownroot said. "Not for the drones."

"But for you . . ." Williams prompted.

"The weak will die, and the strong will thrive. As the strongest of the strong, I'm helping the process along."

He's Like Dr. Seuss on crack, Vinca said.

"So who's getting the horn?" Williams asked.

Who's getting all the horns? Ivy corrected.

"Thanks to me, my grandkids'll be rich as the Federal Reserve, and they'll be untainted—thanks to your fair, hooved beauty. Her skin will let my grandkids survive the toxic air. Her horn will let them eat or drink whatever they want. Nobody'll be able to challenge them in the new world I'll create. My genes will be around for millennia."

Williams paused for a moment, as if assessing Brownroot's plan. "You worried the EPA'll stop you?"

"They haven't yet, and I doubt they'll try. No teeth. Congress yanked them out long ago." Brownroot tossed the plastic refuse from the wire into the forest and added, "The only thing stopping me was this Heart."

"The Heart?" Williams said. "I don't understand."

But Ivy did.

"The damned animals that thrive on its magic hide shit from me," Kellogg said, pausing a minute to wipe the sweat from his brow. "They keep hiding the great coal and gold and titanium deposits. I know there's a huge oil deposit in my Yucatán property—I can smell it. But can I find it? No."

"How unfortunate for you," Williams said. "It must really limit you."

"Well, that property isn't guarded anymore," he said with a cold grin. And Ivy knew he referred to Tchili's mutilation.

Which meant . . . which meant Blaze Williams really wasn't the Mutilator. "I'll find the reserves soon enough."

"What a relief."

"Yes," Kellogg said, apparently missing the sarcasm Ivy thought she heard. "And that's not all. Those damned mutants keep cleaning up the toxins." Brownroot shook his head.

"And that's a problem because . . . ?" Blaze asked.

"If the world gets trashed and my offspring have the monopoly on survival tools—like unicorn horns and skins—they're guaranteed to outcompete everyone else," Brownroot said. "But if the world doesn't get trashed, well, no monopoly. What's the point of that?"

To Ivy, the point of this tirade was clear. Kellogg Brownroot was trashing the world, and Blaze Williams was trying to save it. If she hadn't broken the rope's spell in the bubble, she knew that with this information, her heart and her head could agree. Blaze was one of the good guys.

"Mmmm-hmm," Blaze said, making that noncommittal sound again.

"But . . ." Brownroot let the word trail while he carefully set the battery on the ground. He pulled a bottle of water from his rucksack and took a long pull from it. There was something frightenly attractive about this man's competence, the way he drank. He was cool as a summer lake. "This'll be the end of those damned creatures."

"Yep," Blaze agreed. "Blowing up the Heart's the first step toward making your wish come true."

With a battery-powered drill in hand, Kellogg approached the rock exuding the sexual energy of a bull. He pulled the trigger, and the drill spun. He held it near his crotch and smiled. Flashing Ivy a glance loaded with rapacious intent, he said, "You looked great in the filmy T-shirt, unicorn. Especially with your arms chained behind your back. Great tits. Too bad about the horn. We could've had some fun together."

Blaze ignored Kellogg's comment. "You planning on drilling this rock?"

"I am," Kellogg said. "We've got to bury the dynamite in it to blow it up right."

"Won't work. Not unless you brought a hand drill."

"Why not?"

"Like I explained earlier," Blaze said, "electronics won't work this close to the magic source."

With an expression of disbelief, Kellogg walked purposefully toward the Heart with the drill spinning.

"Kellogg," Blaze said in exasperation, "you said yourself one of the ways you knew about the Heart was that cell phones wouldn't work around it."

"Exactly," Kellogg said. "And now we test."

Sure enough, as he approached the Heart of the World, the drill bit slowed its spinning. By the time he stood next to the Heart of the World, the drill fell silent.

"Guess it's the right boulder," Blaze said.

What are you doing, Blaze? Ivy said.

Get ready to help, Blaze said to Ivy. *I need you.*

Ivy took a deep breath. With her own ears she had heard Kellogg admit to taking Tchili's horn, which meant she could trust Blaze. Didn't it? Could she trust him enough for this?

"Well, goddamn," Kellogg said, wiping his forehead. "I can hardly believe it."

"Believe it," Blaze said with a chuckle. "You're forking over a large chunk of money tonight, Brownroot."

"Money well spent. But what am I supposed to do? Shove the dynamite under the boulder?"

Shove the dynamite under your ass, Vinca said.

"That might work," Blaze said to Brownroot.

But Ivy couldn't let Blaze follow through with this plan. She'd seen enough to convince her that the Heart of the World was in serious jeopardy.

I've got to do something now, Ivy said in Vinca's mind. *Any ideas would be welcomed.*

See what Blaze is up to, unicorn. Trust him.

Brownroot had four fat sticks wrapped tightly together. Before Blaze could help him drill the holes with his antimagic bubble spell, Brownroot shoved the dynamite into a cranny beneath the Heart; then he started walking away, the red wire uncoiling behind him.

Vinca, Ivy asked, *you don't really think I should let them put primed dynamite right next to the Heart, do you?*

"Better come with me if you don't want to get blown to shit," Brownroot said. "And bring that unicorn too. Don't want to ruin her pelt."

"No, we don't." Blaze led her after Brownroot. Apparently he still hadn't noticed the change in the lead rope.

Uh, Vinca answered Ivy. *It's really hard to see how that's a good idea, but Blaze . . . he's a good guy.*

As they approached Brownroot's dirtbike, Ivy knew she had to act now, this very second. If Blaze wanted to lop off her horn and use her skin to keep his children safe from nuclear fallout, her biology would sorely tempt her to accommodate him.

But allowing Brownroot to blow up the Heart wasn't in her biochemical contract. She was the Guardian of the Forest, and her job demanded her best. It was her duty to stop Brownroot by whatever means possible.

What those means were, she still didn't know. But one thing was certain: she couldn't think straight in unicorn form in the presence of a virgin. And if she couldn't think straight, she couldn't trust herself to act appropriately.

Ivy let the Heart's throbbing power pulse through her hooves to her own heart as she embraced her transformation. Her front legs melted into arms, and her hips changed to accommodate bipedalism. Then she stood, firmly, with two booted feet on the ground, her khaki-clad thighs quivering with fear and resolve.

The first breath of air she pulled into her human lungs flooded her system with relief. She wasn't the slave to Blaze Williams's scent she'd been just the heartbeat before this. She was free. Well, freer.

Blaze must have felt the Heart's thrum fluctuate as Ivy used its power. He looked back just as the rope slithered to the ground, useless.

No, Ivy! I need to— he started to say, but Brownroot interrupted him.

"What the Holy Mother?" Brownroot said, perhaps seeing the blond woman rather than the unicorn.

But Ivy didn't care. She didn't want to give either man a second to think. She raced toward Brownroot's dirtbike and leaped on it, slamming her foot down hard on the kick-start as her ass hit the seat.

Ivy! Keep Brownroot near the Heart. I've got a spell to send him to—

But Ivy wasn't listening, couldn't afford to. With the bike buzzing beneath her, she turned the throttle and gunned the thing down the hill.

Vinca shouted in her mind. *Get the red wire!*

Ivy spun the dirtbike around, slamming her foot to the ground for balance as the back tire slid away from her. Then she gunned it back up the hill, looking for the red coils.

To your left! Vinca shouted, and Ivy saw them, the red plastic bright against the dark vetch.

Driving like a rampaging dragon, Ivy leaned over the side of her bike as she sped toward the wire. If she could snag it and drive, she'd rip the wire from either the explosives or the battery. She could stop this.

"Ivy, no!" Blaze called as she leaned over to scoop the wire.

Guilt stabbed at her heart. Blaze wouldn't hurt the Heart of the World. Still, she couldn't go through with his plan. If Blaze were really the savior, together they could come up with a different plan.

A sudden vision swamped her mind—Blaze wielding a gem-studded sword against a massive dragon, evil glinting in its eye. The image was mad, nonsense, but it grabbed her heart, and she couldn't ignore it.

She couldn't ignore it, but she couldn't ignore the Heart of the World either.

Yielding to her head, she jerked the bike into the vetch and snagged the red wire.

Ivy! Blaze called. *We need to keep Brownroot here just another minute. We need to keep him next to the Heart.*

But she couldn't permit Brownroot to stick primed explosives into the Heart. She was its Guardian.

Looping the coils around her wrist, she drove madly away from the Heart. As she sped away, the wire pulled taut, and she shot a glance behind her.

Yes! Vinca shouted as the big, square battery skittered through the vetch, gave a mighty leap, and then fell dead to the ground. The red plastic coils whipped through the air behind the dirtbike. Ahead of her, the dynamite sticks popped useless to the ground next to the Heart of the World.

I did it! Ivy called back.

"Goddamn bitch!" Brownroot called as she flew past, chunks of dirt flying from beneath the back tire of the bike. "Blaze!" he shouted. "Get her."

But Ivy had a different plan. As she buzzed past her high school sweetheart, she used her animal strength to grab his shirt and pull him behind her.

He didn't resist. Instead, Blaze jumped on the bike behind her and grabbed her shoulders. Ivy gunned the bike down the hill, away from the Heart and away from Brownroot.

"Williams!" Brownroot shouted as they drove away. "What the hell are you doing?"

As Blaze buried his face in her hair and snaked his arms around her stomach, Ivy wondered exactly the same thing.

8

The heat of Blaze's body flooded Ivy's veins, and she drove the bike toward a hunter's cabin deep in the woods, revving the engine too high in her distress.

"Where're we going?" Blaze shouted over the whine of the bike.

"Just hang on!" she yelled back. The deep sound of his voice distracted her, and she hit a jagged root. The bike bounced, shoving Blaze snug against her. She might have been resistant to his fragrance in human form, but she wasn't immune to the press of his cock against her ass.

She almost hit a tree.

"Watch what you're doing, cowgirl."

Annoyed with herself, she shook her head, but the vibration of the bike between her thighs did little to help her focus.

You're having some fun, unicorn! Vinca said with glee.

Shut up, Ivy tried to snarl, but the fairy's laughter was contagious. She ended up laughing too, glad the fairy wasn't sharing this information with Blaze.

Finally the abandoned cabin came into view, and something inside Ivy gave. She recognized it as relief.

Kellogg Brownroot won't be able to find this place, Vinca said. *At least, not easily.*

Or quickly, Ivy agreed.

Stopping the bike in front of the shack, Ivy killed the motor. The man in question slid off the bike slowly as though reluctant to break his contact with her. Without a word, he stepped back and looked at her.

And for the first time in over a decade, Ivy really looked at him. It was worth the wait; Blaze looked great. His jeans fit snug over his thighs, highlighting their strength, and his waist seemed just as athletic as the last time she had run her hands over it. A memory crashed over her—a memory of the planes of his chest under her fingertips, the dreamy look in his eye.

And the heat of his lips as they caressed yours, Vinca added. *Don't forget that.*

Fairy, go away, Ivy said, too confused to feel either anger or mirth clearly. *Go find Seal or something. Get out of my mind.*

"Ivy," Blaze said. "Share the joke?"

"No joke," she said, staring at her feet to avoid the heat of his gaze. "There's only an annoying fairy."

"Then look at me."

She did.

Time had polished him. He didn't look like the untried youth of her memory. He looked like a man about to do battle, a warrior. The fan of lines around his eyes, the slight hook to his nose, the strength of his jaw . . . Blaze Williams seemed ready for any trial life would lay before him.

"Who are you?" she asked as his beguiling scent floated to her consciousness.

"You know who I am."

She blinked. Did she?

"Come on, Ivy. You know the truth—you've always known the truth."

"The truth," she said. "Truth can be a slippery thing."

"Look at me, Ivy," Blaze said again.

Marshalling her courage, Ivy met his gaze—and caught her breath at what she saw.

"Your eyes," she said. She remembered green eyes, eyes the color of moss and ferns and deep summer oak leaves. But that's not what she saw. Now his eyes were the exact shade of a tigereye stone, complete with honeyed swirls. "They've changed."

"They did," he agreed. "When I came into my power."

"But they're brown," she said. "They look like tigereye."

"Is that a problem?" he asked. Ivy thought he looked worried.

Looking into his eyes, the eternal song of her kind echoed through her mind, making her long to hear the deep bass of the male counterpart who'd accompanied her that night. The song had completed her. "It's not a problem," she said. It definitely wasn't.

"I'm told they match the color of my soul, but I don't know what my soul stone looks like."

"Who are you?" she asked again. What she really meant was: are you the singer?

Blaze ran his hand through his dark hair so a dark chunk of it obscured his eye. "Don't pretend you don't remember that night under the pier at Kinzua Dam," he said. "You knew me then. You knew my heart."

"People change," she said, stepping away from the danger she sensed here. "Maybe you did too. Like your eyes."

"Ivy."

That she'd just been remembering those nights only flamed her anger. He had no claim to her. He'd foregone it long ago—like his green eyes, apparently. Besides, the past wasn't the point.

"You're a wizard." Ivy got off the bike and kicked the stand down hard. A clump of dirt flew through the air and landed with a solid *plop*.

"Yeah," he said slowly. "Apparently it runs in my family. My dad, his dad, his dad before him."

"Then why're you a virgin? No one's a virgin at, what, thirty-two? The last I remember, you were well on your way to losing it."

He gave her a rakish grin, and she saw how long his eyelashes were. A band of moon gold edged his dark pupils. "Maybe your kisses spoiled me," he said in that rich voice of his.

Her unreasonable desire for him formed a thick fog in her mind, and she had to swallow because her mouth literally watered for him, for the salt of his sweat and the taste of his skin.

"Maybe I've been waiting," he added.

Until now was his implication.

Ivy struggled with her burning hunger as Blaze let the words sit heavily between them. She looked away. The thrall she'd experienced in equine form clung to her. One word from him, and she'd be his, regardless of her human form.

Then anger kicked through her, fierce and hot. "Don't play games with me." She stepped away from the bike and put her hands on her hips.

"Who's—"

"Damn you and your innuendo. Don't suggest I'm the right girl for you unless you're going to throw me on the bed in that cabin and make love to me until dawn. Finally."

He stared at her as though stunned.

"But you won't do it, will you?" She laughed, but it was a hard sound. "You can't make love to me or anyone else because then how would you catch a unicorn? Only a virgin can do that."

Blaze didn't answer her. He closed the distance between them with one long step, and he pulled her to his chest as though she was precious to him. "There's more than one way to catch a unicorn," he said, his voice husky with desire. Then he kissed her.

Only, it was unlike any kiss she'd had before.

This one scalded and delighted, and the shock of it made her freeze. Perhaps Blaze took this for acquiescence, which would have been right, because when he touched her mouth with his tongue, teasing and questing, she parted her lips. She pressed her hips against his.

He tasted as good as he smelled, as good as a warm spring rain that melts the last winter snow. And rational thought fled as he took her mouth, deep and slow, covering her, his warm hand gripping her thigh as he tasted her.

There was nothing tentative about him as he sucked the tip of her tongue, sliding, owning, dominating the kiss, leaving Ivy breathless.

"You've done this before," she said, pulling away from him.

"Yeah," he agreed. "With you. In that grassy patch at Kinzua," he breathed, his mouth centimeters from hers.

"On the shore."

"Mmmmhmmm." Cupping his hand behind her head, he pulled her to him, capturing her mouth again. At first their tongues clashed and tangled, and her knees quivered. Desire coiled through her belly and hissed to her fingertips, her nipples, her lips.

Then they found each other, and clumsiness fled. He slowed, deepening the kiss. His tongue slid slowly over hers. The velvety glide of tongue over tongue promised a deeper delight.

Her legs couldn't hold her, and she collapsed against him. She didn't want to stand. She wanted to lay, legs spread for him, thighs wrapped around his waist. Ivy felt his cock throb against her thigh, and she pressed against him.

"The door," she said. "Open it."

Blaze paused, making Ivy's heart skip a beat. He might do it.

124 / *Lucinda Betts*

He might bust down that door, toss her in the bed, and roll with her until both were satiated. Finally. She could inhale his scent and taste his skin. She could luxuriate in the play of his muscle under her fingertips. She could memorize the silky feel of his hair as it caressed her cheek.

"I can't," he said. "At least not until after I take care of Brownroot."

Ivy laughed, shaking her head. Maybe he hadn't caught Tchili. Or maybe this was all some elaborate ploy. But she couldn't trust this warrior virgin; around him, she couldn't think. She couldn't trust her own decisions. "So what might happen if you lose that precious commodity?" she asked. "The way I hear it, your dad saw plenty of action beneath the sheets."

"If I make passionate love to you, like every cell in your body is screaming for, my ability to work magic will diminish. That's exactly what I need to avoid."

Ivy had been about to say, "Like you'd ever get it," but his cell phone beeped, a precise metallic sound that had no place in her forest.

Blaze didn't look at the phone. Moving slightly away from her, he took it off his belt and tossed it far into the trees.

Ivy stepped back too. "You should answer it," she said. It beeped again from a copse of ferns.

He tried to pull her back to him, but she stopped him. "Your friend Brownroot wants your help." Her gaze was steady on him, challenging him.

"He's not my friend, he's my associate."

"You'd better talk to him anyway," she said. "You've got a road to build and a boulder to blow to bits."

Blaze shook his head. "It's not what you think."

"Oh, and you know what I think."

"You're in the wrong here, Ivy. Not me." The phone had stopped ringing, and the normal forest sounds had quieted as if waiting for a storm.

And she realized—the storm raged within her. Her inability to keep the Heart safe, her inability to stop the person who was mutilating unicorns . . . Her worries blew like a maelstrom through her mind. She'd been able to do nothing—until now.

Now the perpetrator stood right in front of her.

Potential perpetrator, Vinca said. *You heard Kellogg Brownroot.*

Be quiet, fairy. I asked you to leave me.

Her heart cold, Ivy said to Blaze, "You're a danger to everyone and everything I love."

"You've got it wrong, Ivy. Kellogg Brownroot is the guy behind this. He hurt the unicorn in Mexico, and he'll hurt as many others as he can."

"Her name is Tchili," she hissed.

"Okay." Blaze held up his hands in surrender. "But being pissed won't solve anything. If you hadn't interfered at the Heart, Brownroot'd be living in the second dimension, and his explosives would've gone with him."

"What are you talking about?"

"You'd be safe and so would the Heart."

Ivy squinted her eyes, her brain aching. "What the hell is the second dimension?"

"It's—"

But she interrupted herself, shaking her head. "You know what? I think this is more bullshit."

"Really?" With his arms crossed over his muscled chest and his dark eyes slanted, Ivy wanted to eat him up, despite his words, but she refused to yield to her desire.

"I saw you lure that jerk to the Heart of the World," she said. "And for what? Money? Don't give me this second-dimension crap."

"I brought him to the Heart because our power's strongest there. I needed all the power available."

"Including mine?" Ivy said. "You came to my cabin and

forced me into unicorn form and dragged me to the Heart. What were you planning on doing with me, wizard?"

"I was trying to keep you safe," Blaze said. "Kellogg Brownroot is mutilating unicorns."

She gave him that cold look but didn't interrupt.

"Think about it a minute." His voice was calm and deep, reminding her of a forest pond. The beauty of it attracted even the swan maiden.

"Think about what?" She could still taste the tang of his kiss, and the smell of her excitement hung in the air. "How you kidnapped me to watch you and Brownroot blow up the Heart? How you tried to make me an accomplice to the biggest crime against my kind?"

"If I ruined the Heart of the World," he said slowly, "I couldn't use any magic of my own, could I?"

"But you'd be rich as Croesus."

"Ivy."

"You are a virgin." She wouldn't be placated. "A virgin has been mutilating unicorns."

"I know," he said. "My father told me—I mean, the ghost of my father. And not the virgin part, just the horn and skin part."

His awkwardness disarmed her, and she took a step away from him, seeing for the first time that his power over her even in human form made him as dangerous—and seductive—as a snake.

"I didn't have anything to do with Tchili," he said.

"Part of me wants to believe you," she said slowly. "In fact, part of me does believe you."

"Then believe me."

"But only virgins can catch us." She put her hands on the dirtbike, ready to run, to save herself. "And virgins, especially males, aren't exactly a dime a dozen." She straddled the bike. "Kellogg Brownroot is not a virgin, and yet you conveniently are."

"You think I want to be? Jesus, you of all people should know that's not true. If it wasn't for the acorns . . ."

That comment slammed home the memory of his hands on her naked back, the cool, damp scent of Kinzua and Blaze's sweat. He hadn't planned on stopping that night. Nor had she.

"Why exactly did we stop that night?" she asked, a cold realization dawning over her.

"Acorns," he said. "It started raining acorns on us. All over our heads and backs and—"

"And we told my mother about the acorn rain," Ivy said. But they hadn't told her their clothes had been scattered over the shores of the lake.

Blaze laughed. "Your mom said it just happened sometimes."

"Which made no sense," Ivy agreed. "And she got that knowing grin and laughed like a hyena."

"We weren't anywhere near an oak tree."

Ivy looked at him, almost laughing now. "You ever see acorn rain before that?"

"No." He shook his head. "Haven't seen it since then either."

They met each other's gaze for a minute, and Ivy knew he was thinking the exact thing she was thinking. Fairies.

Vinca, Ivy said so Blaze could hear. *Where are you?*

Nothing but silence met them.

Vinca, Blaze said. *We know you're watching. You're always watching.*

Seal probably is too, Ivy added to Blaze. *Vinca!*

What is it? the fairy asked, her voice uncharacteristically chagrined.

You know something about acorn rain? Ivy asked.

The fairy said nothing. Ivy couldn't see her either. She must have been hiding.

Well, do you? Blaze asked.

Maybe. Vinca's voice was small, much smaller than usual. She fluttered over to Ivy and landed on her shoulder. Then she hid herself in the woman's thick blond hair.

Why'd you pelt us with acorns? Ivy asked.

I'm not throwing acorns, she said. *I'm just sitting here.*

Not now, Blaze growled. *Then. Years ago. You know when.*

Oh, Vinca said. *Then.*

Well, what was that about? Ivy asked. She knew the answer to this question was important, would tell her something she needed to know.

It wasn't just me throwing them! Vinca said. *Seal did it too.*

Seal, Blaze said, shaking his head. *He threw acorns at us?*

Where is that cretin? Ivy asked.

He's following Kellogg Brownroot, Vinca said. *Watching him. We need to know more about him.*

More mischief, Ivy said.

Don't blame Seal and me, Vinca said, coming out from behind Ivy's hair. *Both your parents put us up to it.*

Our parents? Blaze asked.

What'd they have to do with this? Ivy asked.

It was our job to watch you both, keep you out of trouble. Your parents wanted you to have normal childhoods. Vinca jabbed Ivy's cheek with her little finger and said, *Your mother in particular knew you were destined for Blaze, but she didn't want you to feel like you had no choice. She wanted you to choose him—over everyone else. Like a normal woman.*

Something inside Ivy's unsettled heart calmed itself. Her mother. She'd known Blaze was for her.

But then why the acorns? Blazed asked, his mindvoice as deep as his speaking voice.

Blaze, Vinca said, shaking her head. *You know the answer to that. If you'd lost your virginity that night to Ivy, you'd never have come into your power.*

Virginity makes my power stronger, he said in Ivy's silence.

Your power.

My father knew he had to get me away from you to train me. For the first year, I couldn't even look at another girl, I missed you so badly, and my father spent all that time cramming magical knowledge down my throat. By the time he was finished, I knew that only you . . .

Only me, what?

But Blaze shook his head, and Ivy could see he wouldn't answer the question. Blaze spoke aloud. "I'm here to protect the Heart."

Ivy couldn't imagine how much more power a wizard needed.

The phone rang again, and he looked at it, then at her.

"And you expect me to believe you're *fighting* Kellogg Brownroot?"

"I believe him," Vinca said.

"I have to answer the phone," Blaze said, his tone apologetic as he walked toward the ferns. "I can't ignore Brownroot forever."

"No doubt."

"Brownroot won't be put off," Blaze said. "We have to stop him, Ivy."

"Mmmm-hmmm."

"*We* have to save him. I need your help."

"Right." Her anger shimmered with frustration because what he said *could* be true. And he had those eyes, all moon gold. She swore they shined with truth.

Blaze picked up the phone. "Williams here," he said.

"Where the hell are you?"

"I couldn't let the unicorn get away," Blaze said as if talking to a slow child. "I went after her."

"Behind her on the bike?" Brownroot's tone oozed disbelief. "Looked to me like you went with her, not after her."

"What'd you want me to do?" Blaze asked. Ivy heard anger creep into his tone, and she realized how masterfully Blaze was playing the oil magnate. "Say, 'Please stop,' and act surprised when she didn't? I had a chance to go with her. I took it."

The man on the other end paused for a moment, and Ivy could almost see him considering. "You catch her?" Brownroot finally asked.

"No." Blaze looked at Ivy. "She got away. She dumped me off the bike in the middle of the forest."

"She jerked you on that bike only to throw you off?" Brownroot said. "What kind of sense does that make?"

"Well, uh," Blaze sounded reluctant, but Ivy wondered if he was only then concocting the tale, "she knocked me in the face first. Guess I'm lucky she didn't run me through with that horn of hers."

"Goddamn," Brownroot said. Ivy heard the grin through the phone. "She punched you?"

"Yeah." Blaze paused again and then said, "I can catch her again."

"I thought only virgins could catch unicorns," Kellogg said. His snide tone cut easily across the airwaves.

"You've been reading too many fairy tales, Kellogg," Blaze said. "You pay for my next hooker. Ask her about virginity."

Blaze winked at Ivy as he said this, and the jolt of jealousy that shot through Ivy surprised her. She didn't want him rolling in any other woman's bed. Not a hooker's. Not a queen's.

Your mom was right, Ivy, Vinca said. *He's the only man for you.*

Shhh, Ivy said. *I'm trying to listen.*

"Well, how'd you catch her then?" Brownroot asked.

"I went to school with her, Kellogg. She's a friend of mine." Blaze looked at Ivy then added, "Or she was before this."

Kellogg laughed, an incongruously pleasant sound. "Catching her a second time might be a little harder than it was the first."

"No doubt," Blaze agreed. "She'll meet with me though."

"You go to school with the fairies too?"

"Jesus," Blaze said. "What kind of drugs you doing?"

"Just forget the unicorn for now. If we demolish that boulder first, it'll be easier to catch her anyway."

"Whatever you say." Both men stood in silence for a minute. "So what do you want to do?" Blaze asked finally.

"Well, why don't you come back here? Bring a hand drill because a battery-powered one won't work, and we'll blow up this rock."

"Fine."

"We'll do it right this time." Brownroot paused. "It was a bad idea to just stick the dynamite under the rock anyway. Might blow up the ground without doing anything to the boulder."

"Wouldn't want that," Blaze said.

"No, sir," Kellogg said. "We would not." Then he added, "Bring more of that red wire with you too. The bitch took it with her on my damned dirtbike."

"Yeah," Blaze said. "Give me an hour or so, and I'll be there with the drill and the wire."

"Make it two hours," Kellogg said. "I've got some stuff to do."

Blaze snapped the phone shut, and he and Ivy eyed each other a moment, Ivy's intellect warring with her biology.

"Why are you working with that pig?" she finally asked. "It's your association with him that baffles me."

"Keep your friends close and your enemies closer."

She blinked at his cryptic answer.

"My father believed that," Blaze explained. "Brownroot was his business partner, but Dad never trusted him. He waited for Brownroot to actually do something, but it never happened— not until Dad died."

"Sorry about his passing," Ivy said, remembering the stubby man wearing the old-fashioned bowler. He'd always had a crooked grin for her.

Blaze held up his hand to stop the direction of the conversation. "When Dad died, Brownroot leaped at the chance to put in the road so he could get at the timber."

"And you became suspicious."

"I did—Brownroot's on the board of several coal companies in the Midwest. Why did he want timber?"

"What'd you suspect him of, exactly? Greed and avarice?"

Blaze shook his head, making a chunk of his black hair fall over his eye. "I didn't get a chance to wonder anything—my dad came back as a ghost and told me Brownroot was mutilating unicorns."

"What?" she asked.

"Well," he said, apparently stalling, "my father actually said— well, recommended, really—that we work together to stop him."

"But not 'work together,' if you get my meaning," Vinca taunted from Ivy's shoulder.

"But—"

"Don't," Blaze said, interrupting Ivy and shaking his head. "I don't want you endangering yourself. I don't want your help. I don't want you near here when I blast him to the next dimension."

"I think that's for me to decide, Blaze Williams."

"You don't know how dangerous this guy is," Blaze said. "Not only is Kellogg Brownroot catching and dehorning unicorns, he also stole the *Canticles Al Farasakh*."

"The *Canticles Al Farasakh*?" Ivy shook her head as if she knew nothing about this, as if she didn't know the book was sitting safe and sound in the trunk of her car. "What *Canticles*?"

Ivy, Vinca said in her mind. *You should tell him.*

I will, Ivy said. *Shhh.*

"All arcane magic available to human magic users was in that book. Other creatures—maybe dragons—would've been able to use it, but it was created for people. Some of the spells go back to the time of Sultan Mehmed II in the Ottoman Empire."

"And the book has a spell for getting rid of shady characters?" Ivy asked, only half kidding. She was finding it hard to believe Blaze was evil, despite the fact she'd found the book in his cabin.

Ivy! Vinca said. *Tell him!*

"The *Canticles Al Farasakh* is—well, was—divided into two parts: the white half and the black. A spell in the black half can shove Brownroot into the second dimension."

"What does that mean, exactly?"

"Two-dimensional space borders our three-dee world."

"Does that mean he'll be flat?"

"I understand everyone's flat there, like the King of Spades on a playing card. And there's no traveling between the dimensions."

Ivy closed her eyes and took a deep breath.

"That's what we need to do, Ivy. I need to get him close enough to the Heart to use that spell."

"You make it sound like something happened to the *Canticles*. Where is it?"

Ivy, tell him now! The fairy bit her ear.

"Ouch!" Ivy said, slapping at the fairy.

"You okay?"

"Something bit me," Ivy said, rubbing the spot. "You were telling me where the book was."

Blaze shrugged, his hands in his pockets. "I don't know. My father died in his study. He'd been reading the *Canticles Al Farasakh*. When I found him, I shoved the book in the drawer and called the paramedics. It was weeks before I went to look for it again, but it'd vanished. Dad's ghost said Kellogg took it. I can only assume he's right."

"So you don't know who took it?" Ivy demanded, feeling guilt for the heavy hand she was using. But she needed to know how important the *Canticles Al Farasakh* was. "Some madman could take over the world with the thing, and you just shrug."

"It's locked with spells."

"Couldn't someone pick it?"

He shook his head. "It's locked with a high-level spell. You need to know the exact words to open it."

"If Brownroot really has it—"

"He has it," Blaze said.

"But could he use it to catch unicorns?"

"Maybe." Blaze shrugged. "But I don't think he can use the *Canticles Al Farasakh*. He hasn't been trained . . . not unless he has some sort of wizard accomplice."

Ivy put her hands on her hips. "According to Tchili, a human man, a virgin, mutilated her. And there aren't a lot of grown men walking around in a state of innocence. Maybe he's using a spell to fool us."

"All the more reason to shove that bastard into the second dimension as soon as possible," Blaze said.

"And the *Canticles Al Farasakh*?"

"It'll come back to me."

"Like a lost dog?"

"That's part of the book's magic—it always comes back to the person most able to use it." But a dark expression crossed his face.

"What is it?" she asked.

"According to lore, getting back the *Canticles Al Farasakh* involves a battle between good and evil."

"And which are you?"

He sighed, more annoyed than angry. "What do you think?"

Ivy realized he'd sucked her in; she believed his story, but she didn't say a word. She didn't trust herself.

"Do you trust me?" he asked.

His scent, thick with crushed ferns and pristine ponds, made it hard for her to think. Ivy closed her eyes and rubbed her face, wanting nothing more than to buy time before she answered.

An image bombarded her, unbidden. Blaze's sword slammed against the obsidian-black scales of a dragon, its yellow eyes glowing with evil.

The vision exploded into near reality.

Behind Blaze stood a herd of unicorns, snow-white coats gleaming in bright moonlight. Pixies and centaurs, dryads and fairies hid behind hooves. Crystal's warm muzzle pushed warm breath on Ivy's flank. A swan maiden fluttered above them, her elegant wings hardly moving. Each creature wore an intent expression, and Ivy became aware of the strange flow of magic.

Each beast worked together to lend its magical strength to Blaze as the long, arched neck of the dragon lashed toward him, fire spewing from its mouth. Each beast trusted Blaze to save them all.

Ivy opened her eyes, and the dream melted away. "Who are you?" she asked for the third time.

Blaze's eyes met hers. "A man running short on time."

Her instincts screamed at her to trust him. But she knew the vision might be a clever spell, and his very presence made her slightly mad. His beguiling scent looped around her, pleading with her to yield.

"I can get the *Canticles Al Farasakh* for you," she said.

Thank God, Vinca said in Ivy's head. *What took you so damned long?*

"How're you going to do that?" Blaze asked.

"I have it," Ivy said. "I stole it—from you."

"From me?"

"Yeah, oh, great savior of the Heart," Ivy said. "I stole it from you."

"Well, it *was* in your cabin," Vinca said, fluttering from one of Ivy's shoulders to the other.

"Bring me Tchili's horn," Ivy said, "and I'll give you back your *Canticles Al Farasakh.*"

"But Kellogg Brownroot has the horn."

"Good." Ivy pushed the dirtbike toward him. "Then you know where to find it."

Blaze took the bike from Ivy, but she could see from the set of his jaw that he was angry. "I'll bring you back Tchili's horn because it's the right thing to do." His eyes were narrowed.

Ivy said nothing for a moment—things were starting to fall into place in her brain. With the help of the tigereye soul stone, she'd nearly found Tchili's horn. In fact, she'd narrowed it down to Manhattan, where both Kellogg and Blaze had been. "I'll go get the *Canticles Al Farasakh* right now," she said in a gentler voice. "No battle between good and evil necessary."

"I'm not worried about the *Canticles Al Farasakh*," Blaze said, kicking on the bike's motor. He tapped the thing into gear with his toe and started down the mountain.

Be careful, she said as he left.

At first, she didn't think he'd reply, but just as he drove out of the cabin's clearing, he said in her mind, *That book will come back to me because it's mine.*

9
_____

We need to get that book, Ivy said to Vinca, squashing the guilt she felt for negotiating with Blaze. She should have just trusted him. The best she could do now was hurry to comply with her end of the bargain.

As she shifted into equine form, Ivy's mane sprouted from her neck, and her forehooves touched the ground. Ivy tossed her mane as she galloped down the trail Blaze had just used. His scent clung to the breeze, not wiped out by either the breeze or the odor of unburned gasoline from the dirtbike. *I don't want Kellogg Brownroot to have the* Canticles Al Farasakh. Ivy ducked under a low-hanging branch. *I looked in that man's eyes, and he's definitely bad news.*

And speaking of bad news . . . Vinca said, clinging to her mane, *where the heck is Seal?*

I thought you said he was trailing Brownroot.

I said that, true, Vinca agreed. *But mostly I was guessing. Unless Seal's having sex with Brownroot, I can't imagine why he's been gone so long.*

Seal likes to flirt with danger.

And Brownroot's hot enough to roast Seal's weenie, Vinca said.

And you're so different from him, Ivy teased. *You'd do Brownroot in a heartbeat.*

Well, not all of us have tall, dark, gorgeous soul mates appearing on the horizon to sweep us off our feet.

Fairy. Ivy's tone was warning. But the words sent a delicious shiver of anticipation through her. Vinca knew exactly how to push her buttons. *Besides, he can't get laid.*

He can't get laid yet, Vinca corrected.

Ivy cantered through a bunch of branches, knocking the fairy off as a warning.

Hey! Vinca cried as the boughs swept over Ivy's shoulder. *Watch out for those branches.*

Ivy was still laughing as she slowed to a trot and then stopped. *We're here.*

Ivy felt Vinca climb up her neck and peer into the glade. *There's your car,* the fairy said. *With the book in the trunk.*

All we have to do is walk over and get it. But Ivy's legs were frozen in place.

That's all we have to do.

Ivy stood at the edge of the forest, looking at her cabin tucked away beneath a copse of beech trees. The fluttering leaves bathed the cabin in shade, and the little building looked safe and inviting. Her car, its green paint gleaming in the afternoon sun, looked innocuous.

Why do I have such a bad feeling about this? Ivy asked.

I don't know. Vinca launched into the sky in a flurry of gossamer blue wings. Her topaz hair rippled behind her as she flew around the edge of the glade. *But I have that feeling too. Let me look around.*

Be careful.

Ears forward, Ivy took a deep breath, searching for any

scent that didn't belong. She smelled earth cooking under the hot summer sun, the evergreen scent of the hemlocks, and the loamy scent of the oak trees. The scent of rain from two days ago was almost gone. She looked at the sky and saw days of clear weather.

You see anything, Vinca?

No, but I still have that feeling and—

Ivy, a voice broke into the conversation.

Hey, Crystal, girl, Vinca said. *How're things in the great Southwest?*

Vinca! Ivy! Crystal said, and now Ivy could taste her surviving sister's panic.

What is it? Visions of Tchili ripped through Ivy's brain. *Are you okay?*

I'm fine, Crystal said. *Just scared. I think he's here—the virgin who hunts unicorns.*

Why? Ivy said, keeping her urge to panic under control. *What makes you think that?*

I can smell him, her sister said. *He smells like . . . nighttime under a spring moon. He smells like a virgin warrior. His smell makes me want to kneel down at his feet and swear my life to him.*

That sounds familiar, Vinca said dryly, flying back to Ivy and landing in her mane.

Have you seen him? Ivy asked, ignoring the fairy's comments. It could be Blaze. Or it could be strong magic that mimicked Blaze. After all, the *Canticles Al Farasakh* had been out of Blaze's hands for days. *What does he look like?*

I don't know. I didn't see him, Crystal said. *As soon as I caught wind of him, I turned to girl form and ran. I'm hiding in a cave near the Pojoaque reservation. It's high up, and I brought in the ladder, and I don't think he can find me.* Crystal took a deep breath and said, *But if I smell him again . . .*

Crystal didn't need to finish that sentence; Ivy knew exactly what she meant. She knew the scent of the virgin warrior could turn the strongest unicorn into her own worst enemy.

That sounds like how you reacted to Blaze, Vinca said.

Who's Blaze? Crystal asked. *Is he the guy who mutilated Tchili?*

I don't think so. Blaze is a wizard, and some madman named Kellogg Brownroot stole his ancient book of spells. Maybe the lunatic is using it to camouflage himself as a virgin.

That makes sense, Vinca said. *Why would Blaze be any-where near Crystal, and how would he get to New Mexico?*

Unless he wants her horn too, Ivy said, voicing the thought she was fighting not to think. Where was Blaze? Did Blaze have a spell to get to New Mexico that quickly? Ivy wished she knew more about wizards and their power.

Who's Blaze and who's Kellogg—

Crystal, Ivy interrupted. *I think you should lower your metabolism, and you should keep it low. So you're almost hibernating.*

I won't inhale his perfume that way, Crystal said.

The creatures under your protection would rather have you out of commission for a few days than dead, Ivy said. *And it'll be only for a few days.*

You sound so certain about that, Crystal said.

That's because we're close to a solution! Vinca said. *Ivy's going to trade the magic book we stole from Blaze for Tchili's horn. He's off getting the horn right now. We'll be able to restore Tchili to her power.*

You're working . . . with the Mutilator . . . to get the horn back? Crystal said, her voice slowing already with her decreased metabolism.

No, Vinca said.

I wish I could say for sure that Blaze Williams is not the Mutilator, Ivy said.

Ivy's in loooove. Vinca cackled with the jibe.

Who ... do you ... think the Mutilator is? Can you ... stop ... him? The questions came so gradually; each word took a heartbeat to form.

It's Kellogg Brownroot. He owns a logging company, and he's a major shareholder in a bunch of Midwestern power plants.

But ... why?

Ivy understood the question, despite the paucity of Crystal's words. *He wants to blow up the Heart so the wilderness won't be protected. Without magic, the guardians die, and without guardians, he'll drill, clearcut, strip mine, and who knows what else. It'll make him rich.*

And he knows ... about unicorns.

Somehow.

And our ... horns?

He wants those too.

Why?

To save his children and grandchildren from the mercury and acid rain he's dumping into the environment. They'll be protected.

Can you ... stop him?

Yes. That image of Blaze wielding his sword flashed through Ivy's mind. Blaze could stop him. *I think.*

I keep having ... the strangest ... dreams, Crystal said.

What of? Ivy asked.

There's a herd of us ... and other ... creatures.

With her slow words, the hair on the back of Ivy's neck began to rise. The dream was too similar to her own vision to ignore. *What else?*

A man ... a warrior. Crystal paused. *He's fighting ... a dragon ... with a sword.*

Ivy paused before she said, *I've had the same dream.*

His eyes change. ... They start green but turn ... brown.

142 / *Lucinda Betts*

Like tiger . . . eye. They have . . . a sliver of . . . gold moon in them. Ivy heard Crystal catch her breath before her sister added, *They have . . . spring moon . . . in them.*

Oh! said Vinca. *We know this man.*

Do . . . you?

I think so, Ivy said. *I've known him for a long time.*

But . . . Ivy, Crystal said.

What?

You must . . . help him. He won't . . . ask, Crystal said. *But he needs . . . help.*

Ivy thought of Blaze buzzing down the hill to meet Brownroot to get Tchili's horn back upon Ivy's demand. The way his ass filled out his jeans, the strong set of his jaw . . . He seemed nothing but determined and competent and capable.

Ivy, he went alone, Vinca said. *He went without you, without the Guardian of this forest.*

But Crystal wasn't finished with them. She said, *In my dream . . .*

Ivy waited, but her sister seemed to have drifted away. Finally Vinca said, *In your dream what?*

He's defeated. . . . Crystal said.

Defeated, Vinca snorted. *What could defeat Blaze Williams?*

The Dragon Uroboros. . . . Crystal said. *It slaughters him.*

The Dragon Uroboros? Why would he want to battle Blaze? And I've had him locked up in Mauna Loa for years.

Volcanoes . . . can't hold dragons . . . for long.

Okay, but why would Blaze take him on? Vinca said. *Why would Uroboros come back here? Ivy has just locked his ass up again.*

Revenge? The word came so slowly from Crystal.

No, Ivy said. *Not revenge. This is a creepy thought, but what if . . . ?*

What if what? Vinca asked.

What if Uroboros wants the same thing as Brownroot?

Why would Uroboros want to poison the planet? Vinca said. *That makes . . . no sense.*

Yes, it does, Ivy said more certainly now. *Think about it. Kellogg Brownroot wants to dump so much sulfur dioxide into the atmosphere from his coal plants. What makes baby dragons grow super big?*

Sulfur dioxide, said Vinca.

And what else?

Nitrogen . . . oxide.

That's right. And carbon dioxide.

And coal plants spew out all these, Vinca said, fluttering in the lovely green branches above Ivy.

Brownroot's ugly world will be perfect for baby dragons.

Don't send . . . Crystal said, dripping each word from her mind, *. . . Blaze alone.*

10

Even as Ivy regretted sending Blaze after Tchili's horn, she hoped she wasn't too late, that Brownroot hadn't done any harm to her warrior virgin.

But how could Brownroot do anything to him? Ivy asked Vinca. *Blaze is a wizard, a powerful one, and we're so close to the Heart—he'll be at the height of his power.*

That's true, the fairy said. *But why would Brownroot show up in your and Crystal's visions as a dragon?* Vinca nervously braided a purple harebell into Ivy's mane. *Maybe the dragon's figurative?*

Maybe Brownroot is a dragon, Ivy said, only half kidding.

That can't be true. We'd know. You'd know. Dragon's don't just show up out of nowhere.

I know. I'm just saying, Ivy said. *It'd make sense. Dragons can use the* Canticles Al Farasakh. *Why else would Brownroot steal it?*

Maybe he's a wizard. Wizards use that book, too. Vinca plaited another purple blossom into Ivy's long mane.

Then we're back to the same problem we have if he's a dragon, Ivy said.

Yeah, Vinca agreed. *Where the hell'd he come from? We'd know. Blaze would know.*

Ivy swished her tail in frustration, still unwilling to venture to her car sitting in the clearing.

Maybe he's just a mortal—and an evil one, Ivy said. *That might be the best we can hope for.*

You think we should go check on Blaze? Vinca said. *Before we get that book?*

Yeah, Ivy said. *Only, I hope we don't need to save him.*

We won't need to save him—

Ivy, a tiny voice interrupted. *Here you are.*

Seal. Ivy would recognize that moue anywhere. *Where've you been?*

Yeah, Seal, Vinca added. *What'd you find out about that Kellogg Brownroot guy? He any good in the sack?*

I've been looking all over the forest for you, Seal said breathlessly, ignoring Vinca.

Why? What's up? Seeing Seal fly from the trees behind her, Ivy trotted over to him, glad for his presence as he fluttered near her face.

Mr. Tall, Dark, and Handsome sent me for you, Seal said. *He told me to give you this.*

What?

In reply, Seal opened his miniature brown vest, baring his tiny chest, perfect in its proportions if not its size.

*I don't underst—*Ivy started to say, but then the fragrance filled her equine nostrils, the spring-moon scent of her warrior virgin. Seal must have caught the essence of Blaze under the vest, and the perfume filled her nostrils. She was entranced.

Where is he? Ivy demanded of Seal. *Where's Blaze?*

What's going on? Vinca demanded. *What'd Blaze give her? Seal, what're you doing?*

You have to save Blaze, Seal said to both of them. *Kellogg Brownroot has him. He's captured!*

But where are they? Vinca asked, sounding unwilling to panic.

They're at the Heart of the World, Seal said, buttoning his vest as he flew toward Ivy's back. *Go!*

With the scent of warriors and crushed ferns and summer moonbeams on a hot night rushing toward Ivy's blood, cool logic fled.

Ivy, wait, Vinca said. *Let's think about this. What if it's a trap?*

But Ivy wasn't listening. Now that Seal had set her on the scent, she found her warrior virgin without effort, the enchanting essence of him. She cantered wildly toward the Heart of the World, her hooves tattooing over hard earth as she followed the tie connected to his heart.

And something else. . . .

Ivy slid to a fast stop, her hind legs far underneath her body.

What is it? Vinca asked.

Go, unicorn! Seal urged, slapping her withers as if she were a draft animal. *You should see what Brownroot's doing to him. He needs your help!*

But Ivy stood for a moment, cautiously exploring the oddity. Something dangerous, something that didn't belong in her forest and never had, had wrapped itself around Blaze's essence.

Something's not right, she told the fairies.

What do you mean? Vinca asked.

Can't you smell it?

Smell what? Vinca asked.

I don't know why you're stopping to smell the daisies, Seal said. *That man needs our help, and he needs it now.*

Vinca snorted. *You keep saying that.*

But something quivered on the edge of Ivy's consciousness, something that gave her pause despite the nearly overwhelming need for her to run to Blaze.

What do you smell? Vinca asked. *We fairies don't get this sense at all. Tell me!*

It hurts, Ivy said, tossing her head and snorting. This new smell twisted up her nostrils and stayed there. *It hurts my nose. It sears like onions or sulfuric acid.*

Weird. Vinca's tiny fingers worked through Ivy's mane.

I'm sure it is, Seal said. *But maybe we should just go? Like, now?*

It smells like pain, Ivy said.

Then go! Seal said.

Ivy obeyed, galloping headlong down the trail toward the Heart, but even as she ran, she analyzed the strange odor.

It's more than pain, she told the fairies. *It's somehow wrapped around Blaze's good smell. It's choking it.*

Seal's right, Ivy, Vinca said. *Run!*

Adrenaline coursed through Ivy, and she galloped toward the Heart. A huge fallen tree loomed across the trail in front of her, and Ivy gathered her haunches under her to clear it.

Maybe Blaze's spell backfired? Vinca said, making Ivy click her hooves clumsily on the giant log.

What spell? Seal asked.

Blaze is going to send Kellogg Brownroot to the second dimension with a spell from the magic book, Vinca explained. *But not until he gets Tchili's horn back and the magic book—which we have.*

As Ivy continued her rush toward the Heart, she said, *Maybe you're right about the spell backfiring. Sending someone to the second dimension can't be easy.*

The second dimension, Seal scoffed. *I bet even the mad scientists at Fermilab and Los Alamos haven't done that.*

Blaze can do it, Vinca said. *I know he can.*

Ivy ignored the bickering fairies as she bolted through a small clearing. The ground here was drier, and her footing gave a little bit as she flew around a bend in the trail. She caught her breath and realized the two smells had grown stronger.

Dear God, Vinca said. *Look at that!*

Where? Seal asked.

In the branches above us!

Ivy saw curling tendrils physically wrapped around the green boughs of the hemlock trees, and she recognized them immediately. *Those are the scents,* she said.

Does the green one stink? Vinca asked.

Yes, Ivy answered. *And the molten brown smells like Blaze.* The acrid scent looked biliously green compared to Blaze's tigereye.

And, Jesus, look at that, Seal said. *Hemlock needles are falling from the tree where that green smoke touches.* Ivy heard amazement in his tone. *That stuff is strong.*

And none too healthy, Vinca said. *It's killing the forest.*

Perhaps even more frightening, the Heart's power throbbed with an insistence she'd never felt before. The hunger to roll in bed with someone nearly swamped her ability to think. Someone strong was using it. The Heart's power pounded through her hooves and to her knees. It reverberated through her horn and heart as she ran.

You feel the Heart throbbing? Ivy asked.

Yeah, Seal said. *What is it?*

I was hoping one of you would know.

Maybe it's Blaze drawing on the Heart to banish Brownroot? Vinca guessed. *Maybe that's what it feels like when you use it to push someone to the second dimension?*

Maybe, Ivy said. *But something about it feels wrong, like the Heart isn't giving power but* . . . She couldn't find the right words.

I know what you mean, Vinca said. *It's like something's stealing power from the Heart.*

Or raping it, Seal said.

I think it's Kellogg Brownroot, Vinca said. *You know, "Brown"? "Root"? How much more obvious can a name be? He's killing the place.*

Ivy ran around a switchback curve, her hooves sending pebbles flying down the ridge. *Maybe it'll be over by the time we get there.*

I don't know if that'd be good or not, Vinca said, clinging to her mane.

As Ivy galloped along the deer path, she saw the mucous-green tendril strangling Blaze's honey-brown Magic, and she ran harder. *I don't get the feeling Blaze is winning.*

That's what I was trying to tell you! Seal cried.

Rounding another curve, Ivy found the foul magic snaking over the ground, and she leaped over it, not wanting to touch it even with her hooves.

That's what Crystal was saying too, Vinca said, finally picking up the panic Seal had brought to them. *She said Blaze needed help. Maybe he's fighting for his life!*

We're almost to the Heart, Ivy warned the fairies. *Get off my back. Go hide in the trees.*

I'm not going anywhere, Vinca said, and Ivy felt her grab her mane in a steely grip.

Stay if you want, but you're insane. I'm out of here, Seal cried, launching himself into the sky in a flurry of wings.

Seal, you always were a coward, Vinca taunted. *I am not afraid.*

Vinca, Ivy said in a cool tone. *Get off me now.*

I'm staying.

Well then, hold on. I'm going in.

Ivy lowered her head as she neared the clearing where the Heart stood, her eyes and ears scanning for Brownroot. The razor-edged spirals of her horn glinted in the sun.

Blaze might have a problem killing the enemy outright, but she did not. She was the Guardian of the Forest, and she'd skewer Kellogg Brownroot. She'd skewer him in a heartbeat.

There he is! Vinca cried from Ivy's back.

I see him, Ivy said, spying Brownroot, his back to her. Dust covered his faded jeans and Western shirt, and his shaggy rock-and-roll hair tumbled to his shoulders.

Get him! Vinca cheered, clinging tenaciously to Ivy's mane. *Get him!*

Hang on.

All around her, power crackled. Drawing on the Heart for speed and strength, Ivy leaped toward Brownroot, killing horn aimed low for his kidney.

Go get him! Vinca cried. *You've got him!*

And Ivy knew the fairy was right. She already tasted Kellogg Brownroot's blood. She could feel the coppery liquid slip over her horn. She'd drink in his death. She'd revel in it. Her hooves anticipated the feel of bone and flesh crunching beneath them.

Go! Vinca cried. *Run!*

And Ivy ran like hell. She ran faster than a thoroughbred at the Preakness; she ran faster than a cloudwolf across the sky. The Heart's power poured through her feet, through her blood and heart. It loaned her the speed of dragonflight.

Go! Vinca cheered again. *You've got him!*

Then all four feet crumpled beneath her, and she fell to the ground, gasping. Ancient boughs framed the skies above her, and the pebbles on the ground seemed overly large. They were inches from her eyes.

Ivy! she heard. *Ivy!*

The sound came from far in the heavens, but nothing made sense, and everything hurt. Her stifles and fetlocks ached. Her entire gaskin felt numb, and her feet wouldn't obey her command to stand, no matter how she struggled.

Blaze! she called. *Vinca. Where are you?*

Ivy! her fairy friend cried. *I'm here! In the trees above you.*

Where am I?

But before Vinca could answer, before Ivy could decipher this terrible new world, Brownroot leaped toward her and landed on her head. He snapped a halter over her nose and behind her ears, and he wrapped the rope from her legs through the halter before she could fight him.

Pinning her ears back, she bared her teeth, ready to bloody this demon's flesh. With satisfaction she watched him jump away from her, but as she tried to snake her head toward him, an implacable force jerked her back.

It was the rope. Her nose was tied to her feet.

"Damned if that old cowboy wasn't right," Brownroot said, shaking his head. He shifted his weight so his ass sat right on her poll, completely immobilizing her.

Ivy! she heard Vinca cry. *Are you okay?*

I'm fine, Ivy said. *But stay away. He's trapped me.*

"You, Miss Unicorn, have been caught in a trap that's worked for cowboys catching mustangs for generations." Cold pleasure laced Brownroot's voice.

Channeling the Heart's power into her neck, Ivy snaked her head toward him again, ready to bite him. Again the rope held her nose to her feet. She couldn't move.

Using all that power, she slammed the Heart's magic through her veins, trying to transform into girl form. She'd slither from this rope.

She poured the Heart's energy into herself—and nothing happened. She poured more energy, and still nothing.

What's going on? she asked Vinca, fighting her growing panic. *I can't change form. Why can't I change?*

It's an enchanted rope! Vinca called. *He's got an enchanted rope on you. But it's not blue like the one Blaze used—it's green. It's mucous green!*

Please run, Ivy implored her friend. *Get away from here, Vinca. It's not safe. The man has magic no man should have.*

I can't leave you, Ivy. I—

"I used a stallion as bait, and you ran right into my ropes," Brownroot said, apparently oblivious to the fairy. "You like my ropes? I know you like my stallion. He's a prime stud, from the looks of it. You'll like me better, I promise."

Ivy wildly fought to move her head, looking for Blaze. What had happened to him? She could still smell him—and that poisonous odor too.

Where's Blaze? Ivy asked Vinca. *Find him and tell him what happened.* And even as she said this, she tossed her head, seeking Blaze. She knew he could save them.

But Brownroot gave her no opportunity to search, to interpret. He pulled a syringe from his back pocket and jerked off the plastic cap with his teeth. Spitting the yellow cap into the weeds, Kellogg pushed the plunger so the pungent smell of the drug overwhelmed the forest scents.

What's he doing? Vinca cried. *What is that?*

He's going to drug me, I think, Ivy said.

That can't be good.

Get out of here, Ivy said, calmer now that she realized this fate could not be fought. *Go find Blaze. Free him if he's captive. Get Seal to help you.*

"I expect," Brownroot said, reaching for Ivy's shoulder, "that your biology is very much like that of a horse when you're in unicorn shape."

With her ears pinned flat against her skull, Ivy tried again to bite him, but Kellogg didn't even flinch. Apparently he was convinced his magic would hold her.

"But still," he said, "I'm not a man to take any chances in that direction, so I've doubled the dose here. When you wake up—if you wake up—I'll have your horn." Then he jabbed the long needle into the flesh of her neck and pushed. "And your skin. I'll have that too. For a rug. Or a shirt."

That bastard! Vinca cried in Ivy's mind.

The drug had an immediate effect. Ivy's heart rate slowed in a way she couldn't reach with her magic. If Brownroot had his way, she would fade out of existence. She'd have no choice.

But he would not win this battle. Blaze would. Blaze would save them.

"I like the gold hues of your horn, Miss Unicorn," Kellogg said. "It's very rich, very classy. That green and red one from the Mexican unicorn looks too Christmassy for my tastes. This gold of yours . . . that's more my style."

She knew she should be angry, but Ivy's emotions were beyond his reach. *Who'll reattach my horn?* she wondered. *Does Blaze have that spell in his* Canticles? *Maybe with Crystal's help . . .*

Ivy? Vinca asked. *Ivy, answer me!*

Get that . . . book . . . back to . . . Blaze, Ivy said to Vinca.

"And don't think Blaze Williams will be running to your rescue either, Miss Unicorn," Kellogg said in his rich baritone.

What does he mean? she wondered slowly. *Has he done something to Blaze? No . . .*

But Brownroot didn't leave any room for doubt. He grabbed her muzzle and pulled it toward him. Too drugged to fight back, too incapacitated to even try to bite him, she had no choice but to look him in the eye.

"Do you hear me, Miss Unicorn?" he demanded.

She didn't want to acknowledge him, but the evil radiating from his gaze was too much to bear. She closed her eyes.

"Good." Kellogg laughed. "I want you to know before you slip off into oblivion that Blaze Williams didn't fool me for an instant. That fucker was never on my side."

Vinc . . . a, Ivy tried to call. *Where . . . Blaze?*

I'm not leaving you! Vinca cried.

Find . . . Blaze.

But her fairy friend didn't answer. Instead, Kellogg laughed again. He dropped Ivy's head, and she flopped helplessly into the dust. A fleck of forest litter landed on her eye, and she couldn't blink. Ivy couldn't move.

"I have a special hell for men who try to trick me," Kellogg said. "And Blaze Williams is in it."

Find . . . him.

As the sound of a saw filled her ears, Ivy let her mind float off into oblivion.

II

Ivy.

The voice came as if in a dream, floating and ethereal. It seemed almost a balm to the ache on her forehead.

Exquisite pain throbbed from her hooves to the tip of her tail. The ragged edges of the torture jawed through to her bones, chewed past her tendons so every inch of her body hurt. The agony separated her mind from her body so she didn't feel real.

Ivy.

She ignored her name, remembering the needle, the promise to lop off her horn, to skin her. Brownroot's threat hadn't been idle then. She'd known it wasn't. And now her horn was gone.

Wake up.

Why? Why would she wake up? The intensity of the pain, both physical and mental, kept her from feeling her skin, her fur. Whether he'd skinned her—mutilated her as he had Tchili—she didn't know. Agony throbbed through her with every heartbeat, and she didn't care if Kellogg Brownroot had taken her pelt or not. She could just float off. . . .

Ivy.

Air rushed into her lungs, but she couldn't feel herself breathing. She didn't care if she breathed.

Brownroot had stolen her magic. Brownroot had stolen her magic. . . .

Suddenly Ivy felt as cold as an arctic night. The silver-maned wolves of her imagination closed in on her, but she didn't want to fight or flee. She wanted to lie down and die. She'd offer them her soft underbelly, let her lifeblood pour from her veins and feed their voracious appetites.

Ivy.

She wanted to die.

Ivy.

Go . . . away, she said.

But the voice wouldn't leave her mind. *Ivy, wake up.*

In her black world, the voice was a point of light. Gently gleaming, it was the only thing of beauty on the bleak landscape. It was nice to be loved . . . but death's embrace would be sweeter.

Ivy.

Go away, Crystal, she managed to choke out. *I don't want to talk to you right now.*

Hot blood ran down her face and puddled beneath her chest. More blood had congealed in the corner of her eye, and a modicum of rational thought returned.

She didn't want her sister to see her like this, hornless and tied.

I need you, the voice said. *Please.*

Ivy reached for the Heart but couldn't find it. She couldn't find it.

Her sister would give up all hope and turn to stone if she knew Ivy's fate, and Ivy couldn't let that happen. The battle against the oil magnate now belonged to Crystal. Her sister would have to rally the magical creatures to vanquish Brownroot. At least Crystal had a name and a motive. Crystal wouldn't have to choose between Blaze or Kellogg. She'd know.

It's your fight now, Crystal, Ivy said. *Leave me be. Go fight it. Go fight Kellogg Brownroot.*

I'm not Crystal, the voice said, warm and melodic. *Now, please, get up.*

Not Crystal then. Not Crystal. The thoughts floated around her mind as insubstantial as clouds. When she tried to grab them, they slipped through her grasp like fog. If not Crystal, then who?

Ivy.

Vinca, Ivy said, finally understanding. *I said to leave me alone. Go find Blaze. Both of you can help Crystal.*

Ivy, the voice said. *Vinca isn't here. I don't know where she is. I haven't seen Seal either.*

Not Crystal, not Vinca, not Seal. *Leave me alone.* Only those words made sense in her pain-filled universe.

Ivy.

With that one word, his otherworldly scent wafted over her, compelling her to obey. The acrid odor of poison, the bilious green that had taken shape on the trail, still lingered in her nostrils, but it had weakened. Neither scent belonged to her sister.

I'm not Crystal, the voice repeated. *And you need to get* up.

Blaze? she asked.

"We have to fight him," he said, his physical voice filling her ears with shocking clarity. "We have to fight Kellogg Brownroot. He is evil—more evil than anything on this planet."

Blaze? she asked again. The solid sound of his voice jarred her back to reality. *Is that you? Are you alive? I thought—*She remembered the bilious coil of magic strangling his magic. She remembered Brownroot's words, his promise that Blaze was now in hell.

She remembered being able to feel the Heart. Had Kellogg blown it up, or was it simply that she lacked her own ability to touch it? Regardless, she'd never channel it again.

"I'm fine." His voice moved like mist through her mind. "I'm very much alive, but you have to get up. He'll be back soon."

I have no horn, Blaze. He took it. He sawed off my horn.

Ivy knew that were she in human form, she'd be crying. But without her horn, she'd never be human again. Like Tchili, she'd be nothing more than a white mare, a mortal white horse with an odd scar beneath her golden forelock, should anyone care to look. She'd be as powerless as she'd been as a child, when Chicory had died at her useless feet.

Soon even her ability to use mindspeech would fade, if she followed Tchili's trajectory. After tomorrow or maybe the next day, she wouldn't be able to speak to Blaze or Vinca or Seal. She'd never save another injured creature.

"Ivy," he said in a hard tone. "You're the Guardian of the Forest. Even without your horn, you're the Guardian of the Heart of the World."

Fuck you. Some Guardian. What mere horse ever guarded anything? Was there anything left to guard?

"Get off your ass and guard," he said. "The trees need you. The creatures of this forest need you."

She thought of the ropes Brownroot had used to capture her. He'd moved so fast, and his magic had been so strong, she hadn't been able to shift into girl form and flee.

That magic. How had Brownroot gotten that magic? And how could she fight someone that strong without her horn? A fly couldn't battle an elephant.

I can't, she said. *I can't get up.*

"You haven't tried." Blaze's voice held no judgment; he'd just stated a fact. A cold fact.

Fuck you. Brownroot had probably blown up the Heart of the World anyway.

"If you want to fuck," he said, "let's do it. I won't object except on the grounds that I'd much prefer to make love to you, that I've always wanted to finish what we started all those years ago."

What?

His words made no sense in her pained mind. What was he saying? Her heart danced a crazy beat as her mind sifted for meaning.

"I don't want a few minutes of pleasure," he said. "I want a lifetime. I want your mind and all that gold hair. I want your dreams and your hopes, and I have since the moment I first laid eyes on you."

The drugs swam through her veins, through her brain, jiggling her thoughts so they made no sense. She believed he was telling her he loved her.

But that couldn't be right, could it? He'd left her. Years ago, Blaze had left Ivy. But he'd had to go, right? Their parents had schemed to separate them to protect his precious virginity. And then she'd accused him of the most horrible things. He couldn't love her. Nothing in this pain-filled world made sense.

Screw you, she said. But the venom was gone. She wished she had a human mouth. She wished she could see his face; then she'd know what he was trying to say, what he meant. She wished she had her magic. She wished magic still existed. *Screw you,* she said again.

"Come try."

She imagined it—not screwing. Loving. She imagined running her hands through his thick, dark hair. She imagined skimming her palms over his muscles, the hard contours of his arms. She'd drink in his strength. She imagined throwing her head back and offering her throat to him, the hot licks of desire matching the heat of his kisses as he worked his way toward her breasts.

"Come try," he said more softly. "I dare you."

She finally opened her eyes, and the world swam. Her stomach churned wildly, and she realized that humans called this nausea.

I feel sick, she said.

"It's the drugs. And the pain," he said.

I don't like it.

"Quit whining and get up."

And your sweet words?

"Think of it as tough love, Ivy. Get up so I can hold you and touch you."

I'm nothing but a horse.

"You're you."

I never knew about this beast-loving side of you, she said.

"Ivy," he said, not laughing at her poor joke. Instead, she heard chagrin. "Get up."

Ivy looked around. The rustic beams of the ceiling seemed absurdly far away. Small patches of sunlight illuminated an earthen room, and the dank air carried the smell of dried apples and carrots—and the delicious scent of her virgin.

Blaze? she asked. *Where are you?*

"Behind you."

Ivy realized the drugs were really hammering her, because his voice sounded weak, which just couldn't be true. Nothing could hurt this warrior virgin. In her vision, she'd seen him wield a sword against the most ferocious dragon, and so had Crystal. Nothing about Blaze Williams was weak.

She would do well to emulate some of that strength. *I'm getting up,* she said.

"Good. Sooner would probably be better than later."

Ivy struggled to stand, but her legs tangled, and she fell hard on her face. The jarring stumble sent dagger blades of pain through her eyes.

Damnit, she said, unable to keep despair from her voice.

"Careful, unicorn. Try again." His voice was calm and even, offering support.

Fuck you, she said as despair morphed into anger. Without her horn, she'd never be able to caress him, to feel his lips over hers. She'd never be able to touch the hard muscles of his thighs. *No one sawed off your horn.*

"Just try again," he said. "Please."

His words displaced the despair and anger with a growing sense of urgency. Blaze Williams had never asked her—or anyone, as far as she knew—for help. Ivy tucked her legs beneath her and struggled to a more natural position. Maybe she hadn't imagined that his voice sounded weak.

Are you okay? she asked as she struggled to gain control of her feet.

"I'm fine," he said. "But let's get out of here."

Where's Vinca? Ivy asked. *Do you know? Or Seal?*

"I don't know," Blaze said. "I wasn't . . . awake . . . when Brownroot brought you in here."

Hell of a time to take a nap, she said, knowing even as she said it that his situation must be more serious than he was letting on.

"I agree."

It's weird that Vinca isn't here. She stuck by my side even when Brownroot caught me and tied me up. Seal flew for cover, that wimp, but I thought she'd come get you. Did she?

"No," Blaze answered. "Can you get up? What if Kellogg Brownroot comes back?"

His rhetorical question lit the fire in her, and Ivy tried again to stand. She rolled onto her legs, and the ropes shifted, loosening around her fetlocks. Her gaskins ached, but it was nothing in comparison to the pain throbbing in her head.

Dear God, she said. *It hurts. A lot.*

"I can imagine," he said, his rich voice soothing the pain. "But you can do it."

Not wanting to disappoint him, she wiggled her legs again, flexing her fetlocks and her hooves. This time the rope gave a little bit more.

Something's giving, she told him, pausing to catch her breath. *The rope's sliding. I think.*

"Good," he said. "Can you get out of them?"

Maybe. Let me try again.

Ivy wiggled and rolled. The effort brought a cascade of pain washing from her forehead to her hooves. Red waves of agony sent a blanket of twinkling stars shimmering behind her eyes. The tips of her hooves started to go numb. Never in her life had she felt like this.

"Can you get up? Loosen the ropes?"

You're a relentless bastard, you know that?

"And you use a whole lot of naughty words for a unicorn."

You have no idea, she said, but the effort sent torment streaming through her. Her body throbbed in torture. Her forehead felt as if it had an ax embedded in it.

"You can do this," he said.

Marshalling her strength, Ivy tried again to wiggle her forelegs. Then she shifted her stifles and—

Goddamn it.

"What is it?"

The rope's off.

"I knew you could do it."

Ivy took another deep breath. She'd have to stand now, and anticipation of the pain sent a shudder through her. *Remind me why we have to do this, Blaze. Because lying down and dying might be preferable to living in a world without magic.*

He didn't answer right away, and she wondered if he himself felt similarly. After all, if Brownroot won the day, the Heart of the World would be destroyed, along with all magical creatures. And without the Heart, Blaze Williams was just a regular man.

"You'd have something," he said finally. "You'd have me."

A strange magic of a completely different type momentarily wiped away the pain of her loss, and she lay there, panting in silence.

"Aren't you going to say, 'Fuck you'?"

But the words from his heart incapacitated her more than the pain.

"Even if you can't talk," he said, "you'll have me."

And still she said nothing. Instead she wondered what it would be like to have him. She could imagine waking next to him in the morning and seeing fat sunbeams streaming over the small hook in his nose, his strong jaw. In the quiet of the morning, he'd reach for her and . . .

And it was probably the warrior virgin in him calling to her biology.

"Ivy," Blaze said. "Talk to me."

Waste of breath, Ivy snorted, a pathetic sound in the root cellar. She needed to stand. *After Kellogg stole Tchili's horn, she and I could mindspeak for only half an hour or so before she became completely mortal. I probably have a day or so because I'm closer to the Heart . . . if the Heart still exists.*

"It's not just the unicorn and virgin thing," Blaze said, ignoring her words to address what was on her mind. How did he do that?

Do you know for certain?

"I knew it when I followed you through the forest when we were kids," he said. "And you knew it when you followed me through the high school halls. Your mother knew it and wanted you to know it with your whole heart. My father knew it, and he separated us so our love—" Blaze's voice cracked as he said *love* before he continued with renewed strength. "My father knew it, and he separated us so our love wouldn't prevent us coming into our powers."

Ivy knew if Vinca were here, she'd make some offbeat comment to fill the awkward silence, but Ivy herself lacked that ability. She wanted Blaze. She craved Blaze.

But would she love him if he didn't have that compelling scent, if just inhaling the air surrounding him didn't fill her with visions of stags dashing through the dark wood, and virgin warriors damp with sweat from swordplay, and moon-soaked spring nights thick with frog song?

He worked a strong magic on her, but she craved a more enduring enchantment.

Blaze laughed at her silence, then he said, "When I lose my virginity to you, you'll know I'm right. Our love will last."

How are you reading my mind? She thought only the fairies had that ability, and then only when they were in their rude moods.

"It's not magic," he said. "At least, it's not wizard's magic."

What is it, then?

"We know each other."

Which was exactly the sort of magic she was looking for. If Brownroot had blown up the Heart and all the world's magic had faded away, this solid enchantment would endure.

"Ivy," he said. "We really should get moving."

Do you still have your magic? she asked. *Or has Kellogg destroyed the Heart?* Ivy could hardly choke out the last words. She should have been able to sense the Heart as easily as she breathed.

"I don't know," he said.

What do you mean?

"I can't feel it." He nearly whispered this admission.

But I'm speaking with the mindvoice!

"So either Brownroot hasn't destroyed the Heart yet . . ."

Or the residual magic's clinging to the area, Ivy finished. *Like the way the magic stuck around Tchili for a while, even after she lost her horn.*

"Either way, we have room for hope—if we hurry. We can stop him."

She put her forelegs in front of her, but they felt wobbly, like those belonging to a newborn foal. *Do you think you can help me? Steady me?*

"I—" He paused. "I can't. I'm sorry."

Something about his tone scared her, and she didn't ask him to elaborate. Instead she focused on her task. She heaved her weight forward, and her feet finally found their way under her.

"Steady," Blaze said. "Breathe and hold it."

When I want a Lamaze class, I'll let you know.

Blaze laughed. "Pain make you cross, unicorn?"

When some madman chops off your . . . horn, she said, *let me know how cheerful you are.*

"I wouldn't be cheerful at all," he said. "And we'll do whatever we can to restore your horn in as little time as possible."

Ivy stood in silence for a moment, unable to speak for the anguish and pain.

"I promise," Blaze said. "We'll get your horn back."

How could she believe him? But his words were kind, and with those words Ivy felt grateful for two things: she had her skin, and she had Blaze.

She had Blaze. The words sent a strange shiver through her nerves, an intense pleasure at odds with all the pain and turmoil.

"Can you stand?" he asked.

I'm doing the best I—Ivy turned to look at him, ready to shoot him a feisty retort. But what she saw wiped words away. She sank to her knees again and then collapsed completely.

Oh, dear God, she said.

"Ivy," he said.

And again the words had an ethereal quality, as if they came not from the man chained in front of her but from some distant galaxy—maybe even a different dimension.

"Ivy, really," he said. "I'll survive this. Get up."

But she wasn't as certain as he.

What'd he do to you? she asked, but she didn't need to hear Blaze's explanation. The answer was right in front of her, staring her in the face.

Kellogg Brownroot had burned out Blaze's right eye.

"He didn't like being taken as a fool," Blaze said. "This was his idea of punishment."

It was Ivy's idea of punishment too.

A branding iron stood to one side, looking like a normal barnyard implement.

It looked normal, except for one thing: white ooze dripped across Blaze's cheek and down his shirt, and smoke coiled from the still hot tip of the iron.

12

The shock of black hair hanging into Blaze's face did little to hide the damage Kellogg had wrought, and the horror burned an image into Ivy's brain she knew would stay with her forever. The terrible odor of seared flesh made her want to gag.

Dear God, Blaze, she said, her mindvoice quaking. *What's he done to you?*

"Ivy, I need you to focus," he said, his expression calm. "Untie me."

Kellogg might have poisoned her magic—and Blaze's—but Blaze was a virgin, and Ivy was a unicorn, and Blaze's scent beguiled her. To do other than obey him would take more strength of will than she had at the moment.

Besides, he was right.

She stood, the eggy scent of his destroyed eye clinging sickeningly to his warrior scent. Her legs quivered, and her stomach churned, but she steadied herself with pure willpower. She needed to help him.

"Can you do it?" he asked. "Or are these ropes too much for you in horse form? The knots are tight."

I can untie you, she said, relieved to examine the binds rather than his eye. Kellogg had tied Blaze with thick hemp tractor ropes, and while the ropes might have been difficult to handle in human form, they were thick enough for equine teeth to grab.

She started toward one of Blaze's bound hands, but her gaze slid sideways, and the ruin of his face struck her again. The seared flesh of his eyelid was crinkled and red. Some of it was charred, especially the tender flesh below his eye. What remained of his black eyelashes was gooed together across his cheekbones, and the place where his eye should've been was sunken into his brain. Blaze's eye was gone.

Without a thought, Ivy reached for the power of the Heart, already twisting it into a healing rope—but she got nothing. No energy. No power.

In that heartbeat, she was once again that helpless child looking at her sister dying at her feet.

My horn, she wailed.

"Ivy." More chagrin filled his tone. "We'll live another day, okay? I'm not going to die from this, and neither are you."

But if I had my horn, I could cure you! She approached him, planning on touching him with her stump. Maybe the residual magic would be enough to heal him.

"Stop," he said, perhaps guessing her intent with that mind-reading knack he seemed to have. "Just untie me. If you have any magic left, we need to save it."

This was her worst nightmare, come to horrible life. Blaze needed healing, and she was worse than useless. *My sister!* she cried. *My mother! They can help you. Can you reach them with mindspeak? I can—*

"Ivy, please. Just untie me." He spoke as a virgin to a unicorn, and she could only obey.

Let me see what I can do with the binds. The tractor ropes held him spread-eagle against the ancient earthen walls, his arms tied to the beams of the high ceiling.

"Yes," he said. "Please untie me. There's a rock digging right into my shoulder blade. It's killing me."

Fine. Pinning back her ears, she dug her teeth into one of the ropes shackling his ankle and pulled. Stubbornly it held, and she pulled harder, which sent pain shooting from her forehead to her knees. Blood began to ooze from her wound. It ran into her eye. She refused to give in to the pain. She might be nothing more than a mortal horse now, but she was no slacker. She pulled the rope with her teeth, jerking hard at the thing.

"Don't hurt yourself," Blaze said. "Stop a minute to breathe."

I've got it, she said, tugging. But when it gave, she flew backward, her hindquarters hitting the supporting column of oak. Above them, the ceiling shook.

"Ivy! Are you okay?"

She wasn't, but she went back to the rope at his ankle. *Yes,* she said, grabbing the rope. *I'm fine.*

"I'm not sure I believe you."

And he was right. Unconsciousness threatened again, sending those terrible stars exploding behind her eyes. *Tell me,* she said, longing for distraction as she jerked at the rope, *what happened? How'd he catch you?*

"When I drove down to the Heart for our meeting, the bastard shot me with some sort of dart. Knocked me out cold."

He used the same drug on me, but he roped me like a mustang first. A wave of nausea washed over her, leaving her weak, and the hemp slid from her teeth. How could this have happened to her? Her days would slide away into oblivion, uselessly.

"When I rope you," Blaze said, his voice loaded with intention, "there'll be no drugs. There'll be nothing but my hand. . . ."

Which would be gentle and sure, Ivy thought, panting for breath. But how could he? He needed all his power to banish Brownroot. And he'd have to work alone. What use was she?

"And my mouth . . ." he added.

Despite herself, an image of the ecoguerrillas flashed through Ivy's mind. The way Clay had chained Ann to the trailer, and the way Ann had loved it. The chains binding Clay to Ann were stronger than the steel links.

Brave words for a man tied to a barn wall, Ivy said to mask the sudden rush of emotion. *Even braver words for a man bound to his virginity.*

"And my heart . . ."

Why? Ivy cried before he could say another word. *Why are you doing this to me? I might be stuck in horse form for the rest of my life. And you can't make love—to me or to anyone.*

"Things will work out," he said. "You'll see."

Ivy looked at him, blood from her forehead trickling down her face. Blaze's words were at such odds with what stood before her—a man with a seared eye tied helplessly in a barn in the middle of Cameron County. No one would help them. They were barely able to help themselves.

I hope you're right, she said, her knees feeling stronger. She began to work at the knot again. *You know why he did this to you?*

"Brownroot figured he could use me for bait. I think he didn't truly believe in unicorns until he saw me with you."

Or maybe when he saw me with the Greenpeacers.

"Maybe."

Ivy tugged. The second rope gave more easily than the first, and she didn't go flying this time. Her flanks were lathered with sweat, and her heart was racing from the pain. Still, she eyed the third rope, which was far above her head. She would have to stand on two legs to reach it.

Every unicorn story has a virgin, so he figured you're a virgin? she asked.

His derisive snort met her ears rather than her mind. "Oh, he certainly did," he said. "Thought it was pretty funny."

Ivy took a deep breath and reared up, balancing her forefeet against the wall to which he was tied. Gold and silver sparkles lit behind her eyes, and she felt a small trickle of blood run toward her neck. *He tortured you . . . to get me? Or for something else?*

She felt him hesitate before he answered. "Couldn't say for sure. But I know one thing—he knew if he hurt me badly enough, you'd come running. And you did."

Damn, she said, cursing both the truth of the conclusion and the stubborn rope. She yanked hard and then yanked hard again. Finally the rope slithered loose, freeing his arm.

Blaze groaned, standing almost on tiptoes, one wrist tied to the ancient beams of the root cellar.

Ivy rushed to support him, and they stood together, drawing strength from each other. The heat of his body pressed against her withers, soothing her like a warm blanket on the coldest winter night.

He wanted something else too, didn't he?

Again he hesitated. "Yes." She heard him swallow, then he added, "Jesus, that hurt."

He wanted the Canticles Al Farasakh? she guessed, shifting to support more of his weight. She wanted to keep his mind off his body, off his pain. *The book I stole from your cabin and hid.*

"Yeah, he did."

And you couldn't tell him where it was because I never told you.

"That's true," Blaze said, "but don't beat yourself up. Even if I'd known, I wouldn't have told him, not even to save my eye."

But didn't you say he needs a spell to open it? she asked. Because Blaze was leaning against her, she could feel him gulping for breaths. She knew he was battling the pain.

"I did say that," Blaze said, wrapping his fingers through her mane. "I can only figure someone's helping him."

Who? Ivy couldn't believe it.

"I have no idea."

If someone helped him, he must have tortured or tricked them, she said, holding still to give Blaze as much support as possible. *No one would do it on purpose.*

"You have a good heart, always thinking the best of people."

And you don't?

"I know no person off the street could just open the *Canticles Al Farasakh* and use the spells," Blaze said, shifting his weight. "I know all the wizards personally, and Kellogg Brownroot isn't a wizard."

I think it doesn't matter if he has someone helping him or not, Ivy said. *I have the book, and he doesn't.*

"That's a good point. Does anyone beside you know where you hid it? Vinca or Seal, maybe?"

Vinca helped me find it and put it in my tr—

"Don't tell me," Blaze said. "There's a mind-reading spell in the book, and I do not want him using it on me."

Sorry. I still don't think he could have the Canticles.

"Who else besides Vinca knows?"

No one, Ivy answered. But then she remembered Vinca had thrown a slew of information at Seal, who might or might not have been listening. *Except, Seal might know.*

"Seal?"

The man fairy with the chocolate skin and silver wings?

"No," Blaze said, shaking his head and wincing. "I know who he is. It's just that . . ."

What?

"Jesus," he said, rubbing his forehead. "My head hurts and we have to get out of here."

But what were you remembering?

"I have this vague memory of Seal being here with Brownroot," Blaze said. "When Brownroot was tying me up and . . ."

Burning his eye out, Ivy thought to herself. She didn't blame him for not wanting to say those words out loud.

That's not a vague memory, Ivy said. *Seal* was *here. He found us so we could help you.*

"Okay," Blaze said. "Sure."

But Ivy sensed an uncertainty in his voice. *What?* she asked.

"Nothing. I was drugged, and it's time to get out of here. I can untie the last rope now." His voice was a thick croak.

You want me to try it?

"Save your strength. We'll need it to get us out of here. Just help me. Let me lean on you."

Okay, she said, shifting to accommodate him.

With a stifled groan, he reached above his head, and she knew that fumbling with the thick rope must hurt. He had to stretch to reach the rope, and slime dripped from his face to her coat. The heat from it nearly burned her flesh.

If only I had my horn!

"Shhh," he said. "We can do this."

Even without her horn, she couldn't put away a lifetime of healing without a struggle. Instinctively she imagined her strength pouring into Blaze, saw the golden puddle of it flowing from her heart into his veins. Normally she'd dip the very tip of her horn into the wound, and it would close up magically, like time running backward. But she couldn't do that now.

"Wow," he said, pausing in his struggle with the rope. "What'd you just do?"

Nothing. I stood here so you wouldn't fall.

"No." His tone was adamant. "You did something. Something warm washed over me, like sunlight. And the pain went away, not completely, but a lot."

She flashed a look at him, but his horribly maimed face remained maimed. Ivy didn't know what to make of this. She hadn't healed him. His eye was still a seared hole.

I wished you healing thought, she said. *That's all.*

"I didn't feel it draw power from the Heart," Blaze said. "And I can't feel the power now."

She nodded, unable to speak, even in her mind. Ivy knelt on the ground then and there, inviting him to mount. Her horn should've been tipped to the ground, but the meaning was clear regardless: she was his to command—with or without magic.

13

As Blaze moved to climb on Ivy's back, the hole where his eye had been throbbed. Without Ivy's healing, it would have been excruciating, so he counted that blessing even as he hissed at the existing pain.

Perhaps sensing his discomfort, Ivy moved closer, letting him lean on her broad, smooth back. Her equine temperature, higher than that of her human body, warmed and soothed him. And his mind forgot his pain.

It focused on hers.

How had he let Kellogg Brownroot chop off her horn? He'd known Brownroot was an evil bastard. He just hadn't seen how dangerous he was. He should have protected Ivy better, gotten her away from this godforsaken town—at least until he'd banished Brownroot to the second dimension.

Funny, now that he'd lost his eye to that bastard, he saw things much more clearly. Brownroot wasn't a rattlesnake; rattlesnakes had much cooler temperaments and made predictable sense. Brownroot wasn't that kind of snake. No, Brownroot was a black mamba, a pit viper, something liable to strike at any moment, with or without provocation. Brownroot was a king cobra possessed by the devil himself.

Now that he'd lost his eye, he saw Ivy more clearly, too. She'd risked herself to save him. She'd rescued him because he'd needed it. And she still wanted him after all these years.

It wasn't just the virginity hanging around his neck like an albatross either, because he knew he'd been too far away from her to compel her with his scent. She just wanted him.

And, God, he wanted her too. He wanted to hold her and love her, forsaking his skills and training. But he needed his power. The Heart needed his power. His father would tell him the world needed his power.

If the Heart of the World still existed. . . .

Blaze hated it that he was so weak Ivy had needed to risk herself on his behalf, but she amazed him nonetheless. He'd thought the intervening years might have left her bitter, but her heart was bigger than he'd imagined.

Suddenly his world slid away, and he realized he was on his knees, the hard-packed earth inches from his face. But his hands were warm, warmed by the solid horseflesh beneath his palms. He understood then that Ivy had lain on the ground so he could more easily get on her back.

Again her courage astounded him. That bloody wound on her forehead couldn't make it any easier for her to maneuver than it was for him. As she lay down, all that blood must have rushed to her wound.

Blaze managed to lay his chest over her broad back and slide his calf over her side. Then he settled his ass over her spine, the girth of her withers supporting his thighs with blessed relief.

Are you okay? she asked.

"I'm fine," he managed, sitting up.

Can you hang on while I stand?

He gripped her mane with his fingers and her sides with his thighs. "Yeah," he said. "You're too nice to me."

I'm a sucker, all right, she said.

He let his mental chuckle fill her mind. *We'll discover sucking abilities and who has them soon enough.*

Are all men such pigs? she asked, but he could hear her laughter. *Watch your head. The ceiling's low in here.* She snorted. *I'd hate for you to hurt yourself.*

Blaze wrapped himself around her warm neck, burying his nose in her mane as she stood and scrambled up the narrow stone steps out of the root cellar.

Thank God you know how to ride, Ivy told Blaze as they entered the small yard around the ancient farmhouse.

"My dad had to drag me to my first lesson," he said. "I didn't want to go. When I looked at horses, all I saw were teeth and hooves."

Ivy gave a weak chuckle. *Smart boy, to be careful around hooves and teeth.*

"No doubt Dad knew riding skills would become necessary when I reached my powers, but I don't think he knew how much I'd love it."

Well, you better hang the hell on because I smell Kellogg Brownroot, she said, breaking into a flat-out gallop, *and I'm not sticking around to see what he wants.*

Without thought, Blaze found himself balanced lightly above Ivy's withers, his calves clamped on her bare sides. Adrenaline kicked some strength into the wall he'd built for his pain, and he hoped Ivy had similar resources.

A branch whipped by his face as she rounded one of the perilous switchbacks. "Are you sure you smell him?" But even as he asked the question, he knew it was stupid.

Can you find Vinca? Ivy asked. *Do you know how to do it?*

"Um." Blaze stalled, leaning back as she raced down a steep grade. He raced through the spells he knew, and found fairies wasn't among them. "No, I don't think so."

Find her soul stone in the ether. She's topaz and a gossamer blue.

Sure. Nevermind his injury, he'd just slip into the ether while riding pell-mell down this mountain riding bareback and bridle free. Once he was in the ether, he'd use a type of magic he'd never tried before and find a missing fairy.

"You don't ask much of a man, do you?"

You came back to Cameron County to be a hero, cowboy, she said. *Time to put your money where that luscious mouth is.*

"You think my mouth is luscious?" he asked. "I'm going to make you prove it when we're done with this bastard."

Vinca wouldn't have left me by choice, Ivy said, ignoring his weak jest. *I'm worried for her, and she could help us. She would help us.*

Blaze had no idea what the mouthy fairy could do to aid their cause, but he trusted Ivy's judgment. "I'll do it."

I'll take care of your body. When you get to the ether, think of the vinca plant, visualize it, and that should lead you right to her soul stone.

"I can't wait for you to take care of my body."

And you're a virgin? Not planning on staying that way long, are you? The unicorn beneath him snorted just like a feisty mountain pony. *You're as bad as the fairies, the way you've constantly got sex on your mind.*

"Not sex," he said. "Love. And adoration. And if you'd been celibate for as long as I've been . . ."

He's getting closer, Blaze. Find Vinca.

Programming his thighs, calves, and hands to ride like a three-day eventer, Blaze slipped his mind inward into the meditative state. He'd never used the ether, but he knew about it. He knew that to find it, he'd have to visualize it. And it was hard to visualize something he'd never seen. Damn, he needed help.

Blaze paused for a moment, remembering the last time such a desperation was on him. His dad had helped him then, and maybe he'd help him now.

Dad, Blaze called into that inward space of his mind. *Dad, I need your help. If you can, please help me.*

Blaze. He heard his father's voice. *You've made such fantastic progress. I'm proud of you, son.*

What are you talking about?

You've asked for help, and that's not easy for you. Never has been. And after that crazy Vinca smashed herself at your request, well, I thought you'd never be able to ask for help again.

Dad, I—

Shhh, his father admonished. *We must hurry. Let me show you how to find the ether.*

Okay, Blaze said, his complete attention on his father's voice.

Imagine the woman of your dreams in a formal gown of black velvet.

A vision of Ivy easily came to mind, but instead of her usual Timberlands and Levi's, she wore formal black velvet and heels. She even wore long, black, velvet gloves that came to her elbows. Her long blond hair was twisted into something fancy at the top of her head, but those tendrils escaped and framed her face. With that playful look of hers, she brushed a wisp out of her eyes.

I've got the image, Blaze said.

Yes, his father answered. *Her face is beautiful, but think of the dress, think how much you love the curves it covers. No time to be modest. Lust after the girl!*

For years you've been telling me not to!

Desperate times call for desperate measures. Now do it.

The task wasn't difficult. Unabashedly, Blaze admired her curves, the way the velvet clung to her hips and her breasts. He walked around behind her while she laughed, and he admired the back of the dress. The dress dipped very low, just centimeters above the curve of her ass. He reached to touch that seldom seen bit of skin and—

No, his father said. *Not her skin. Her dress. Look at the fabric. See where it's smooth, and see where it's not. You need a fold. Find one. A small one is fine.*

Along Ivy's ribs, just above the curve of her waist, the velvet rippled. Blaze reached to run his index finger along the ripple, fully expecting to find the grooves of her ribs.

No, his dad said.

It's good to hear your voice again, Dad.

Shhh, his father said. *Shrink yourself. Become an inchworm or something. You need to fit into that fold. You need to want to be in that fold. You need to have Ivy's velvet surrounding you.*

Blaze was game, but he didn't want to be a worm, not even one inching all over Ivy's body. Vinca came to mind. The idea of that sexy little fairy tantalizing Ivy's perfect curves was hard to ignore. Some girl-on-girl? He wasn't proud of the thought, but as far as he knew, it was every man's fantasy.

You're right, but you're missing the point, son, Blaze's dad admonished. *Get in that fold. And hurry, because Kellogg Brownroot is nearly here, and you need to find Vinca.*

Can't you just tell me where she is?

Blaze, his father said. *You know what the cosmic forces would say about that. Now get to work.*

Okay, Blaze said.

And then he imagined he was his fingertip, a thought he knew would make no sense if he ever tried to explain it. When his full-size self touched the beautiful curve, his fairy-size self stayed on the rich fabric. For a moment, he stood in the fold, inhaling Ivy's feminine scent. He touched the velvet above his head, and it caressed his palm, as soft as kitten fur.

The ether, his dad said inside his head. *It looks just like this. It's filled with as much magic as this place is. And there's more than just a hint of lust. Imagine it.*

Blaze did. Within a heartbeat, a black, velvet universe surrounded him. Just beneath the surface pulsed the most precious thing in his life—the woman who'd always held his heart in her hand.

What Blaze noticed in the second microsecond of his voyage into the ether was the complete absence of pain. Subduing his fear, he touched his face, tentatively, as if he were touching boiling oil or a poisonous spider. As his finger touched flesh, he breathed a deep breath of relief.

His eyelid was there, right where it belonged, smooth and broad. It wasn't sunk into his skull. His fingertip brushed over his lashes. But his eye was there. He opened both eyes and saw depth—the ether had restored his missing eye!

Don't get too excited, son, his father said. *The ether's like your dreams. Your true self appears here. Only, back in the physical world, you're still missing that eye.*

Damn, he didn't have time for this, but he couldn't help himself. He rubbed his eye, assuring himself it was really there.

But you may yet regain a way to see things, son, his dad said, sounding fainter. *If you learn how to look.*

Are you saying I'm going to move to the ether permanently?

Mmmm, his dad said, making that noncommittal noise for which he was famous.

Blaze really didn't have time for guessing games. Ivy wanted Vinca, and Blaze had to find the pesky fairy. Every minute he was in spirit form, he was leaving Ivy to fend for herself and burdening her with his physical body clinging to her back.

Remember to keep your focus, son.

Blaze recognized father speak when he heard it. Translated, his dad meant: keep your cock in your pants, son. Blaze ignored the comment.

Blaze looked around, but all he saw was velvety black that exuded both love and lust. In the blink of an eye, soul stones appeared all around him. They gleamed like the brightest stars set against a sultry summer night. A pink and green amalgam glittered to his right, and right next to it he saw something white and navy, and just below that a green and blue soul stone sparkled. More glittering combinations blinked in each direction.

The soul stones, Blaze asked his dad. *How do I sort through them?*

But no one answered.

Dad?

Blaze sensed he was alone again. His dad had helped him find this place, and then he'd gone back to wherever the dead go when they die.

Thanks, Dad, Blaze said into that space in his mind, hoping his dad could hear him.

Blaze scanned the sky above and below, looking for topaz and blue, but it was hopeless. There must have been thousands of souls pulsing around him. He found topaz gleaming above him, but it was teamed with emerald. And when he scanned for blue, his mind reeled because so many blue choices sparkled around him: light, dark, opaque, transparent, opalescent.

With so many to choose from, Blaze could spend hours sifting through the soul stones. But he didn't have hours, he had heartbeats.

And then he remembered Ivy's advice. *Think of the plant,* she'd said.

Closing his eyes, he tried to envision a vinca, which wasn't nearly as easy as calling up an image of Ivy in formalwear. He had only the vaguest idea what vinca the plant looked like.

Focus, he told himself. Surely he could call up an image. Maybe from the forests of his youth or the gardens around Manhattan's brownstones?

As he sought an image of the plant, a vision of the fairy appeared in his mind instead: her topaz hair and skin, shining gold in the afternoon sun, her green skirt made from some sort of plant, her raspberry lips and perfect breasts, her hands on her tiny hips as she teased him. *I'll grow on you,* the feisty fairy had said when she'd first told him her name, *like the plant.*

And then he had it. Vinca the plant was a ground covering. It was a weed, an invasive species.

Breathing a sigh of relief, Blaze let the image come into focus. Glassy evergreen leaves edged with creamy white. Lavender-blue blooms. Five petals. The tiny yellow stars in the center. Vinca might be an invasive weed, but it was beautiful.

Vinca, he called into the ether. *Where are you?*

He didn't get an answer. Instead a shooting star whizzed past his face and crashed into the nothingness just in front of him. When he blinked—with both eyes—he saw that her soul stone gleamed almost within reach.

Her soul was the golden topaz of her skin, a soft, amber color, and it was mated with a blue more turquoise than he'd been imagining. The blue was almost fuzzy, like gauze curtains. It was the same color as her wings. That's what Ivy must have meant about gossamer, he realized.

Blaze reached for Vinca's orb, an image of the fairy firmly in his mind. But as he touched the soul stone, the strangest sensation zipped through him. If he'd been sucked like a spider through a vacuum cleaner, it couldn't have felt any weirder. Vinca latched on to his soul like a drowning person grabs a life raft, and she pulled him through the ether.

Why wasn't he surprised at her forwardness?

His spirit self landed in a place he recognized—Kellogg's cabin. Blinking both of his spirit eyes, he looked around, grateful for the absence of pain and his ability to see in-depth. The logged sides of the cabin came into perfect focus. So did the small field in front of the little house.

But where was the fairy who'd dragged him here?

Vinca? he asked.

Mmmumnphff! he heard in response.

Blaze couldn't decipher the word, but he pinpointed the sound as coming from inside the cabin. He walked toward the door and tried the knob—and his hand slid right through the door. Interesting. He let his entire self fall into the cabin, sliding like a cartoon ghost from one room to the next.

Then all sense of wonder fled.

Vinca had been captured in a bubble spell, green as pus. For a moment he stood, part of the door, staring at the sphere. He reached out a mental tendril toward it and then pulled back as if he'd been burned.

It smelled like Kellogg. But how was that possible? Kellogg wasn't a wizard, hadn't gone through years of intensive training. Kellogg had been an associate of his father since Zachariah had left Cameron County, and although Brownroot had always been greedy—slick in the way he manipulated the lobbyists and the White House so the oil and coal industry always came out on top—he'd always been clearly mortal. Not a whiff of magic had ever floated around him.

But there it was. Brownroot had made that pus-green bubble in front of Blaze, and Vinca could not escape it.

Floating from the door, Blaze stepped toward her. Freeing her without magic seemed like a good idea. Any wizard worth his salt would feel thrumming in the Heart's power—if the Heart still existed—as Blaze used it, and he didn't want to alert Brownroot. Although Blaze still couldn't imagine how the man had come into his power, especially since he hadn't even seemed to really believe in fairies and unicorns until yesterday. Weird bastard.

Blaze crossed half the room, but the fairy began shaking her head wildly. Her hands were tied behind her back, and someone had put a tiny piece of duct tape over her perfect lips, but she was clearly trying to tell him something.

Mmmumnphff! he heard again from behind the tape, which must be spelled itself, he realized, since even her mindvoice was muffled. Simple duct tape wouldn't have that effect.

What is it? he asked. This bubble spell, and the thing with the duct tape, was too creepy, too dangerous for caution. Blaze would use magic to free her. He began the slight preparation needed to banish the bubble spell. He'd take on Brownroot if it came to that.

Mmmumnphff! Vinca said again. She was kicking at the bubble, which only covered her in mucous green.

Seriously concerned now, Blaze began his subvocal singing of the spell that would break the bubble, hoping there was enough residual magic left from the Heart to cast an enchantment—but Vinca gestured wildly with her shoulders, banging without effect against the bubble's walls. Was she pointing at something?

Still singing his enchantment under his breath, Blaze looked behind him. And for a moment, Blaze was just confused.

Seal fluttered near ceiling height just near the kitchen, and he looked pissed. What in the world had made him so angry? Who'd made him so angry? Was Brownroot here?

Blaze started to scan the rest of the room for whatever had made Seal so angry, but just before he could speak the final words of the spell, the tiny brown fairy above his head waved a huge wand at him, a grimace contorting his handsome features.

Even as Blaze realized the fairy was pissed at *him,* a shot of spirit adrenaline zinged through Blaze, and he whipped himself back to the ether.

Which was a good thing. Because the last thing he saw as he evaporated from the cabin was a lightning bolt sizzling from Seal's wand right toward his head.

Seal had tried to fry him.

14

Bathed in the velvet blackness of the ether, Blaze could draw only one conclusion: Seal had helped Brownroot trap Vinca. Jesus. Seal must be working with that greedy bastard.

Blaze had to rescue Vinca now, he knew, but Blaze paused in the ether for a second. How was he going to tell Ivy her lifelong friend had gone evil?

He pushed that problem to the background. It'd be a lot harder to tell her if Seal and Brownroot managed to hurt Vinca first. He wouldn't let them hurt the mouthy fairy, not on his watch.

Part of his wizard's training involved memorizing a handful of useful spells, and one of these included a place-switch spell, in which one being swapped physical location with another. He should be able to rescue Vinca this way.

But the fact that Seal held a magic wand—amazing—made the spell trickier. For one thing, Blaze had never seen an actual magic wand. He'd thought wizards lost their abilities to make wands generations ago. Had Brownroot given the wand to Seal? Where the hell had Brownroot gotten it?

Blaze wouldn't let this concern stop him. He imagined the wand falling harmlessly to the carpeted floor as Seal and Vinca switched places.

Confident that he was ready to bust Vinca out of the enchanted sphere, Blaze grabbed on to the fairy's soul stone and landed right back at the cabin, the arcane Persian words of the spell rolling easily through his mind like a favorite song.

Again he landed in the small yard, but he didn't rush through the door. He didn't use the door at all. Instead, he walked through the chimney, like some vengeful Santa Claus.

Seal's back was turned, focused on the door, as Blaze silently entered the room, and he took a minute to study the fairy.

Blaze realized the wand must be magicked for Seal to hold it. It was at least four times the fairy's length, and it looked metallic, but Seal held it as easily as a stalk of grass.

Blaze shot a quick glance at Vinca, his fingers at his lips so she wouldn't arouse Seal's attention. She slowly nodded, huddling into herself.

Before Seal saw him, Blaze let the words of the enchantment unravel in his mouth and fall gently from his lips. The ancient words were so quiet any background noise would have obscured them.

But there was no noise in this room, only silence—and a hyperalert fairy on the lookout for a vengeful wizard.

As Blaze's spell blossomed in the air, power should have rippled from the Heart of the World. Any magic creature—any wizard or fairy—should have sensed it. Blaze himself couldn't feel it, but the fairy fluttered his silvery wings as he turned toward Blaze, wand poised to unleash its terrible wrath.

Cold hatred filled the tiny fairy's eyes, a hatred directed at Blaze. And perhaps that loathing slowed the fairy just a heartbeat, because it seemed to Blaze that the fairy's abhorrence took Seal's breath away.

Blaze didn't care—the overwhelming emotion was something to use. Before Seal could flick his wrist to unleash the wand's vicious magic, Blaze sang the final ancient syllables, and his enchantment coalesced, filling the cabin with the chocolate and gold vapor of his magic. Power from the Heart should have reverberated its beauty through the room, but Blaze couldn't see it.

For a moment, he had to trust that his spell worked, because he couldn't see through the richly colored mist. Leaving no room for panic, he visualized Seal in the bubble and Vinca flying free. Within a heartbeat, the vapor cleared and he saw success. Had he used residual magic?

Seal's tiny silver wings were beating madly against the mucous-green walls, and Vinca fluttered over the door where Seal had been, her hands still tied, her mouth still taped.

Maintaining his calm, Blaze scanned the carpet by the door for the wand. It wasn't there. His spell hadn't worked quite as he'd hoped, because the brushed-nickel thing wasn't anywhere on the floor—not by the door or the fireplace or in the hall.

Where was the damned wand?

Then he spied it—in the bubble. With Seal.

Mmmumnphff! Vinca said, but Blaze ignored her.

Keeping his emotions under wraps—that wand was dangerous in Seal's hands—Blaze cast a quick spell, one that froze Seal in place.

His spell didn't work, and for a moment he was worried that all the residual magic was depleted. Or maybe the wand gave the fairy some sort of immunity. Blaze sang the arcane words, but Seal continued to whip his hand back to discharge the lightning.

Blaze used all his training to overcome whatever protection Seal had against Blaze's spell, pulling from whatever remained of the Heart's power. He willed Seal to freeze. With preternatural clarity, he imagined the fairy frozen, completely immobile.

Opening his eyes, Blaze examined his efforts. His spell had

wrapped around the green-mucous bubble, strangling it like some crazed octopus. His amber-gold and chocolate-brown tendrils of magic obscured the foul green.

But had the spell worked?

Blaze waved the air around the sphere, dissipating the mist. And what he saw made him want to celebrate. Seal was frozen, his grimace of loathing immobilized on his face. His tiny fist was flattened against the sphere's wall, green mucus dripping down his wrist.

Vinca, Blaze said with relief in mindspeak. *Take that wand from him.* Blaze wasn't at all sure that his spirit form could physically manipulate anything. He hadn't practiced that skill since he was a child.

Mmmumnphff! Vinca said, buzzing around his face.

Seeing the problem, Blaze let another quick spell float from his lips, and her bindings fell away, vanishing in the air before they touched the ground. Rubbing her lips and wrists, she buzzed over to Seal like an angry bee.

I told Ivy you'd be more powerful than your dad, and I do believe I'm right.

Please, Blaze said. *Can you get the wand?*

Yes, she said. And Blaze could have sworn her voice was quavering. When she got to the mucous bubble, she looked at Blaze, her diminutive, fox-colored eyebrows raised in a question.

"Can I—" She shrugged, making those tiny breasts jiggle, and she pointed at the sphere.

It won't keep you out, only Seal in, Blaze explained. *Hurry, though, Brownroot's chasing us, and that freeze spell on Seal won't last forever.*

Vinca reached into the bubble and grabbed the wand. And while she was there, she slapped Seal with all her tiny might. "You stupid, stupid little man," she said; then she turned back to Blaze and asked, "Could he hear that?"

Yes, Blaze nodded. *He did.*

She turned back to her captive and said, "If you think size is so goddamned important, you've been surfing that damned Internet too damned long. Fool." She stopped for a minute and wiped her brow. Then she lit into him again. "No one cared that you're small! I loved you small!" She threw her little arms in the air. "Ivy loved you small! What, you never wanted to fuck another fairy as long as you lived? Because that's what would have happened if you'd gotten your stupid little way!"

Blaze could see she'd berate Seal for a long time if he didn't stop her. *Vinca,* he said.

"That Kellogg Brownroot guy said he'd make Seal human-sized if he helped him get the book back—and that fool fairy believed him!"

Vinca, Blaze said. *Get out of here. Go find Ivy and tell her what's happened.*

"You want to boss me around now?" She whirled toward Blaze, her green skirt flaring, showing off her lovely thighs. "Open the goddamned door for me."

Blaze didn't take the tone personally. Vinca was scared and pissed off. *I can't. I'm a ghost.*

"You fool," Vinca said in that tiny, acerbic voice. "Use a goddamned spell to open the door. Hell, just open a window."

Um, Blaze started to say. He didn't consider himself to be a man who was easily embarrassed, but he was embarrassed now. *I—um, yes.* Then, before she could come up with any pithy replies, he sang the arcane spell that sprang the door open, and hot afternoon air poured into the room.

"Thank you." Her words were polite, but the inflection was biting.

Let's not fight, fairy, he said, holding up his ghostly palms. *You completely rock, and we're on the same team.*

"Don't be nice to me, Blaze Williams," Vinca said, her hands on her hip, the wand pointing to the ground. She looked like a stern schoolteacher, but deep emotion filled her tiny blue eyes. "You might make me cry."

Betrayal by a trusted friend is something to cry about, he agreed. *But maybe you could do it later. Brownroot is hunting us down.*

"It's worse than that."

What do you mean?

"I told Seal where your book was, and he told Brownroot where Ivy and I hid it—that was a while ago. Brownroot was going to get it, but Seal was keeping me captive until Brownroot knew the book was still there—in the trunk, I mean."

So we can assume Kellogg has the Canticles Al Farasakh—*again.*

Vinca looked defeated suddenly, and Blaze's heart went out to her. He was supposed to save her, not make her feel worse.

"I shouldn't have told him!" Vinca wailed. "This is all my fault!"

No, honey, it isn't. He wished he could scoop her up and comfort her. *You trust your friends. You're supposed to trust your friends.*

"I have a big damned mouth." She shook her head angrily and wiped her nose with her wrist.

As Blaze thought of Ivy's bloody forehead, shorn of its glory, Blaze's spirit hand went to his restored eye. He knew all about guilt and failed responsibility.

I think we can assume that even if you hadn't told Seal, Brownroot would've done whatever he could to get the Canticles Al Farasakh *back.*

Vinca didn't look convinced, but she made an attempt to collect herself, taking a deep breath and asking, "What do you want me to do?"

Is that wand too heavy for you to get to Ivy?

"No," she said. Vinca tossed the thing from one hand to the

other, the flat shine of it catching the afternoon sun. "It's not heavy at all."

Good. Can you catch up with Ivy? Give her the wand and let her know what happened here.

"You want me to tell her about Seal?"

He could hear reluctance in her tone, and he didn't blame her, not one bit.

I'll tell her, he said. *I'm sure I'll catch up with her first.*

"Okay." She fluttered toward the open door, sunlight pouring through it, and asked, "You know where she is?"

Last I saw her, we were galloping away from the Heart of the World with Kellogg Brownroot hot on our trail, down those switchbacks that lead to town.

"We?" Those fox-colored eyebrows were raised almost to her hairline.

Yes, Blaze said. *I'm riding her as we speak—*

"Blaze?"

A searing and sudden pain lacing from the small of his back to his right shoulder made him flinch in pain. *What the*—he started to say, but the hurt flying across his flesh and through his nerves broke his hold on the ether.

15

The pain tore Blaze's spirit form from the cabin. He landed back in his own body with a suddenness that left him breathless. The scent of sweating horseflesh filled his nostrils, but it didn't obscure the other smell—the smell of his roasted skin.

Ivy, he said, feeling her mane between his fingers in addition to the swamping pain in his eye and up his back. Between his thighs, her body heaved with Herculean effort, and her foamy sweat soaked through his khakis to his skin. *What happened?*

I'm glad you're back, Ivy said. *Sorry you got hit. Brownroot was throwing lightning bolts like they were confetti. I caught one—well, you did—when I jumped the creek.*

You okay? You didn't get hit?

I'm fine, and I think I lost him when I jumped the creek—I can't hear the dirtbike now, and I don't think he can cross it on a bike.

Blaze looked behind them, squashing a longing for perfect vision. With his poked-out eye, Blaze couldn't judge the distance between them and the stream, but it looked pretty far. *I think you're right*, he said. *I can't see him.*

Did he hurt you much?

Blaze felt his back. It hurt like sunburn. *I'm fine.*

I don't suppose you can spell us to my cabin or something? she said, slowing her run to an easy lope.

No, Blaze said, leaning forward to ease her ability to run up the hill. *Teleporting a horse is beyond me, even in a world of infinite magic.*

You calling me fat?

Blaze laughed, his thighs clasping her sides. *No,* he said, admiring the curve of her neck and the way her mane practically floated as she galloped. *You're perfect in every way.*

I hope you mean that. Ivy burst off the deer path and jumped over a huge log with all the grace of a steeplechaser at the Grand National. Blaze grabbed her mane as she leaped, amazed at her strength. *Because when this is over, you might be stuck with a new horse for your stable—and I eat a lot of hay.*

Ivy tore through a bunch of low-hanging evergreen boughs, and the green needles ripped at Blaze's face, chewing at the tender flesh where his eye used to be.

You'd be worth every oat. And I suppose we really have to run right through all these branches?

I'm sorry, she said, trotting into the woods, thick woody vines banging his thighs. *But this is the fastest way away from here.* A jagged branch, as fat as Blaze's leg, smacked his knee.

Ouch, he said as thorns from something else ripped at his arm.

Watch out, she said. *Now duck!*

Taking her at her word, Blaze ducked into her mane—and caught a mouthful of fairy wings.

"What the hell?" he tried to say, but it came out more like, "Hah-ha haaw?"

"Spit me out, Blaze Williams!" Vinca said. "You'll make me drop this damned wand."

Vinca! Blaze and Ivy said at the same time. Careful not to raise his head, he extracted the butterfly-sized fairy from his mouth.

"Who'd you think it was?" Vinca said in that snotty way, wiping Blaze's spit off her wings. "The head of the EPA?"

Very funny, fairy, Blaze said. But it was difficult to think of a smarter comeback because it seemed as if the forest were trying to eat him alive as Ivy galloped off the trails; the branches bruised him through his clothing and tore at his exposed flesh.

I think I'm funny, Vinca said.

Finally he looked at the fairy, who wore a teasing smile on her raspberry lips as she sat where Ivy's bridle path would have been shaved, were she an actual saddle horse. But the smile melted when she saw his face.

She gasped. *Oh, my God. Oh, my God.* Her own tiny hands fluttered like her wings to her face where she touched her own eye. *Oh, my God,* she said again. *Your eye.*

And then the tiny fairy climbed to Ivy's poll and saw the bloody mess where her horn had been just hours ago.

"Oh, my God, Ivy!" Vinca said out loud for every creature, magic and mortal, to hear. "What's he done to you?"

I don't want to talk about it, Vinca.

"We have to get your horn back!" the fairy said with outrage. Both her hands and wings were madly fluttering. "We have to do it now!"

"Vinca, that's enough," Blaze said.

"But—"

"Enough." Blaze didn't quite growl, but almost. "Just give it a rest for a minute, fairy. We need a second to regroup."

"I just can't believe it!" Vinca wailed.

He ignored her shock. There was nothing he could do about it. "I think," he said slowly, "Ivy and I will need all the help you can give us."

"Then let me try this." Vinca stood tall on the tips of her

toes and shook the wand at Blaze like she was trying to get the last drop of water off it. As she waved the wand, she said, "Wand, do what we need most."

And once again, Blaze found himself ripped through the ether, Ivy in equine form still between his thighs.

As her hooves left the ether and hit the earth, Ivy recognized the glade immediately. She sometimes slept here in unicorn form. The grass grew thick, and it cushioned the fall of her feet, which was good because it seemed every part of her ached.

What would she have done without Blaze's generous gift of his own strength? She wanted nothing more in this moment than to lie down in the tall grass and drink in the earth's power.

"This was a good place, Vinca," Blaze said. "Thank you."

"Thank the wand," the fairy said. "I'm not sure I had much to do with it."

"Either way," he said, "the glade is safe." Feeling Blaze's spine and ass shift on her back, Ivy knew he was looking around. "No one can come at us from above. It's well protected."

"It's pretty, too," Vinca said. Ivy guessed she was doing her best to wear a cheerful face, but the fairy would be struggling. "This wand is a strange thing. Why'd it bring us here?"

"Maybe it bought us some time," Blaze guessed.

This is a place of respite, she said. *The creatures of this glade allow no discord here, only rest and pleasure.*

"No dragons, then," Blaze said.

What do you mean?

"They feed on strife and conflict. That's how you make baby dragons big and fat—hatch them on a battlefield."

I had no idea. But Ivy was too tired to care.

"I still think this wand is amazing," Vinca said. "But why didn't it fix your eye? Or your horn?"

You asked for what we needed most, Ivy said. *That must mean a reprieve.*

"Speaking of a reprieve, why don't you lie down for a minute?" Blaze suggested, his muscular thighs sliding over Ivy's side as he dismounted. "The grass looks soft."

He was right about the location—it was nice. When Ivy ate in equine form, she loved the grass here best. It tasted sweeter and more tender than anywhere else, and a tiny mountain stream trickling from the steep hill above quenched her thirst. Even now in the late afternoon, hot sun dappled the green blades, and fat, white clouds invited daydreamers.

I keep the water in that stream clean, Ivy said, kneeling in the thick grass, *even from acid rain. So if you're thirsty. . . . And I have a pack in the hole of that oak with a blanket and a few human provisions.* She sank completely into the sea of long, green blades. *If you're hungry.*

Ivy would've retrieved the pack herself, but hands—not hooves—fit into the tree's hole. That she'd have to go through the rest of her life at the mercy of others to open her doors sent a pang of frustration and fear through her veins.

And the fact that she'd never be able to use her horn to keep this water clean again, to heal or protect . . . that thought left her bereft. The totality of her helplessness nearly stole her ability to breathe.

"Let me get the bag," Blaze said. He reached into the thick oak and pulled out the pack. "Before I open this, Ivy, I need to ask you something." Each word he spoke seemed to hold an anchor's weight.

What? she asked, missing her ability to speak as much as her hands.

"Would you rather spend your life as a white mare in my stable—or any stable for that matter—or running free on BLM land in Nevada, or—"

She interrupted his awkward rant. *Blaze?*

"Sorry," he said. He took a deep breath and shoved his

hands in his pockets, looking as abashed as a schoolboy despite his ruined eye. "Now that the time's here," he said, "I find I'm all tongue-tied."

What time's here? Ivy tossed her head, which sent a cascade of pain sparking through her. *I'm confused!*

"If we get stuck in a world without magic—I'm saying *if*— do you want to spend it as a horse or as a woman?"

It's a stupid question. I'm stuck as a horse unless some miracle happens.

"I can compel a change." His eye burned with intensity as though his universe rested on her answer.

"You did it before," Vinca said, back to her snotty self. "Against her will."

"I should've asked your help then," Blaze said, his good eye never wavering from Ivy's, "and I didn't. If I had asked for your help right from the start, Kellogg Brownroot might already be in the second dimension, and the *Canticles Al Farasakh* might be back in our possession."

"Yeah," Vinca said. "That's right. You really screwed it up."

But Blaze's gaze still didn't leave Ivy's. "I'm sorry, Ivy."

"What about me?" Vinca said. "Are you sorry about all the terrible things that happened to me? I mean, my wings were smashed, and I was caught in a snot bubble, and—"

"Yes, Vinca, I apologize to you too. I should have enlisted your help right off the bat too."

In the warm grass, Ivy sighed. *I was too angry with you. I wanted to believe you'd become a greedy industrialist. It made it easier to hate you for leaving me.*

Blaze sat on the grass next to Ivy, and his spring-moon scent wafted over her, still delicious, although not compelling since she'd lost her horn. Or since the Heart's demise.

"Would you choose to be a horse or a woman?"

Ivy tried to think about the question, but her head hurt, and she felt thirsty. She just wanted to close her eyes for a few minutes. The grass beneath her cheek smelled so sweet.

"Ivy?"

"Why does she have to choose?" Vinca asked. She'd found a cloth napkin in one of the rucksacks Ivy had ferreted away, and she was gently dabbing at the wound on Ivy's forehead.

Having the blood washed off her face, from the corners of her eyes, from around her nostrils, felt like heaven to Ivy. She wanted to sleep for a year in the warm sun.

Yes, Ivy said. *Remind me why I have to choose.*

"Here," Blaze said, reaching for the napkin and missing the fairy. His depth perception had been completely ruined, Ivy saw. "Let me do that." Vinca placed the cloth right in his hand.

He began cleaning Ivy's face and neck, wiping her legs, expertly relieving the tension in her tendons as he would have with any performance horse who'd had a workout like hers.

"It's like this," Blaze said finally. "A final confrontation with Brownroot is inevitable. I have to—no," he corrected himself, "*we'll* have to take him on."

"Damn straight we have to take him on," Vinca said with her usual spunk. "And that rat bastard Seal tóo."

Seal? Ivy asked. She hadn't thought she had any capacity for sorrow left, but she found she did. *What happened with Seal?*

"Honey," Blaze said, stroking her neck, "he's helping Brownroot."

No, Ivy said. *I can't believe it. Not Seal.*

"It's true," Vinca said in her jingle-bell voice. "He thinks Brownroot'll turn him into a human-sized fairy when they're finished with all this."

But if Brownroot destroys the Heart, there will be no magic to change him. I mean, if the Heart still even exists.

"Maybe he thinks Brownroot will change him before all the

magic dissipates," Blaze said, still running that soothing hand down her neck.

"Or maybe he's lost all capacity to think with his big head," Vinca said.

"For all we know, Brownroot already changed Seal to full size."

Ivy couldn't even consider Seal's defection, had no place left in her mind to process that loss, and Blaze didn't give her time to worry—not about that.

"The point is, any number of terrible things might happen during this confrontation," Blaze said.

Like?

"Like Brownroot might kill me. He might capture you again—and maybe you'd better decide what form you'd like to be in, should the worst happen."

"Oh, my God!" Vinca said. "That creep is not going to kill you or blow up the Heart of the World! I'll poke his eyes out myself—" And then she must have realized what she said because she glanced at Blaze and blanched. "I mean, I'll stop him! I'll—"

"Vinca," Blaze said in his warm voice, "it's okay. I watched you attack that Hummer, and I know you're fearless, but we don't need crazy bravery here."

Besides, we think he already blew up the Heart.

"Blew up the Heart?" Vinca asked. "But all the magic we've been using . . . Of course it still exists."

But can you feel its power?

Vinca paused, thinking. "I—I don't remember! Oh, my God! Did that bastard blow up the Heart too? Are we using residual magic?"

I don't think we'll know until we get there, until we actually see it.

Vinca's hands were flapping, and her voice rose to a screech. "But—"

Then her voice fell silent, although Ivy could see her lips moving.

Vinca, there's no strife allowed here. You have to stop, or the magic of the glade will remove you.

Ivy watched the tiny fairy drop her hands in resignation. Her lips were still moving without sound, but then her chirpy voice filled the glade. "I'm sorry."

Next to Ivy, Blaze shook his head. "An amazing place."

A place of respite.

"I need to know what you want, Ivy." He pushed that shock of hair from his good eye. "Do you want to stay a horse, or would you prefer your human form?"

Ivy's head hurt too much, but she knew what she wanted. She wanted him. Like she always had. She wanted her power back. She wanted to lose this feeling of helplessness.

But it was not possible. Now, more than ever, Blaze Williams belonged to the Heart of the World, to the world itself.

She should choose equine form, just to offer the last protection she could to the Heart. She should, but she couldn't.

A woman, she answered finally.

"You're certain?" Blaze shifted uncomfortably, his hands still in the pockets next to his lean hips.

Perhaps when this drama was over . . . perhaps then she could hold him. *I'm sure,* she said.

Then he began to sing the same words she'd heard before in the car by her cabin.

The forced change hurt, but it was worth the pain. If she had to spend the rest of her days as Blaze's pet, she'd die. She wasn't a pet—she was his equal.

Her hooves retracted into hands, and her tail retracted into her back, but long after she'd normally have regained her human form, her equine traits were still evaporating. And it hurt. Blaze's spell didn't create a smooth transition; it jerked her through the transmutation. And during a prolonged moment where no unicorn attribute gave way to a girl feature, Ivy wondered if she'd get caught forever in a half-horse, half-girl state.

When her silvery horse mane finally gave way to her gold-colored human hair, Ivy found herself standing. Her knees quivered, and her thighs trembled. She rubbed her aching forehead, but the throb of power that usually pulsed there was gone.

It was gone.

She would've fallen, collapsing into the dirt at her feet, if Blaze hadn't been there to catch her. But he gathered her in his arms, surrounding her with his strength, protecting her from the ruin of their world, from the ruin her life had become.

His lips touched hers as gently as a butterfly laps pollen, his touch more tender than it had ever been all those years ago, more tender than he'd been earlier today.

"We can't do this," she said.

But he didn't answer. He simply kissed her more deeply, cupping her face in his hands. She gave herself to his kiss, yielding their fate to him.

Ivy pushed his dark hair out of his face. The sight of his ruined eye filled her with a longing to make him whole, slamming home once again the entirety of her helplessness.

Her fingers, palms, her nails savored the silky texture of his hair. As she caressed the smooth nape of his neck, she realized she'd been such a fool to suspect him of trying to hurt the Heart or her sister unicorns. Blaze Williams's soul shone with purity and truth.

With a shiver of delight, she twined her arms around him. Years of feeling the Heart of the World left her sensitive to its presence and fluctuations. But even without her horn, she realized that in his arms she still felt that familiar thrum of power—only now it felt exactly like human desire.

Ivy's lips sought his, wanting his warmth and strength. Tasting the salt of his sweat and tears, she sucked in a bit of his bottom lip, remembering how he'd used to love when she bit him, sometimes hard.

But there'd been enough pain today, for him and for her.

As slowly as a flower opening with the warmth of spring, she ran her tongue over his lip. Her shallow, quick breaths mingled with his, and she swam in the luxury of his masculine scent. The image of a sword-bearing warrior virgin invited rather than compelled.

As he kissed her with a deliberate slowness, holding her as though she could save him, Ivy wanted him to herself.

Blaze withdrew for a moment, just long enough to look closely at her face. His eye shone in the afternoon sun, sparkled, it seemed, just for her.

"We can't do this," she said again. "The Heart of the World needs you, and—" And then she couldn't speak. Her lips moved, but no words left her mouth.

"Respite," he said. "This glade offers only respite."

And she quit fighting; she trusted Blaze, trusted his need to help her save the Heart.

As slowly as an oak leaf drifting on a spring breeze, he tucked a tendril of her hair behind her ear and kissed her again. He didn't demand anything from her. He didn't need to take possession. She was his.

And he was hers.

He touched her mouth with his tongue, teasing and questing. Embracing the comfort he offered, she parted her lips again. Heat from his body enveloped her as he wrapped her in his arms.

The somnolent feeling of their kiss didn't last. In the face of this desire, she knew it couldn't. With a budding awareness of the ache between her thighs, she returned his kisses with growing passion, tangling her tongue in his, surrendering her body to his.

Blaze tilted Ivy's head back, asking her to yield. But he was asking for what she'd already given. She opened her mouth to him as her pebbled nipples pressed hard against his chest, and he ran fingers through the length of her hair.

His magic thrummed through the balls of her feet, through her knees. Sending a thrill through her nipples and lips, the enchanted sensation settled between her thighs.

But in her human form—without the innate magic of her horn—she was free from him. The hold of the virgin over the unicorn was gone.

What she had left to give him now came from her heart.

His chocolate-brown eye gleamed with desire as she looked at him. The golden moon in the sea of brown glowed gently in the afternoon sun.

Ivy stepped back, missing the strength of his arms around her. She pulled her T-shirt over her head and stood vulnerable before him. Her eyes were open, and she was his.

"We'll keep your virginity intact," she said.

As he pulled her toward him, the warmth of his palms as they slid over her skin electrifying her, she wanted to explain this to him, tell him she had no reservations. But his lips dipped to the hollow of her throat, and her words floated away.

Words seemed to fail him too. "We'll see" was the only sound he could mutter as his mouth explored the curve of her neck. She leaned her head back so he could kiss the entire length of her neck.

Stepping back from her, Blaze opened the pack and shook out the blanket. He laid it on the thick grass and said, "It's not the shores of Kinzua."

"It's more," she said.

"More what?"

"More enchanted."

And suddenly she was right. Vinca had apparently called in all her fairy friends. No acorn rain this time. The fairies were blessing this union.

Sunlight gleamed through their crystal and gossamer wings,

filling the meadow with jewel-toned purples and blues. They fluttered through shafts of sunlight with one purpose in mind—to fill the dell with wonder.

And, as Ivy looked around, she saw how the fairy folk had succeeded. Bright dashes of pinks and orange danced through the evergreen boughs, flirting with splashes of turquoise and emerald.

But didn't they know? Blaze couldn't lay with her, not and save the Heart.

Surrounded by twinkling fairy wings, Blaze wrapped his hands around her wrists and pulled her to the blanket. Her skin, aching for the glide of his touch, savored the fleecy texture beneath her thighs.

As Blaze bent toward her to kiss her, Ivy melted into his arms. If she could never do anything but remember how beautifully they'd sung together, at least she had that—their souls had created the most perfect song she'd ever heard.

His lips trailed the tears to her mouth, and there he drank in her sorrow until none was left. He left nothing, save desire. He sucked her lips and rolled her tongue over his until she returned his ardor, and it didn't take long. As his hands found the small of her back and pulled her snug against him, the air between them crackled, tight with possibility.

"Ivy," Blaze said, his good eye locked on hers. His voice was husky, filled with the vibrant energy of a man aware of his strength. The power of his voice matched the strength of his thighs and shoulders.

But she'd had enough words, and she'd waited long enough to have him. "Yes," she said. That one small word filled the meadow.

Blaze knelt before her like a knight kneeling before his queen. He brought her hand to his lips and kissed her palm, sending that wave of desire to her core. He looked up at her, his eye luminous. "I promise to love you, Ivy, with my whole heart."

At his pledge, words failed her.

16

With a deliberate slowness, Blaze unlaced Ivy's boots and slid her feet out. Then, his eye locked on her, he unbuttoned her fly. Her khakis slithered to her ankles, and he stood, holding her hand as she stepped out of them. For a moment he simply admired her, and she almost felt self-conscious as that rakish grin lit his face.

"These things used to scare me to death," Blaze said. He traced the peach-colored strap of her bra from the top of her shoulder to her breast.

The way time seemed to have slowed in this glade of respite sent a shiver through Ivy. He was hers—this warrior virgin was hers.

"And now?" she asked.

Ivy wanted to reach behind her and unhook her bra, but he'd left her heavy with desire. The palpable existence of her need weighed down her arms. The fog of it filled her mind. Her breasts and thighs, each of her chakras, were heavy with it. She couldn't move.

But he could. As if savoring the texture of her skin, his hands slid along the length of her back, stroking and caressing until his fingers reached the clasp. And then she stood naked, save her panties.

"Dear God, you're beautiful," Blaze breathed, palming a breast with enough admiration to satisfy a goddess. There was no mistaking the desire in his voice.

She leaned toward him, letting the tips of her nipples graze his T-shirt as her lips touched his. She tugged his shirt off without a word and let it float away.

Ivy let her finger drift over the planes of his chest, over his stomach as he traced the outline of her areolae.

Ivy groaned, and he dipped toward her breast, flicking his tongue over her skin. Her awareness of the warm fairy colors, the very forest that housed her heart . . . all of these faded away as he sucked.

His mouth touched her so lightly at first and then more insistently. Cushioned by the soft grass beneath their blanket, she arched toward his mouth until she couldn't bend farther, feeding him and herself—and even that wasn't enough.

She thought of the way Ann had offered her breasts to Clay, and a thrill coursed through Ivy. Blaze unabashedly savored the gift. The sun might have set and risen again, for all she cared. He became her world.

But her hunger expanded. She'd been craving nothing more than his mouth on her breast, his hand on her skin. But now her mouth craved him, and her core cried out for satisfaction.

She lay on top of him, the breadth of him, the solid feel of his muscle and flesh beneath her making her feel as weightless as a spring blossom carried on a breeze. Her breasts slid over his naked chest as he leaned on the blanket, into the grass, and his warm palms caressed her shoulders.

Wanting to close the small distance between them, she leaned toward him and kissed him. His lips drank her in as though they couldn't get enough of her, searing lines of pleasure into her heart and between her thighs.

Blaze's hands traveled lower down her back, toward the curve of her ass. She arched, inviting his fingers to explore the aching warmth of her core, but her panties were in the way.

Ivy laughed a little and straddled him so her heat pressed hard against his cock. Only two layers of cloth separated them.

One layer must always separate them.

His hands found her breasts. As the pads of his thumbs traced her nipples, she groaned but pulled away. She bent down and grabbed his snap with her teeth. It gave easily, and she undid the fly. She pushed his jeans away.

Tracing her hand down the hard ridges of his stomach, she slid her hand over his cock. The velvet heat of it was something she hadn't expected. Running her hand from the wide base to the very top, Ivy spread his pearl of liquid over the tip. Her fingertips memorized every contour, every change in texture. She licked him, savoring his musky male scent, and he lay back, yielding himself.

Her panties were just about to slide off in a puddle of desire, but she wasn't through pleasuring him yet. With his length in her hand, she leaned forward so the tip of her breast caressed the tip of his cock. He throbbed in her palm.

His thumbs hooked over her waistband and tugged. The feel of his knuckle over the soft skin of her waist, the promise of it, sent another wave of desire right to her core. She couldn't take any more teasing. Her panties were gone, and she needed satisfaction.

He did too.

"Come here," he growled. Then he rolled her beneath him. The liquid silk of his skin over her breasts, the weight of his body covering hers . . . She sighed and knew the world would always be a place worth living in as long as Blaze was in it.

Ivy stretched her hands high above her head and arched her back as Blaze straddled her, his cock pressing hard against her. She thought he might fuck her there and then, like a pirate or a Viking, but instead he savored her.

The warmth of his hands explored every detail of her waist and hips, the soft curve just under her belly button. She lay in the warm, soft grass, naked before him. The weight of her desire left her weak for him, completely subject to his adoration.

Without crushing her, he leaned over and captured her mouth in his. His tongue danced over hers, and she felt the promise of it. He promised something more lasting than she'd ever felt in the hands of the fairy folk.

With his gaze locked on hers, he didn't say a word, but fidelity poured from his expression. When he licked the tip of her tongue, Ivy knew there wasn't anything she wouldn't do for him. This kiss held significance and hope. Even if the world crumbled like dried earth between their fingers, they'd have each other.

"Please," she said, barely recognizing her voice for the way desire had weighted it. "Your jeans, they're still in my way."

He stood, and despite his lean hips and muscular planes, he looked self-conscious as he finished taking off his jeans. Laying in the lush grass looking up at him, she could think of only one word to describe him: adorable.

"Gorgeous," she said as fairy light painted him in jeweled colors.

"No acorns," he said, and Ivy laughed.

"Vinca seems to have given us her blessing."

Then Blaze was embracing her, his chest caressing her breasts. The scent of the crushed grass beneath their blanket floated around them, mingling with his delicious fragrance, and Ivy could imagine no headier perfume.

Rolling on his side, Blaze kissed her, gently rolling his lips over hers. With the lightest touch, his tongue teased. His fingertips caressed her face, telling her with his every movement that he wouldn't hurt her, that she was sacred to him.

"I wish I had a coronet of gold to put in your golden hair," he said, his voice melodic as he wrapped a tendril around his finger. Then he took her left hand and said, "Or a ring for your finger that sparkles like your eyes."

"I don't need a crown or a diamond," she said.

"Would you take my heart instead?" he asked, burying his face in the curve of her neck.

"If you take mine."

His hands slid along her shoulder blades, and she arched toward his hungry mouth, the strength of his hands keeping her safe. As his fingers traced their way from her breasts across her midriff, her stomach tightened in anticipation.

When his fingers finally slid between her thighs, her breath caught in her throat. She couldn't breathe. The pleasure was too intense, too shocking. Ivy thrust her hips toward him, wanting more, wanting something deeper. The ache between her thighs couldn't be denied.

His fingers dipped in enough to tease, enough to ask. But she was ready, and his cock throbbed against her thigh.

Her desire filled her, weighed her down, leaving her weak and lusciously unable to move. She was his, and he showed her the delight of being his.

Lie back, his fingers commanded, *and enjoy the enchantment cast by our souls and our bodies.*

And she did.

His fingers caressed her labia with a featherlight touch, so close to her clit, close enough to tease but not satisfy. She thought she might die from desire, and she flexed her hips toward him. Burning, she craved the relief of his touch.

His mouth traveled up to the tender spot behind her ear. He bit her earlobe as his fingers slipped over and around her throbbing clit.

She fought back a moan and the urge to press against him. Enslaved by the delicious ravishment that overwhelmed her senses, Ivy yielded herself completely. If he stopped now . . .

Passivity was no longer an option. Ivy began moving rhyth-mically against his hand and shifting to show him exactly the right angle. *Here?* his touch asked.

Yes, her body answered. *Just like that.*

He added more fingers, and suddenly it felt like he had a fingertip slithering around every slippery inch of her.

Her body stiffened, and she knew she was so close. He didn't miss a beat. Suddenly she cried out. She knew every creature in the forest heard her, and she didn't care a bit. Her muscles pul-sated against his fingers, and he expertly pressed against her, satisfying her. Behind her closed eyes, her orgasm tore through her.

"Ivy," Blaze said, his eye locked on her, but suddenly the late afternoon sky blackened, reminding Ivy of tornado weather. The light breeze around them began to blow erratically. Even her human nose, lacking all magic, smelled the impending rain.

At first she thought—irrationally—that her orgasm had done something to the sky. Is this what happened when a wizard got too close to losing his virginity? "What's happening?"

It's the Glade of Respite! Vinca said. *It's objecting to some-thing!* The fairy glared at Blaze and then said aloud, "It's prob-ably you."

"Me?"

How long do you really think you can hold out? Vinca looked at Blaze and then looked at her wand. *You've waited too long.* She waved it at the two of them.

Ivy found herself naked on top of him. Once again, the blue afternoon sky arced above them.

I really like this thing. Vinca laughed. *Now I'll leave you in privacy.*

Ivy tried to wiggle out from underneath Blaze, but he was heavy, and the delicious sensation of her breast sliding over his weight didn't encourage her to actually leave. His cock pressed against her.

"We can't go through with this, Blaze. The Heart ... If we're to have any chance at all. . . ."

"If we're to have any chance at all," Blaze said to her, kissing her face, "we need to trust our love for each other. We've not trusted that love enough."

"But your powers."

"This feels too right," Blaze said to her. "And my father . . ." He shook his head and laughed.

"Your father what?"

"My father had a habit of telling me to do the opposite of what I was inclined to do."

"Why?"

"So that when I committed myself to doing it, I was completely committed, that I did it to the best of my ability."

"And that's relative to us how?"

"He told me specifically not to make love to you, which means," he said, stroking her inner thigh, "I'm going to make mad, crazy, passionate love to you." He stopped suddenly and looked at her. The vulnerability in his expression grabbed her heart. "I mean, if you want me to. That is, if you want me at all."

Collapsing against his muscular chest, she inhaled his musky scent, wanting it to fill her nostrils for eternity. She thought of the Heart of the World, the cold, granite boulder that had sat for millennia in this forest. Could their love save it? Could she trust her love for Blaze?

"Yes," she said. "I want you. And I love you."

He buried his face in her neck and nibbled behind her ear. "Then I'm yours, unicorn."

"I'm not a unic—" she started, but he shushed her with a kiss that left her squirming with desire.

She wanted to purr like a kitten as the rough skid of his cheek tickled her soft flesh, and he added, "We've started something that needs to be finished. Come here," he said, pulling her closer to him.

His mouth was on her neck, and his hand was on her breast, and his arms were wrapped around her. Tilting her head to offer him the full length of her throat, Ivy realized the Heart hadn't diminished in its importance to her—it was only that Blaze had become more critical.

She was wet, and she was ready, but he didn't rush. He pulled her so that she straddled him, giving her the power to stop at anytime. Her knees pressed against his sides, his cock pulsated against her sex. He moved his mouth from hers downward.

Knowing what he wanted, she leaned forward and pushed a breast to his mouth. She was so willing, so willing.

As he licked and sucked and bit at the stiff nipple, desire coiled in a tight ball in her belly. She twisted to present her other breast to his mouth, enjoying the shift in pressure of his cock against her clit. He obliged, hungrily, grazing his teeth against the other nipple and pressing harder against her.

Closing her eyes, Ivy focused on his fingers, his lips, the muscles of his chest as his touch burned over her skin, teased her abdomen, made her muscles pull tight.

Lost in a tangle of pleasure, she sighed and parted her thighs, letting the tip of his cock slide over her clit. She wanted his magic, his scent surrounding her, the heat of his muscled body pressing along hers, the gentle, careful way his hands moved over her.

"Yes," she moaned. His hands encircled her waist and pulled her fully on top of him. He thrust his hips upward in an invitation she accepted. She pressed against him, electrified by the sensation of his shaft pressed so intimately against her body.

"Hurry!" Ivy said, thrusting against him. "Now, please!"

Still, his hard, swollen cock pressed against her sex. Shifting so the tip was poised for entry, Blaze thrust into her, and she began to lead the way, sliding his cock right over her clit.

Ravenous now, Ivy lowered herself completely until he sank even deeper into her, spreading her, filling her. She shuddered.

She felt him shudder too.

"God, Ivy . . ." Blaze pushed her onto her back. Blaze was over her, making her feel safe and protected. His musky scent, as deliciously pungent as the hemlocks around them, filled her. She felt her muscles clamping on to him.

The magnitude of his desire for her filled her. Under him, she began to work, meeting each of his thrusts. She could hardly bear the pleasure of the penetration, and she hoped he was as close to ecstasy as she was.

Gasping, she couldn't look away from his face. She saw his jaw flex in an effort to control himself. Forced to keep her strokes short with his body on top of hers, she let his cock sink deliciously inside her. Suddenly she knew she was one nudge, one feather touch away.

For a moment, Blaze's body was as taut and tight as the trunks of the ancient oaks surrounding them. Then he quivered. When he shuddered with a yell, Ivy yielded. Within seconds, she came with him.

Blaze roared, "I need to . . . !"

Ivy thrust herself down, and he thrust up for one more fulfilling drive.

"Blaze!" she cried as the orgasm sizzled across her nerves in a delicious explosion.

Deep inside her, she could feel the pulsing of his thick cock.

Time stood still for a moment while Ivy's heart thudded in time with Blaze's. The pace of his breath matched hers, and their blood pumped in tandem. Spasms still delighted her body when she opened her eyes, longing to see the expression on his face.

But an orange sphere, translucent as a soap bubble, caught her attention instead. It had appeared above them.

"Blaze," she said into his ear. "What is that?"

17

A bolt of lightning cracked from the blue sky above them as the ginger-colored bubble came closer and expanded. The wind blew, bitter cold and out of nowhere, raising goose bumps over Ivy's body.

As Blaze rolled off her, Ivy watched the wind whip her T-shirt through the air toward the bubble. Her shirt slammed into the sphere, but the bubble didn't pop as she thought it would. Instead, her shirt bounced off and whipped toward her.

Trying to rein in her fear, she caught the shirt and shrugged into it, braless.

"Where's Vinca?" Ivy shouted to Blaze over the outrageous windstorm. Ignoring the approaching sphere, she scanned the branches whipping above them but saw no fairies. "Is she all right?"

"I don't know—"

"Here I am!" Vinca shouted, careening toward them from the top of one of the huge evergreens, her wings pressed tightly against her sides. The nickel-colored wand was tucked under her left wing.

"Catch me!" The wind took Vinca's words and tossed them so Ivy wasn't sure she'd actually heard them. But fast as a blink, Blaze whipped out his hand and caught Vinca.

"Thank God you're safe," Ivy said, taking Vinca from Blaze's hand.

"What is that thing?" Vinca shouted, pointing toward the orange bubble. It had moved closer to Blaze and Ivy, but Ivy still didn't know what it was.

"Did you make it with the wand?" Ivy yelled.

"No! Why would I do that?" Vinca put her hands on her tiny hips. "Maybe you did something to piss off the Glade of Respite!"

"I don't think so," Blaze said. He grabbed Ivy's khakis and bra and gave them to her. The bubble was just above their head now. "But I don't know what it is." He grabbed her panties, which were skittering across the glade.

As Ivy pulled on her clothes, shoving her bra into her pocket, the bubble descended toward them. Along with Blaze, she tried to dodge it.

"What *is* it?" Ivy yelled again.

"I saw a green one like that!" Vinca shouted, hardly audible above the wind, "and it was bad news. Stay away from it!"

But Blaze shook his head as he pulled on his jeans. "I don't know what it is," he said. "But Kellogg Brownroot didn't make this."

"How do you know?" Ivy asked. Blaze stepped aside as it tried to fall upon them again, and Ivy stayed right next to him, hating the feeling of helplessness that swamped her. Magic had never in her life worried her. "How do you know?" she asked again.

"It doesn't have his smell."

Vinca crinkled her tiny nose and shouted, "None of those bubbles have a smell."

"Maybe not to you," Blaze answered, again stepping north,

away from the sphere that was pursuing them slowly across the meadow. "But I can smell it." Then he shrugged into his shirt, which threatened to blow away in the wicked wind.

"Then why're you running away from it?" the fairy shouted.

"Good question."

"Blaze, I don't like this," Ivy said. "I can't sense anything about it."

He looked at her, understanding in his expression. "Then trust me!" Blaze shouted over the wind, which was howling even more insistently now. The wind threatened to rip their clothes from their bodies.

"What?" she yelled. "I can't hear you."

"Trust me!" He grabbed her wrist and pulled her toward him. The orange sphere drew closer, and although Ivy's head told her to move away, she listened to her heart and stayed at his side. His arm held her waist; his hand protected her head.

The amber-colored sphere descended toward them. Ivy told herself her fear was irrational, based only on the fact that she was blind to magic, but logic didn't still her mind. With the wind blowing leaves around them, trepidation left her cold. She buried her face in Blaze's chest.

The bubble dropped over them, its slightly slimy skin embracing Ivy's skin for a brief kiss. And then they were inside. Before she opened her eyes, an incredible ache raced through her forehead, replaced immediately by a deep and relentless throb.

"Oh!" she cried, putting her hand to her forehead.

"What is it?"

"My magic! Something touched the place where it should be."

"Something touched something," Vinca said, not shouting but audible nonetheless.

"I don't understand," Blaze said, ignoring the fairy.

But the pain had subsided in Ivy's head. "I don't know. For a second, the center of my horn's power really hurt."

"Listen," he said, looking around them. The bubble had brought quiet and calm with it. Despite its filmy appearance, it filtered out the howling wind. Even as leaves and branches swirled around them, Ivy heard nothing but the sound of Blaze's breathing.

"What is this thing?" Ivy asked, tapping the side. It dimpled but didn't break. In fact, it seemed pretty rubbery.

Vinca squirmed out of Ivy's hand. "Take this," she said, handing the wand over. "I don't want it anymore." Then she buzzed toward the bubble's wall and back into the growing storm. The wind grabbed her and whipped her away from them, but Blaze was faster, catching her as if she were a fly ball.

"What the hell do you think you're doing?" Blaze asked her.

"Let me go, you big brute," the fairy said to Blaze. He released her, and she fluttered over to Ivy's shoulder, grabbing Ivy's long hair to steady herself.

"Are you trying to kill yourself?" Ivy asked.

"I wasn't trying to kill myself," Vinca said, brushing a small twig from her mussed hair. "I was stuck in one of these damned things once already. I don't want to get stuck again."

"What are you talking about?" Ivy asked.

"That green sphere was Brownroot's creation, Vinca," Blaze said.

"And you're so damned sure this one isn't?" Vinca demanded. "I just wanted to make sure we weren't all trapped."

"Well, I guess you know," Ivy said. "You still want to leave?"

Above them, they watched as a huge branch shook, cracked, and began to fall.

"Watch out!" Blaze shouted, tackling Ivy out of the way. Vinca grabbed on to Ivy's earlobe and shrieked. The branch hit the edge of the bubble and slid off. If his quick action hadn't saved the women, the magic sphere would have.

"You still want to leave?" Ivy asked again, more softly this time.

"Um," Vinca said, letting go of Ivy's earlobe. "No. That's okay."

Ivy nodded and looked at her warrior. "There's something strange about this bubble, Blaze. I think you made it."

"Why?"

"It smells a little like you."

"Hmmm," Blaze said. That shock of hair had fallen in his eye, hiding his expression. "Let me try something." Blaze's gaze became focused, and then he said, "I can feel it!"

"The Heart? Can you feel the Heart?" Ivy asked.

"Yes!" He turned toward her, his one eye blazing with intensity. "I can feel its power better than I've ever felt it." He stepped left. "Dear God!"

"What?"

He stepped right and then turned in a circle. "Brownroot has some sort of dampening spell around the Heart, but I can actually feel gradations of its power sneaking out around the edges. In fact, I can feel the power oozing out more clearly than I could ever feel the Heart when it wasn't dampened."

"Does that mean—" Vinca started to ask, but Blaze wasn't finished.

"Look." He closed his good eye, turned in several circles, and stopped, facing a random direction. Then he paused and said, "I'm facing northeast."

Ivy looked at the sun hanging in the sky. "You're right," she said. "How'd you do that?"

"Your power's increased, hasn't it?" Vinca said.

But he was off on some inner journey again, Ivy could see by his look of concentration. He hummed a few bars under his breath, and just as the notes wrapped around her heart, the orange sphere surrounding them flared, doubling in size.

"What the hell?" Vinca said. "How'd you do that?"

"Hang on to that wand, fairy," Ivy told her. "I think it does amazing things."

"It's not the wand," Blaze said, laughing. The deep sound filled the glade. "It's one of my father's misdirections—he always told me making love to Ivy would decrease my power, but it's done exactly the opposite."

"But I know for a fact your dad lost his powers when he lost his virginity," Vinca said. "He loved your mom with a passion, but he definitely took a hit."

But Blaze smiled, his eye locked on to Ivy. "My mother wasn't a unicorn."

Then Ivy understood. "Something he told you not to do, so you'd do it even better?"

"Exactly."

Ivy had a hard time imagining a more attentive lover than Blaze had just been, a more sensuous lover. Blaze's spring-moon scent clung to Ivy's skin, and her breasts still ached deliciously from his touch.

"But I can love you even better than that," he said as if he'd read her mind. Blaze fell to his knee. "Ivy L'Engle, after we rid the world of Kellogg Brownroot, after we've restored the safety of the Heart of the World, Tchili's horn, and yours, will you marry me?"

Vinca madly clapped her hands and giggled, her wings brushing against the orange bubble surrounding them. "Say yes! Say yes!"

And Ivy couldn't help but laugh. She threw her arms around Blaze and kissed him, letting his scent fill her lungs and give her life. As she leaned into him, her chest against his, their heartbeats matched each other. "Yes!"

"Yay!" Vinca cheered even as the wind increased its howling outside their protective sphere.

"Now," Blaze said, "let's stop Kellogg Brownroot."

"Smite the bastard," the fairy said.

"Smite?" Blaze asked. "Did you just say 'smite'?"

"That's what I said." She laughed. "Smite that ugly bastard."

A huge branch crashed down on the orange sphere, and another lightning bolt cracked above them. "I think Brownroot is planning on smiting us," Ivy said. "I'm assuming he's doing something to cause this weather."

"Wait here a minute," Blaze said, walking to the other end of the bubble. The bubble stretched for a moment and then popped into two, so that one surrounded Blaze and the other protected Vinca and Ivy.

"I have to tell you something, unicorn," Vinca said. Her unusually somber tone gave Ivy pause.

"What?"

"I had a vision while that bastard Seal trapped me in the snot bubble."

"What kind of vision?" Ivy remembered her own—and the one Crystal had described. "Did it have Blaze and a sword?"

"Yes." Ivy felt rather than saw Vinca nod on her shoulder. "And a dragon, a huge dragon. Bigger than any I've seen around here. And evil."

"Did Blaze win?"

Vinca paused, and fear—as physical as spiders on her human flesh—crawled up Ivy's spine. Finally the fairy said, "I don't know. The vision didn't show me."

"What did the vision show you?"

"Nothing we didn't already know," Vinca said, returning to her normal self with a giggle.

"And what's that?"

"He's going to need our help."

Ivy looked at her virgin warrior—no, her warrior—across the glade. He didn't look like he needed help.

"Even with all his new power?" Ivy asked.

"Yep," Vinca said. "He still needs us."

The amber glow of the protective sphere bathed Blaze. She guessed from his look of concentration that he was casting a spell. His spread legs were planted firmly in the earth beneath him. His broad shoulders were relaxed.

Something flickered in Ivy's vision, something strange. His jeans and T-shirt vanished, giving way to leather armor padding his chest and thighs. A long sword appeared in his hands, and he easily stepped back into a warrior's pose, balancing his weight on the ball of his back foot. He arced the huge sword above his head in a graceful swoop as effortlessly as if he held nothing heavier than a broomstick. The blade glinted in the light of the rising moon, flashing a gold the exact color of the amber in his eye.

"You see that?" Ivy asked Vinca.

"What?"

Ivy sensed rather than saw a huge dragon coiled just beyond sight. The evil radiating from its black soul permeated the glade, sinking in even to Ivy's magic-deprived heart. Never in her life had Ivy felt such cold evil, such heartless malice, and the spiders of fear crept along her spine again.

But then Blaze's long sword sent its golden light flickering through the darkening glade again, and Ivy knew: the gleaming sword curving above Blaze's head was meant for the dragon—the dragon she couldn't actually see.

"Where's the dragon?" Ivy asked the fairy.

"What dragon?" Vinca asked.

"That one!"

"I don't see anything." Vinca shifted her weight on Ivy's shoulder to look where she was pointing. "You mean the one from my vision? I don't know. I figured it was a figurative thing, you know? Not anything real."

"Then what the hell is Blaze doing in armor wielding that huge sword right this minute?"

"Honey," Vinca said, "that injury went to your head. I have no idea what you're talking about."

Ivy blinked and looked again. Blaze was back in his jeans and T-shirt, the white cotton stretched across the expanse of his back. His hands were empty, no sword in sight. "I don't understand," Ivy said.

Blaze walked toward them, exuding power. "I've got the spell ready," he said in that melodic voice.

"Does it involve a sword?" Ivy asked. "A long sword?"

Blaze blinked his good eye. "I can't use a sword without depth perception."

"That's not what she asked, wizard," Vinca said.

Blaze stepped close enough for the separate orange spheres to reconnect with that strange popping sound.

"Is Brownroot a dragon?" Ivy asked.

"I've no idea, but you are so goddamned gorgeous." He pulled a leaf from Ivy's hair.

Vinca put her hand over heart and pretended to swoon. "Love is in the air," she said. "That's the strange weather."

"Vinca, shut up," he growled. Then he turned toward Ivy. "Are all your friends this annoying? This one won't shut up, and the other's plotting with an axis of evil the politicians haven't even dreamed of."

"You are so avoiding my question, Blaze Williams," Ivy said. "What are we supposed to do now? How're we going to stop Brownroot?"

"Shhh," he said. "We've got each other. We can do this." Blaze brushed her forehead with the pad of this thumb, toward the place where her power had been centered before she'd lost her horn. "What's this?" But as his thumb slid over the spot, that penetrating pain shot through her again.

"Stop! Damn," she said, clutching her forehead as the ache spread behind her eyes.

"What is it?"

Another branch crashed toward them, but the bubble deflected it. "I don't know," she said. "It feels like—like when I

change from girl form to horse, only even stronger than that."
She threw up her hands. "I can't explain it."

"It's glowing," he said, looking at her forehead but not
touching it again.

Vinca fluttered right in front of her, examining her forehead.
"He's right!" she said. "There's a jewel in your forehead. It's
very pretty."

"Like a—" She didn't dare say the words. "Like a new
horn?"

But Blaze shook his head. "I don't think so." He brought his
hand closer and then away again. "It's like a gemstone of some
sort but lit from behind."

Ivy explored the area with her own fingertips. It didn't hurt
when she touched it herself. "I don't know, Blaze. What color
is it?"

"It's . . . beautiful."

"But what color?"

"It keeps changing from an emerald green to some greenish
blue color," he said, squinting at it with his good eye.

"It's turquoise!" Vinca said. "It's weird."

"Coming from a woman whose skin is the color of topaz,
that's saying something," Ivy said.

Blaze brought his hand closer but still didn't touch her. "It
gets brighter as my hand gets closer."

"It's pulling me," Ivy said. "Did you do this?"

Blaze shook his head. "Maybe it was the wand."

Ivy looked at Vinca, who shrugged and said, "I have no
idea."

"I think it's time to hunt down that bastard Brownroot,"
Blaze said. "Let's go to the Heart and send him to the second
dimension."

Ivy led Blaze through the deer paths toward the Heart, the
purple sky howling around them. The wind whipped birds and

squirrels from the trees. She turned to help them, but Blaze stopped her. "We need to hurry."

Realizing he was right, she asked, "You have a plan for when we get there?" The orange bubble added an eerie glow to the early evening. It cast strange shadows on his face.

"Not sure," Blaze said easily, keeping pace with her long stride. "It depends what he's done to the source. Can you sense the Heart?"

"Not without my horn."

"But with that gem on your forehead, does it help? It must *do* something."

Ivy concentrated on the pull that had been her center since the beginning of time—the tug of the Heart of the World on her being. She didn't feel that, but something kept calling her. The sensation was similar, sort of. It wanted her to go southwest, which wasn't the straightest path to the Heart.

"No—" she began to say.

Ivy. Crystal's voice in her mind was clearer than it had been in ten years. Had her sister somehow come to Pennsylvania to help her?

Crystal? Ivy asked. *Are you here?*

Help me.

You sound like you're right here. Where are you?

That man— Behind Crystal's voice, Ivy heard panic. *Kellogg Brownroot—he's—*

And then her voice was gone.

"What is it?" Blaze asked. Ivy had come to a complete stop in the center of the trail.

"He's doing something to my sister." Ivy started racing down the path. "He's doing something terrible. I think he's brought her here."

As Ivy and Blaze approached the glade where the Heart of the World stood, an amazing thing happened. A dryad had emerged before them, her face beautiful in its angularity, despite the appearance of her skin, which looked like hemlock bark.

"Hello?" Ivy asked, walking alongside her. Her twiggy legs carried her remarkably quickly through the gale. The girl-shaped creature twitched a long, pointed ear in Ivy's direction but kept walking south toward the Heart.

Keeping pace, Ivy reached out to touch the creature's narrow shoulder, and almond-shaped eyes met hers. They were exactly the shade of evergreen needles, and for a moment, Ivy lost herself in the quiet green of them.

But then the dryad broke the spell. "He needs to know where the hardest, straightest trees grow in our forest," the dryad said in a voice as soft as a summer breeze. "He needs the best ones."

"Who?"

"The great magician. The dragon." Not slowing, the creature walked purposefully south, leaves swirling in her hair. "He needs to know. I must lead him."

"Is he a dragon or a magician?" Ivy asked the dryad, but the creature was already walking down the path with that glazed expression.

"Hey!" Vinca shouted to the creature. "You can't just walk away from Ivy! She's your protector!"

"Shhh, Vinca," Ivy said. "I can't protect anyone." But she met Blaze's gaze over Vinca's, and the alarm she saw in his expression matched that growing in the pit of her stomach. She asked, "What do you think—"

But a water nymph appeared, her silvery hair cascading down her cerulean back like a waterfall despite the crazy wind. "He needs to know the source of the life-giving outflow of springs here in our mountains," the creature said without prompting.

The creature's watery eyes never left the path ahead of her, and when Ivy touched her cool back and asked, "Who?" the nymph kicked one of her webbed feet at Ivy and jerked away from her.

"The great magician, of course," she said in a voice that sounded like waves crashing over rocks. "Now, get out of my way, unicorn."

"I'm not a uni—" Ivy began, but the nymph wasn't listening.

The nymph scurried beneath Blaze and Ivy, looking intent on her goal. "They look like rats following the Pied Piper," Blaze said.

"It's like he's calling them somehow," Ivy agreed. "Calling them and tricking them to hand over the things they guard. I wonder if this is what Crystal was talking about." She looked at her fairy friend sitting on her shoulder and asked, "What about you? You feeling the need to hand over any of the treasures you protect?"

"Nope, my coal deposits are safe from him." Vinca shook her head. "The only thing he makes me feel is the overwhelming urge to poke his eyes out with that wand," she said.

Ivy snorted as the wind blew another huge branch against their orange sphere of protection.

"How about you?" Vinca asked. "You feel any strange compunction to hand over the Heart of the World?"

"No." Ivy shook her head. "Maybe he's got no way to lure me in without my horn. Besides, he's got no magic of his own."

"If he's got no magic, how's he luring the dryad and the water nymph?" Vinca asked.

"Good question," Ivy answered as they continued down the path toward the Heart. "How can he lure any magic creature?"

She'd asked the question rhetorically, but Blaze had an answer. "The *Canticles Al Farasakh*."

A gleam of scarlet caught Ivy's eye. "The *Canticles Al*

Farasakh," she repeated, looking into the glade where the boulder containing all the world's magic sat.

"That's what I said."

"No," she said, pointing into the glade they hadn't quite entered. "That's it there, isn't it?"

Kellogg Brownroot was sitting cross-legged on top of the Heart staring into his lap. A fat tome rested on his legs, its red cover and binding just barely visible.

His shaggy hair was unruffled by the howling wind.

18

"I'm going to kill him!" Vinca said, grabbing the wand and swooping away, but Blaze caught her midair, quick as a snake.

"Didn't you learn anything when you attacked the Hummer, you brave fool?" he asked as the wind bashed leaves and sticks against the orange bubble. "Some things are just too big for you to tackle alone."

"You learn that lesson *now?*" she asked, one fox-colored eyebrow arching in derision.

Blaze ran his hand over his missing eye. "I've seen the error of my ways."

"Shhh," Ivy said, leading them all away from Brownroot's line of sight. She hoped all the blowing forest detritus would mask their movement if he caught it from the corner of his eye. "You'll get us all killed."

Blaze brought the captured fairy up to his face and said, "The minute you leave this sphere, you'll fall victim to whatever spell he's using to compel all the magic creatures, and I can't protect you." He gently set her on Ivy's shoulder and told her, "Stay here."

"Unless you think Cameron County would look nice with a few strip mines," Ivy added.

"No offense to the unicorn," Vinca said with a saucy grin, stroking Blaze's shoulder, "but I'd rather stay in your pocket, wizard. I love it when you get all manly."

And then Ivy noticed the wind wasn't working alone. Cloudwolves had gathered in the sky above Kellogg, slathering and gnashing their doglike teeth. Long, gray tails lashed the sky, and cold, hard hail fell as their jaws worked. "We'll do your bidding," they bayed toward Brownroot. "We'll bring rain to whatever crop you desire. We'll bring hail and snow too, when you want to kill."

"The way he's compelling all the magic creatures, that's an enchantment from the dark half of the *Canticles Al Farasakh*," Blaze said, seeing what had caught Ivy's attention.

"And look what he's done to the Heart," Vinca added. "Is that from your book too?"

Ivy looked. An opalescent red bubble shimmered around the Heart, encompassing Brownroot while he read. As cloudwolves roiled in the sky, the sphere took on gray and ruby hues. Brownroot's face took on a demonic appearance in the scarlet bubble. She figured it was the dampening spell Blaze had detected.

Not that Brownroot appeared to notice. He didn't look up as Ivy and Blaze stood on the glade's edge. Which was probably a good thing. Blaze took Ivy's arm and pulled her back into a thicket.

"We need a plan," he said.

Ivy tried to think of something, but her attention kept getting pulled in a southwestern direction. Still, whenever she looked over there, she saw nothing that didn't belong. "Got any ideas?" she asked, longing for the sensitivity her horn would've given her.

"What about this wand?" Vinca said, spinning the thing in her fingers. "Can we use it on him?"

"That wand is ancient," Blaze said. "We don't know what it does or how it works."

"Hey, I saw it shoot lightning," Vinca said. "That seems like a good thing to toss at Brownroot. Fry the bastard."

"But you can't really tell it what to do," Ivy said. "It's almost like it has a mind of its own."

"I think with Brownroot, we'd better stay in control as much as possible," Blaze said as Ivy looked southwest again.

"That was weird," Vinca said to Blaze, pointing to Ivy's forehead. "Did you see that?"

"Wait," Blaze said. "Ivy, turn your head again." She did, and he pointed in the opposite direction. "Now that way."

"What is it?" she asked after she complied.

"Weird," Vinca said, fluttering in front of her, apparently to get a better look.

"What?" Ivy said, forcing her voice to keep quieter than her emotions dictated.

"The gem on your forehead. Whenever you look over there," he said, pointing southwest, "it glows."

Ivy rubbed the nub. It felt more solid now. "Strange."

"What?"

"The nub's pulling me in that direction, and all I see over there is Brownroot's dirtbike."

"Maybe our first plan should be to see what he's got on his bike," Blaze said.

"But how—" Ivy began, frustrated with the hundred ways their hands were tied. "How're we going to fight Brownroot? He's got the book and the Heart. I have nothing. Do you have enough power to take him on after we . . ." she ran her fingertips over his chest, ". . . you know."

"When you fucked like bunnies, you mean?" Vinca asked.

"You've got a mouth, I'll give you that," Blaze said. He might have been referring to Vinca's way with words, but his gaze was on Ivy's lips. "And, no, I don't feel any different. But when I cast a spell . . ." He touched his eye, which was now completely scarred over like a year-old wound. "That's when I expect a difference."

"Not if he's hogging all the magic," Ivy said, pointing at the man sitting on the Heart like some demonic yogi.

"Even if Blaze can't bust through that enchantment, Brown-root can't have all the magic," Vinca said. "Look at all the creatures here now."

Ivy looked. A swan maiden fluttered near a centaur, who stepped around fairies and pixies under his feet. Each wore an expression of blank devotion.

"They all have their magical reservoirs," Blaze pointed out. "If I ask, maybe I can draw on them."

"I'll give you mine," Vinca chirped, shimmying her breasts suggestively.

Ignoring the fairy, Ivy said, "That might work, but only if the creatures *can* give it to you. What if they can't? What if they're in some sort of thrall?"

"They do look like zombies," Vinca said.

But the vision Ivy had been having since she'd scented her warrior came back. She saw both her magical friends and creatures she'd never encountered helping Blaze fight a monstrous dragon. Why did Lord Uroboros keep coming to mind? He was locked away—and she would have felt if he'd busted out of her prison.

Unless he'd busted out after her horn had been sawed off.

"Vinca, Crystal, and I each dreamed the creatures lent you strength," Ivy said.

"That may be," Blaze answered. "But I won't take anything without their permission, and they don't look like they're in any position to give me anything."

"So what are we going to do?" the fairy asked, her voice sounding even smaller than usual.

"I think we should see what's on that dirtbike. Maybe it can help us," Ivy said.

"Lead the way, unicorn."

Ignoring the way Vinca's words put her heart in her throat, Ivy walked outside the glade to the bike, passing two enthralled pixies, their pink and green dresses fluttering madly around their thighs. Their thrall was so complete they didn't flinch as the wind swept a bunch of leaves over them. They didn't even flash a grin at Blaze.

Ivy followed the deer path, not worrying about stealth. No noise they could make would be audible above the freak storm and the ruckus caused by the cloudwolves. When the bike was just a few feet in front of them, Ivy stopped.

On the far side of it sat a canvas rucksack. No cover grew between where they stood and the bike. The last few steps would expose them.

"It's the bag," Ivy whispered, rubbing the jewel on her forehead. "There's something in it."

Blaze looked at the rucksack, and Ivy could almost read his thoughts. If he retrieved it, Kellogg would see him.

"I can do it!" Vinca said. "Let me bring it back here. I'm so small he won't see me."

"But then you'll fall in his thrall," Blaze said. "And I can't cast a spell, or he'll know we're here."

"What if he already knows we're here?" Vinca shot back, but Ivy looked at the oil magnate, and his eyes hadn't left the book. He hadn't moved in the slightest. Blaze must have had the same thought because without another word, he walked over to the bike, the orange bubble stretching between them, picked up the bag, and brought it back.

As he picked it up, though, a searing pain shot through Ivy's head—but it wasn't pain, exactly. It was longing and desire and a need to feel whole. She clutched her forehead and nearly doubled over with the weird sensation.

"What is it?" Vinca asked, stroking Ivy's cheek.

Blaze looked at her. "Your entire face is bathed in the light from that gem."

Suddenly she knew her fate had somehow been tied up in that backpack. The nub on her head needed the contents, needed to bathe in it. "Open the bag," she said.

Blaze was beginning to unbuckle the thing when a neon-red lightning bolt struck the orange bubble above them. Their protective shield crackled and faded for a heartbeat, but then it reappeared as strong as before.

"You looking for your horn, unicorn? You smell it in there?" Brownroot asked, his gaze oddly reptilian. Leaving the *Canticles Al Farasakh* on the boulder, he strode over toward them, his opalescent red bubble connecting him to the Heart.

My horn, Ivy thought. *Even to hold it.* But the glowing nub on her forehead, so bright now that she could see the turquoise light it shed reflected on her hands, ached for it. "Blaze," she said. "Maybe you can reattach it."

"Yes!" Vinca said, waving the nickel wand around in her excitement.

Before Kellogg took another step closer, Blaze whipped open the bag and pulled out the ivory spiral. Small golden loops swirled around it, sending hungry tendrils toward Ivy. She reached for it, longing to make herself complete.

"Yes," Brownroot said as her palm wrapped around the warmth of the ivory. "Put it on."

Something in his tone froze Ivy's blood, and it must have had a similar effect on Blaze because he put his hand over hers, stilling her for a moment.

"It's your horn, unicorn," Brownroot said.

"And if you put it on, you'll be in his thrall," Blaze said.

A moan, filled with despair, met Ivy's ears, and she realized it came from her throat. Her brain knew Blaze was right, but her hand longed to bring the spiral to her head, to caress her forehead with it, to drink in its purity. "Let me just hold it," she said. "I just want to—"

"Just do it!" Vinca cried. "The bubble will protect you!"

Realizing her fairy friend was right, Ivy began to retrieve the horn and—

Ivy! Crystal cried. *Ivy, don't do it!*

The desperation in her sister's voice froze Ivy's hand, bringing horror where logic was too weak. Ivy tore her eyes away from her beautiful horn, the lovely swirls of it that shone with the delicate pinks found in the insides of seashells.

"Crystal."

Her sister wasn't in New Mexico hiding in the caves. Somehow Brownroot had found her, and now she stood right behind him, her silver mane hanging to her knees. Her head was dropped in submission, but her coat gleamed an icy white. Brownroot's hand rested easily on Crystal's pale blue horn.

"Ah," Brownroot said. "I love a happy family reunion. Crystal's going to show me the way to the richest coal mines in New Mexico, aren't you, my sweet?" His broad hand stroked Crystal's neck possessively.

Crystal nodded her head in submission, but Ivy saw a glimmer in her eye. Her sister wasn't in a complete thrall. Unicorn magic was stronger than that of the other creatures. Only dragons were stronger; only some dragons.

This wasn't much consolation, though, because Crystal retained very little of her own freewill.

"You're great at casting evil spells," Vinca said, launching herself from Ivy's shoulder with a flutter of blue wings. She danced in front of Brownroot's nose like some possessed dragonfly. "What've you done to Seal?"

"Seal came to me." Kellogg laughed, the deep sound reverberating off the walls of his brothel-red bubble. "There's no spell on him."

"But he was nice until you showed up," Vinca said, hands on her tiny hips.

"He was a seething ball of jealousy, and I promised him his heart's desire: size. He wanted to be human so he could fuck the unicorn."

"I don't believe you," Ivy said, but she lied. Seal had complained about his size for so long Ivy didn't even hear it anymore.

"I don't believe you either," Vinca said in her songbird voice. "Where is he?"

"You, little fairy, would be much more fun in full size than would Seal," Kellogg said, stepping closer. "And you have something of mine." He reached for the wand, the red skin of his bubble touching their orange sphere.

"I'm sorry, Kellogg," Blaze said. He sang something under his breath and then paused and said, "I don't know what you did with Seal, but I can't let you touch Vinca." He finished his chanted song, and an amber-colored sphere, nearly the same shade as Vinca's skin, appeared around the fairy. Blaze snagged Vinca in his fist and, singing another short melody under his breath, he threw her. Nolan Ryan never threw a ball as well as Blaze threw the fairy. She—and the wand—whizzed through the wind so far and so fast that Ivy couldn't tell where the fairy landed.

Vinca, Ivy said. *Are you all right?*

Yes, the fairy said. *But, Jesus, that man can throw.*

"You really shouldn't have done that," Kellogg said to Blaze.

"And you shouldn't have lied to me."

"Why ever not?" Kellogg answered, his voice cracking.

Blaze shook his head. "You really are a greedy bastard, aren't you? How many coal plants are you running? How much oil is at your disposal? How many refineries and pipelines have you built?"

"Whoever has enough money or power, man? Get real."

"And once the magic creatures have handed over all their precious things," Blaze said, "what then? The world will be ruined, and your grandchildren will have to live and breathe through unicorn skin."

"You worry too much, Blaze, and so did your father."

"Forget killing all the magic creatures," Blaze said. "You ought to just catch them all and start a captive-breeding program."

Ivy had heard the heavy sarcasm in Blaze's suggestion, but Kellogg just stopped and stared at him. Then he said, his voice coming out almost gravely, "You are a brilliant man. A sap, it's true, but a brilliant wizard. It seems such a shame to kill you. Join me instead."

Kellogg must have gone mad, Ivy realized. Or maybe he was certifiably bipolar. Whatever his condition, it certainly didn't stop his actions.

If he's not bipolar, he's channeling Satan, Ivy heard Vinca say from some distance.

That her friend was still tuned in to her thoughts gave Ivy comfort, but she didn't want Brownroot reading any of their minds. *Shhh,* she said to Vinca. *And block yourself. We don't want Brownroot getting any help from us.*

But he's mind blind, Crystal explained. *I might be in his thrall, but I can tell he—*

Her words broke off, and Ivy looked at Brownroot.

He muttered some words Ivy couldn't hear, and the opalescent red bubble around him and the Heart of the World vanished.

"See how much I trust you?" Kellogg asked, opening his arms to show Blaze how vulnerable he was. "Together we'll be rich as the devil himself."

As if Blaze wanted money. Ivy expected her warrior to blast

Kellogg down with his newly enhanced powers, but Blaze just stood there, hands on his lean hips as if considering.

"Join me," Brownroot urged the pair, his voice quavering between reedy and something odd.

Ivy saw the set of Blaze's shoulders relax, and for a moment she wondered if he was buying in to Brownroot's madness. But, then, no. She knew Blaze's heart.

"Go ahead," Brownroot said to Blaze. "Drop your sphere of protection."

You've come into your power, Blaze. You'll be stronger than him. Do something, she urged him in her mind, hoping Crystal was right about Brownroot being mind blind.

I will, he said, his voice caressing her mind.

And he did. He dropped the orange sphere protecting them.

"Congratulations," Brownroot said to Blaze. "We'll work so well together, now that we know each other's true strengths."

"I don't want money, Brownroot," Blaze said, fishing for time, "and I don't want to be your partner. Let's end this once and for all, right now." Blaze shoved his lover's beautiful horn into the backpack, and he gave the bag to her.

Blaze sensed a strong magic there, and it had a wild flavor, unlike anything he'd read about or felt. And that wand... what was going on here?

Don't fight him with spells, Crystal said in both Blaze and Ivy's minds. *He's got something truly evil in his mind. I—But* her voice was gone.

What was that? Blaze asked Ivy.

I don't know, Ivy answered. *I think she's linked with him somehow, but getting past the thrall is difficult.*

Brownroot's cold eyes narrowed. And with a muttered word, flames leaped from his fingertips. He flicked his hand, and the fire shot toward Blaze.

"Wait," Blaze said to Brownroot and then sang a quick phrase in that ancient Persian. The flame turned to snow, which floated gently to his feet. "Let's do this like men, Kellogg. No enchantments."

But the oil magnate laughed. Then he motioned at the icy flakes laying at Blaze's feet, and they turned into tiny red scorpions scurrying toward Blaze and Ivy.

"Don't be a fool," Blaze said. "You've had the *Canticles Al Farasakh* for hours, and I've been studying it my whole life." He sang another phrase, and the scorpions changed to tiny lobelia blossoms.

I could use some help here, Blaze said to Ivy. *Any ideas to convince him to fight without magic?*

Brownroot twitched his fingers and started yet another enchantment, but Ivy interrupted him.

"No!" Ivy shouted to Blaze. "Fight with magic. Your eye. You can't see right. Don't do the macho-man thing!"

And the reverse psychology worked. Sort of.

"Let's fight with fists, then," Brownroot said, curling his fingers and grinning maliciously. He threw a wild haymaker, crackling with magical energy. Electrical sparks spun behind his closed fist.

But even Ivy had seen the punch coming, and Blaze stepped neatly out of the way, bringing up his knee and swiftly rolling his hip and snapping his leg outward from the knee. With the ball of his foot, he struck Brownroot on the thigh as hard as another man might swing a baseball bat.

Purple sparks flew off Brownroot's thigh, and yet Brownroot stood unruffled. "But we'll use magic, Williams," he said, that evil grin still lending him a crocodilian aspect.

Blaze didn't understand. Brownroot should've gone down like a tree under an ax with that kick. However, keeping his face untroubled, he said to Brownroot, "When I kick your ass, I don't want you thinking I took advantage of my training, which you've not had."

"My photographic memory puts us on even ground, Williams. I know every spell you know and maybe more. I've read the whole book."

"I've known you for years, Brownroot. You don't have a photographic memory."

But Kellogg laughed maniacally. "I do now!"

From the corner of his eye, Blaze watched Ivy rub her horn in the rucksack nervously. *It's okay,* he told her.

Purposely keeping his body language confident, his legs spread and his arms crossed, Blaze looked at Brownroot and said, "Practiced without intelligence, the spells are useless."

"Without intelligence?" Kellogg barked something resembling a laugh. "I think you just called me stupid." He muttered something almost under his breath and threw a fierce uppercut toward Blaze's chin.

Blaze ducked out of the way without effort, but something confused him. Kellogg had just used the Heart through some sort of masking spell.

What spell did he just cast? he asked Ivy and her sister even as he answered Brownroot's blow with a jab of his own, snapping out an efficient punch without moving his feet or hips.

The strike hit Brownroot on the jaw, and his teeth clacked together as Crystal said, *He's blocking you from the Heart, and he's masking his block. He thinks he'll trick you into using power that's not there. The dampening spell is a red herring.*

"Problem with a jab," Brownroot said, tilting his head to the side to stretch out the muscle in his neck, "is that it's not a very authoritative punch. Now, a power punch is a different matter altogether."

Kellogg's arm, shoulders, hip, and legs worked together to bring snakelike velocity to the movement as his entire body delivered his fist to Blaze's stomach. Electric-blue power from the Heart augmented the punch, blinding Blaze like a brilliant camera flash.

The bastard was fighting dirty, but Blaze was no neophyte. He pivoted in a full circle, swinging out his leg. But rather than trying to injure Brownroot, he went for a more subtle strategy. He swept Brownroot's feet out from under him, and the logger-cum-wizard fell flat on his ass. A branch blew over his head in the pounding wind.

He's getting ready to throw a huge spell, Crystal warned.

Blaze stood over Brownroot, looking down on him, but Brownroot wasn't ready to give. Both men stared at each other before Kellogg started muttering and flexing his fingers.

High above them, a funnel cloud formed, agitating the baying cloudwolves, and the air took on the sickly scent of putrefied flesh. The magical creatures, all in his thrall, moved in closer, reminding Blaze of the zombies in *Night of the Living Dead.*

Do something, Crystal urged.

Don't you dare use your horn, unicorn, Blaze said, ignoring Brownroot's prolonged muttering. Crystal must have been right—the guy was preparing one hell of a spell. *This wild magic will destroy it if you do.*

But how can I protect you?

I'll do it! Vinca screamed into their minds. Reminding Blaze of her attack on the Hummer, she dive-bombed Brownroot in her orange bubble of protection. The nickel-colored wand was outstretched, green and blue streaks of lightning crackling around the tip. *Here I come!*

And Blaze knew there was nothing he could do to stop her, the brave fool.

As the lightning bolts flew from Vinca's wand, Kellogg stopped his muttering and flicked his fingers, tracing some intricate pattern into the air.

But jagged green and blue bolts raced toward Brownroot before his magic could coalesce, before he could protect himself or cause more havoc.

Vinca's wand had done it.

"No!" The man was on his feet and shouted so loudly Ivy put her hands over her ears. The shrieking wasn't a human sound. It was—

But Brownroot was gone, vanished, and something huge had taken his place. The shrieking had given way to roaring, a roaring so intense several large oaks began to shake—and then topple. Was it an earthquake?

Blaze blinked, trying to make sense of what he saw. Falling trees, crumbling boulders (but not the Heart, he saw with relief), scattering creatures, both magic and mortal. Then he spied a dragon. Yes, a dragon sat curled around the Heart of the World, and Blaze was wrong—it hadn't replaced Kellogg Brownroot. It hadn't eaten the evil man. Something about Kellogg Brownroot shone from the dragon's eyes.

He realized this dragon had possessed the oil magnate's soul—and probably had for some time. The dragon had subsumed Brownroot's soul.

But Ivy apparently recognized something different in the creature. *Uroboros,* he heard her say to the dragon.

Very good, unicorn, he said so all could hear. His words were so loud they filled Blaze's entire skull. *I'm glad to see that losing your horn hasn't turned your brain to mush.*

Uroboros, she said again. *What are you doing here? What do you want?*

Want? the great dragon scoffed, its smoke-colored scales winking in the setting sun. *What do I want? Why, little unicorn, you know what I want. I want more.*

19

I want more, the dragon said in his gravelly voice. The calm menace emanating from Lord Uroboros frightened Ivy.

When every factor lay in Ivy's favor, the mighty dragon was still more powerful than she. Just a hair more powerful, but that was enough. And now, today, not a single factor was in her favor. Her horn was gone. Her allies were zombies. Blaze was missing his eye, and Seal had crossed over to the dark side, like Anakin Skywalker, and then disappeared. And Vinca, well, her weapon was so small compared to the might of the dragon.

And worst of all, Lord Uroboros was wrapped around the Heart of the World. Even if someone else were available, no one could access its magic.

More, indeed, Ivy said. *You have it all.*

Which is why Kellogg Brownroot and I are such soul mates. The more he took, the more he wanted. His greed wraps around his soul in a vicious circle.

Just as yours does, dragon.

Lord Dragon, to you, Uroboros said. *The world Brownroot*

wants to establish will be perfect for my eggs, for my babies—save one fact.

Distract him. Light as the sound of a butterfly wing, the command from Ivy's sister was softly whispered in her mind.

Ivy nodded to the huge dragon lord, wanting to placate him, as no other option seemed available.

What fact is that? From the corner of her eye, she noticed the centaurs and dryads were blinking, blank expressions giving way to puzzlement. Had Vinca's wand freed them? *And I thought you were Lord Dragon. Are you really Lady Uroboros?*

You were always quicker than the rest, Uroboros said. *And, yes, your fairy freed the others with that wand of mine, which I want back, by the way.*

Take it up with her, Lady Dragon.

The state of mind of the lowlier creatures is of no concern to me. No one—not you or your warrior wizard or anyone here—can access the Heart of the World while I've got it. His—no, her—massive slate-colored tail slashed the air around the Heart.

It's rude to read my mind uninvited, Ivy reproached.

Then invite me, unicorn. Invite me into your mind.

You wouldn't like what you saw there—you'd see your demise. A truth was always better than a lie.

Uroboros snorted, sulfuric smoke billowing from her nostrils.

Ivy filled her mind with positive thought, something Lady Uroboros could not ignore. She filled her mind with beautiful images—clean oceans, sections after sections of ancient forests, rivers so clean fish leaped in joy.

Lady Uroboros answered with a vision of her own, slamming the image into Ivy's mind. Four dragonettes flew from their nest, fat and happy, luxuriating in the smog from the blackened sky. Their sooty scales gleamed even in the smog-

244 / Lucinda Betts

ridden light. Dead tree branches arced into the gray haze, and the babies laughed.

I never took you for the maternal sort, Lady Uroboros.

In this pristine world you insist upon maintaining, how could I spawn? But now, the dragoness smiled, a terrible thing to see, full of sharp teeth and gangrenous gums, *but now Brownroot will help create a perfect world for my little darlings.*

Ivy tried to fill her mind with despair; she tried to make the dragon believe she believed her. Ivy wanted the undivided attention of Uroboros while her friends did whatever they were doing. If the dragon skimmed her sorrow, perhaps she wouldn't dig too deeply.

Don't despair yet, my little unicorn, Lady Uroboros hissed. *Brownroot hasn't done all my work for me—not yet, at any rate.*

What do you mean?

Kellogg Brownroot's activities fostered war and strife, and all that strife—

Yes, Ivy broke in. *I know. That conflict feeds your babies.*

Don't worry, little unicorn. I'm starting small, smaller than global warfare. The dragon opened her huge claws, and Ivy saw Seal, frozen with some spell. He was naked, but a huge erection protruded from his groin, his cock twice the size of his body. It dragged in the dirt at his feet. Seal wore a horrified expression on his frozen face.

You are a monster, Ivy said, hoping Vinca didn't see this. The fairy would be damning the torpedoes and attacking the mighty dragon, regardless of the odds.

A monster? Me? Uroboros asked with feigned pain in her tone. *The little fairy wanted to be big. I granted him his wish.* She closed her huge claw, its smoky scales winking in the twilight, and Seal was obscured again.

You know that's not what he wanted.

He should have been careful what he wished for, Uroboros

said, blowing smoke rings from her black nostrils. *When I'm finished with you and your little wizard and all your little friends, the fairy is my treat. I may grant him his wish yet and make his whole body large—large enough to pleasure me. Now, how is that monstrous?*

Hold your horn, unicorn. The melodic sound of Blaze's voice caressed her mind, even in this sea of fear.

Ivy stared at the dragon, keeping the horror and shock she felt plastered clearly on her face. The sound of her beloved's voice made it very difficult.

I've got it, she said to Blaze, filling her mind with pictures of baby dragons breathing in cool, clean air, healthy green foliage spreading beneath them. They were dying in her world's purity. She directed the image to Uroboros.

Just don't let it go, Blaze said. *Under any circumstances.*

But Ivy hadn't let go of it since he'd handed her the backpack, and now it grew extraordinarily hot in her palm. *I've got it,* she repeated.

Good.

All around her, magical creatures beset the dragon. Tiny pixies threw acorns. The cloudwolves pelted her with golf-ball-sized hail. A dryad let a huge oak fall on the dragon, who lashed her tail angrily but did not leave her spot.

You'll not get me to leave, Lady Uroboros said. Then she flashed an image to Ivy. Tanks and jeeps moved across a desert surrounded by burning oil fields. People exchanged gunfire next to the bed of a dried river. Uroboros's dragonettes cavorted through the toxic skies, the air gray with pollution.

Ivy couldn't move. Burning a path from her hand to her mind, images danced through her brain, leaving her unable to move or speak or think.

An oak dryad imbued Ivy's horn with the strength of her solid tree. A water nymph sent all the power of her stream, flooded with snowmelt and spring floods. A swan maiden gave

246 / Lucinda Betts

Ivy the freedom of flight, and in her mind she took wing across clear, blue skies. The cloudwolves gave her the might of a hot summer storm.

But even as all the magic coalesced in the horn in Ivy's hand, she wondered what to do with it. The nub on her forehead called for her horn, but she couldn't satisfy that longing, she knew. What if Uroboros took her over? The dragon had the strength to overwhelm her.

"Blaze!" Vinca yelled across the glade. Her wand was raised.

"Here!" Ivy heard her beloved shout, but she couldn't turn to see. More images were pouring into her brain. War plagued the deserts, fueled by Brownroot's machinations. War spread to Africa and Eastern Europe. Central America took up arms against their northern neighbors.

At the same time, dozens of pixies sent the strength of spring flowers pushing through the cold, near winter earth to her. The strength of hundreds of growing crocuses deluged her horn.

"Blaze!" Vinca shouted. "Watch this!" She pointed the wand at a nearby centaur man, who blinked in surprise at a weapon that suddenly appeared in his hand.

"Give it to the wizard!" Vinca shouted to the centaur, her own wand still outstretched. "I don't want my wand's magic to bounce against his damn bubble!"

"Heads-up, wizard!" With muscles rippling across his naked chest, the centaur man tossed Blaze the sword, his long red hair whipping in the wind. This new weapon wasn't a long sword as Ivy had expected from her visions; it was a curved thing, a shamshir. With a running step, Blaze caught the grip with breathtaking grace.

As more magical creatures lent their residual magic to Ivy, she watched Blaze examine the weapon, awe on his face. Emeralds in the pommel gleamed in the twilight, looking like eyes to

Ivy. The gems made the sword look intelligent. "Thank you," the wizard said with amazement.

"My wand is amazing!" Vinca said.

"Yes," the centaur man agreed, nodding at Blaze. "Chop off Uroboros's head with that new sword, and it's dead, wizard."

I wish you much luck, Uroboros growled, clacking long nails against the Heart of the World. With each tap of her talons, creatures shrieked, including Ivy. It felt as if someone were dragging nails across the inside of her skull.

Do you know how to use that sword? Ivy asked, trying to block out the amazing pain.

Blaze looked at her and nodded, his good eye locked on hers. But he deliberately pushed that shock of hair away from his injured eye, and she caught his meaning.

Chopping off a dragon's head—especially the head of one as smart and old as Lady Uroboros—was going to be very difficult for a whole man. For a man without depth perception . . .

And then untamed magic filled the glade as Uroboros launched herself from the Heart of the World in a huge draft from the sweep of her massive, coal-black wings.

The Heart, Ivy called to her friends, tightening her grip on her horn. *Use it,* she urged, wondering if she should attach her horn or . . .

Uroboros climbed high in the sky, up past the trees, nearly to the cloudwolves. Then she began her terrible descent toward Blaze, talons outstretched. Her reptilian mouth was opened, and her sharklike teeth glinted in the fading light.

But Blaze was prepared, shamshir held at the ready, his weight balanced perfectly on the balls of his feet. Ivy could see from the relaxed set of his shoulders and jaw that his chakras were perfectly aligned. She could almost see the power he drew from the earth, from the Heart.

He could take on the dragon.

As Uroboros swooped toward Blaze, he calmly let the blade arc. It crossed the space with perfect precision, with deadly force. But it crossed the space a microsecond too early, missing Uroboros completely.

Without his eye, Blaze couldn't see how close the razor-sharp teeth were.

Do something, Ivy told her friends.

Lady Uroboros laughed and climbed the skies again, toying with Blaze as she'd toyed with Seal.

Help him, Ivy implored again.

We can't, Ivy, Vinca said. *She's got some sort of spell around the Heart. You've got all the magic of the world stored there in your horn.*

In that instant, she knew it was up to her and Blaze.

She didn't think—she acted.

Taking all the power with which she'd been entrusted in her palm, she sent out tendrils from the horn to Blaze, linking her mind with his. Ivy knew a more intimate bond had never existed between two beings. Sending a grateful thought to each of the beings who'd contributed their residual magic, she gave her mind over to Blaze.

All her hopes and dreams flooded into his mind, and she felt him start, surprised and a little afraid. *But I love you,* she said, losing herself in him. *Don't be afraid.*

Then all her adoration of him and her fierce desire to protect the Heart and this forest and all the world's natural beauties swamped him. And Blaze and Ivy ceased to be separate. She felt what he felt, and he felt what she felt.

When those overwhelming emotions settled, when the confusion gave way to acceptance, he saw her gift—he could see through her eyes.

Like a kamikaze pilot, Uroboros barreled toward them. Blaze filled the longing ache in Ivy to use magic, and Ivy filled

Blaze's overwhelming desire to see. Together they completed each other.

They balanced their weight and centered their chakras, the shamshir singing its desire to drink the blood of Uroboros. Through the being that had been only Ivy, Blaze thanked each of the magical creatures for their aid and told them good-bye. They didn't expect to live the moment, but they could die wrapped around each other's souls and hearts. Through the being that had once been only Blaze, Ivy sighted the dragon homing in on them, and together they inhaled.

Exhale.

Blaze and Ivy slashed. And when the shamshir drank dragon blood, it sang a dark song that filled the glade.

Uroboros shrieked, and trees fell. Where her blood splattered to the ground, the earth sizzled and darkened. The scent of sulfuric acid pervaded the glade. As one, Ivy and Blaze realized the sword had slashed Uroboros's left wing, which now dragged on the ground.

But the mighty dragon wasn't giving up. Her future hung in the balance. Her eggs. Her babies. Rearing on massive hind legs, she lunged for them, casting a spell as she did so.

As Ivy and Blaze stepped easily out of the way, neither of them recognized the enchantment, but both felt the draw from the Heart. The draw was larger than either of them had ever pulled or felt pulled by anyone else, and fear rippled through both of them.

Through Ivy's eyes, Blaze saw the way Uroboros favored her shoulder. The weapon had sliced more than the wing. Through Blaze's feel for the Heart, Ivy recognized the need for a counterspelled shield. She drew more magic from her horn, which was still burning the palm of her hand.

Using Ivy's store, Blaze coolly held his hand to launch the counterspell. Uroboros's spell bounced off the shield, and the air around them crackled. Long plumes of golden sparks shot high into the sky. Blaze and Ivy fell back, staggering from the strength of Uroboros's magic.

"I'm warning you, Kellogg," Blaze and Ivy managed to rasp through Blaze's mouth as they prepared to unleash the spell of the second dimension. "Stop now. All the magic we used here is without the help of the Heart. Once we draw on it . . ."

You can't draw on it! Vinca told him. *It's blocked. You can't send her to the second dimension.*

And Uroboros took a step forward, a smug grin on her crocodilian face. *You're losing, Williams. Go ahead. Use that rock.* And drawing on the Heart again, Uroboros snapped off a second spell.

The spell ripped Ivy away from Blaze, leaving her with no magic of her own. Just as she'd longed for his song when they'd hunted for Tchili's horn, she ached for his touch in her mind. But more than that, she ached for Blaze's heart.

And now Blaze couldn't see properly. How could he fight a dragon when he was like this?

Uroboros threw a spell of pure energy. Ivy didn't need magic to sense it because it looked just like a ball of lightning, and it hit Blaze straight on.

Without her, Blaze had almost no power to deflect it.

He staggered and nearly lost his feet. His face had gone pale, and Ivy could see his good eye was nearly closed—although whether it was from concentration or exhaustion, she couldn't say.

Above Blaze, Uroboros muttered the long phrases necessary to cast a killing enchantment, and then a spell flew from her claws.

Ivy did the only thing she could think of, and even as she did it, she knew her actions would damn her for the rest of her days.

She flung her burning horn hard. She threw it so it would hit the exact spot where Uroboros's spell would intercept Blaze's dimensional spell.

The beautiful spirals coiled through the air like some strange child's toy. The golden horn took with it all Ivy's hopes to ever again serve her forest, to heal, to speak with her mind—to be useful.

When her horn intercepted the spells, her life would be over. Her magic gone.

And it hit, just as Blaze's spell met that of Uroboros.

I've got it! Vinca called, still safe inside her orange sphere of protection. Lightning bolts from Vinca's wand intercepted the spells too, and wild magic ricocheted between the Heart of the World and off the magical creatures.

The bizarre amalgam of spells bounced off Ivy's chest, sending her ass into the dirt. It hit Blaze on his shoulder and sent him skidding as he tried to keep to his feet. It hit the Heart and seemed to double in size. The centaur who'd given Blaze the shamshir collapsed to the ground with a grunt as the magic hit him.

And then it hit Uroboros.

For a heartbeat, her black scales lit up, as though she'd been illuminated from the inside. Black light filled the moonlit glade. Her wings extended their full length, and her tail straightened stiffly, as if rigor mortis had set in. It looked like someone had electrified her.

And then she fell to the ground, her massive head inches from Seal's tiny body.

The dragon wasn't dead, though. Her evil oozed around the Heart, which crackled in response. The green moss growing up the side of the Heart blackened and died as the dragon's sides heaved and her sulfuric stink filled the air.

A strange silence fell.

Seal blinked and looked at Ivy. "What is this?" he asked in a voice no louder than an egg cracking.

"It's Uroboros," Ivy said. "She possessed Kellogg Brownroot for a while."

"No," Seal said, shaking his head. He looked down at his groin in disgust, his overlong penis dragging in the dirt. Then Seal held up the long golden spiral, which belonged only to Ivy.

"It's my horn, Seal."

Beside Seal, the dragon blinked.

"I need it now, Seal. I need to use my horn." Ivy nodded to the dragon, who blinked again.

"Can I help you?" the fairy asked. "Can I do this for you?"

Ivy nodded, grateful to have no need of words.

Beside the fairy, a gigantic eyelid blinked again. The reptile sent another image to Ivy—a nest made of junkyard cars and razor wire, four fat eggs oozing sulfur dioxide. And Ivy knew the dragon was pregnant now with those eggs.

We need to use it now, Ivy told Seal so the others couldn't hear. *We need to use my horn.*

"No!" called Blaze. "Don't do it, Seal! It'll destroy her horn!"

I am the Guardian of the Forest, of the Heart of the World, Ivy said for all creatures to hear. *Seal, I command you. Use my horn.*

"No!" cried Blaze.

And Seal stabbed the horn into the dragon's eye. Seal stabbed—just as Blaze sang a song. But the notes were dark and frightening. They were incomplete and hurried.

But still, the song and the horn destroyed the dragon.

For a moment, as Ivy's horn sank into the dragon's eye, it was as though all her magic flashed before her. Every spell she'd ever cast, every healing she'd ever worked, every trip through the ether, every song she'd sung with every soul—she remembered these in lightning-fast sequence.

Then Lady Uroboros flattened to a paper-thin facsimile of

herself and disappeared from the face of the earth—leaving only the eye and the horn.

Ivy felt joy race through the hearts of all the creatures around her. A swan maiden sang her heart-rending song as her friends winged in unison. The cloudwolves joined the chorus, lending a dark note to the rhapsody.

Ivy felt all this, but she couldn't take her gaze from her horn. Buried three-quarters of the way into the vitreous humor of the dragon's eye, it had never looked more beautiful. The rising moon bathed it in its golden glow, reminding her of the golden moon in Blaze's eye.

Blaze reached for her horn, wanting to help her, no doubt. She wanted to tell him no. She wanted to stop him. But it was like stopping time. If the end didn't come in this heartbeat, it would come in the next.

In the second before Blaze's fingers grazed her horn, the golden spiral—weakened by holding all that residual magic, weakened by intercepting all that untamed magic—burst into a million tiny shards.

Amidst the joyous celebration at the dragon's demise, Ivy's world exploded all around her, the shards of her horn raining down on her, peppering her cheeks and hair.

And then something worse happened—Blaze followed Uroboros, flattening like the King of Hearts in a deck of cards, and then vanishing.

Into the second dimension.

20

A bug was crawling on Ivy's nose.

A bug was crawling on her nose, and it was annoying her, waking her. She didn't want to wake up. She didn't want to face the nightmare before her. She couldn't bear the pity she'd see on the faces of all the creatures who still had their magic, who still had their loves. She thought of Vinca and Seal and found she couldn't stand the taste of her jealousy.

"Ivy!"

The voice was tiny, as if it came from a bug. She swatted at it.

"Don't do that, Ivy!" the bug said. "You'll hurt me!"

"Vinca," Ivy said.

"Yes, it's me, and I'm braiding in the harebells, so please be careful."

Ivy let the fairy braid her hair, soothed by the repetitive feel of it. Warm summer sun beat down upon her, and the swan maiden sang somewhere close by. Her beautiful melody called to Ivy's heart, her empty, forsaken heart, and she wept, remembering the soul song she and Blaze had wrapped around the ether.

* * *

Many tiny hands worked in Ivy's hair, weaving and braiding. "Wake up!" she heard. "You've been asleep for hours!" They sounded like the mice from *Cinderella.*

"Jesus," she said, sitting up, bleary eyed. Bluebells and daisies fell from her hair. A harebell fluttered to her lap. "How many flowers do you need to braid in here?"

"Our crown!" a fairy cried. "You've wrecked it!"

"She didn't wreck it," Vinca said. "Look. See? It's fine." A feathery touch accompanied her friend's assurance to the other fairies.

"Why do I need a crown?" Ivy asked, brushing the white and blue petals from her lap.

"We thought they might make you feel better, unicorn."

"I'm not a—"

But a visceral ache hit her in the stomach—and it wasn't for her horn. It was for him. She craved the luscious feel of Blaze's lips over hers. He'd taste like strawberries and rain. He'd taste like heaven. She craved his strength and the way his scent had coiled around her heart. But he was gone.

"Blaze," Ivy said to the fairies. "He's . . ." But she found she couldn't finish her question.

Vinca fluttered to Ivy's shoulder and stroked her cheek. "We don't know, honey. He just turned flat and evaporated. Like the dragon."

"The second dimension," Ivy said. "His spell didn't work quite right. Only Brownroot was supposed to go. Only Uroboros."

"Can't you bring him back?"

Anger washed over Ivy, not at her friend but at herself. She might have been able to live without her magic. She could have handed the guardianship over to Crystal. But living without her heart . . . What if she'd listened to him when he'd told her to stop?

"Can't you bring him back?" Vinca asked again.

"I can't." Ivy felt her lips tighten, the tension in her jaw grow. "Even if I had my horn, I don't know the spell. And even if I had my horn and the *Canticles Al Farasakh*, I don't know how to crack that book. And I don't have the book. And I don't have my horn." And Blaze was gone. "I can't do anything."

"But there's so much you have to do," Vinca said. "You have to fix Seal's cock, and you have to find Tchili's horn and put it back on her head. And you have to—"

"Stop!" Ivy said, hating the bitterness in her voice. "Please," she said more quietly. "Please, just stop." She rubbed her eyes as if she could rub away this terrible world in which she found herself. "Can you help me find Crystal? I'll hand over the guardianship to her. She'll solve your problems now."

"Crystal went back to New Mexico."

"What?" Shock finally made Ivy look around. The glade was filled with enchanted creatures: tiny creatures with goat hooves and rainbow hair; creatures that looked like rocks with faces, their craggy features visible only from the shadows cast by the setting sun; dryads from trees with which she wasn't familiar; and a horselike creature who had foamy seaweed for a mane and a tail that looked like driftwood.

But she knew the most magical creature of all was missing. And he'd be gone forever.

The fairy who'd been using Ivy's nose as a landing pad lit there again. His wings shone with a metallic green she'd seen once on a beetle. "We wanted to say thank you. We know the great wizard couldn't have defeated Lady Uroboros without your bravery."

Blaze. The great wizard. After watching him overcome all the odds to defeat Uroboros, Ivy could only agree that he had been great.

Brushing the fairy away from her nose, Ivy stood, still

amazed by the crowd that had gathered, all the fairies, the nymphs. In the lake to the east, even the merfolk swam around.

"We made you a new dress," a little gnome said. His skin was the color of obsidian. "Your clothes were covered in blood."

"From your horn," another added.

Ivy touched her nub, and the gem still pulsed there, but it didn't call in any particular direction. How could it? Her horn had been obliterated. She'd seen it shattered into a thousand pieces.

"Do you like the dress?" a fairy asked, her wings like gossamer violets.

Ivy looked down while she ran her hand through her hair. The dress she wore had long sleeves and a fitted bodice. The cut was so low the very edge of her areolae peaked out, a light pink in contrast to the blue dress. The full skirt fell to her ankles.

"It's . . . lovely."

"And the braids?" asked the fairy with the green wings, flitting too close to her nose. He handed her a gilt hand mirror.

Ivy glanced around the glade; all the creatures seemed to be hanging on her words. She looked in the mirror. Someone with miniscule hands had woven braids as tiny as gold chains into her hair. She'd been crowned with a daisy chain. Blue harebells added a dash of color.

"They're lovely too," she said as the fairy took the mirror from her, laughing with glee.

But Ivy herself felt no joy. The only person she had ever wanted to admire her and love her and lust after her was gone.

A centaur woman with auburn hair flowing to her withers approached Ivy and kneeled before her. "We want to thank you," the creature said in a husky voice.

Ivy stepped back. She'd only been obeying her birthright by protecting the Heart. But she said, "You're welcome."

"And we have a gift for you," the centaur maiden said. She stood and offered a small box carved of cherrywood. "To thank you for your sacrifice." With a shimmy of her breasts, the centaur placed it in Ivy's hands.

Her sacrifice. Oh, Ivy's heart ached with it. There was nothing in this box she wanted—Blaze wasn't in it.

And although she knew no gift could replace her loss, their gesture touched her. She was the Guardian of the Forest—or she had been—and she'd done her job well.

"Open it," a fairy demanded, her wings like gossamer violets.

Ivy opened the box—and gasped. Atop a velvet cloth the color of spring grass lay so many pieces of her horn. Each glimmered in the light of the rising moon with the warm shine of a pearl.

"All the pieces are there," the gnome assured her in an earthy voice.

"We found them all," said a pixie.

"But—"

"You healed Blaze a little bit without your horn," Vinca said. "We thought maybe you could do the same to glue the pieces back together. And if that doesn't work, Crystal said she'd add her healing powers."

"Crystal knows about the pieces?"

Yes, Ivy, Ivy heard from across the miles. *And I know you can put it back together—or we can help each other do it.*

But what if she didn't want to? What if life without Blaze was too much to contemplate?

But what if your horn helps you get Blaze back? Vinca asked.

You're so rude reading my mind like that.

Sorry, she said, not sounding it. *But I'm right.*

Ivy looked at the box of shards, her horn. Could her magic pull Blaze back? Would she be able to live with herself if she didn't try? And there was the forest. . . . The creatures here needed her.

You're no coward, Ivy, Crystal reminded her. *You've never in your life refused to tackle something difficult.*

And Crystal was right too. Ivy was the Guardian of the Forest, and she must guard—even if her life held no joy.

All right, Ivy said. *Let's do it.*

Letting the earth ground her, Ivy concentrated on her horn, visualizing it as it'd been when it was whole. She saw the play of sunlight over the spirals. She saw the razor-sharp edges and the needle-sharp tip. She saw healing energy pouring from it, always in the aid of others.

And she felt healing energy coalesce around her.

"Look!" a fairy shouted.

Ivy looked. Before her eyes, the pieces of her horn slid into place, some finding their neighbors with an audible *click.* Soon all the bits were in place, and Ivy could see Vinca was right. The magic folk had found all the pieces. And then all the pieces of her horn melted back together into a golden spiral.

"Dear God," Ivy said, touching it. The spirals were warm, almost pulsing, and so smooth. "It's whole," she said. Unlike her.

As she said those words, she felt the nub on her forehead heat and pull. The turquoise glow from the nub lit the spiral in the cherry box.

"Put it back on," a velvety voice called from the crowd. Ivy recognized the centaur maiden.

"But I'm in human form. I don't *have* a horn in human form."

Maybe you'd better try anyway, Crystal said, her voice traveling across the miles from the Sangre de Cristos Mountains.

It was true that the strange nub on Ivy's forehead was calling to the horn. Tentatively Ivy took the spiral, catching her breath to be holding it again. But she gasped as the glowing nub sucked the horn onto her head, internalizing it somehow.

"Dear God!" Ivy said, feeling as if her world had just tilted. Around her, colors brightened and fairy wings sparkled. The centaur maiden's auburn hair nearly glowed in the sunlight.

"Try shifting your shape," the centaur maiden suggested.

And that too seemed like a good idea. The earth beneath Ivy's feet vibrated with the strength of the Heart of the World. She sensed the magic around her for the first time since Kellogg Brownroot had sawed off her horn.

"Yes," she said. "I'll try."

The centaur maiden took the box from her as she tried to channel power from the Heart. At first, nothing happened. The Heart didn't respond to her plea. But then the Heart answered, filling her with blessed relief.

Her wrists became fetlocks; her ears grew mobile and pointy. A tail sprouted from the tip of her backbone. Within a heartbeat, she stood before everyone, all four hooves solidly on the ground.

Ivy walked around the forest, tossing her head while her friends cheered her on. Pixies and dryads and fairies lined up, clamoring for healing from the injuries they'd sustained during the windstorm, the battle with Uroboros.

And for the first time in Ivy's adult life, no thread of doubt tickled her mind. The ghost of her unfortunate sister was finally laid to rest. Ivy could heal any creature that needed her without seeing Chicory's face. And as the green healing coils looped from her horn onto the first pixie, Ivy knew she should've felt whole, complete.

But the most important part of her was missing.

Vinca and Seal came to Ivy's cabin. Vinca was toting Seal's penis so he could fly, and despite herself, Ivy had to laugh.

"My wand won't fix it," Vinca said. "I shake it at him, and it doesn't work."

"Well, when I shake this at you," Seal said, pouting, "you know for sure it'll work!"

Vinca laughed, the tiny tinkling sound filling the cabin.

"You're not a nice fairy, Vinca," Seal said. "You didn't even try to fix me until now."

"Hmph," Vinca said. "You needed to learn a lesson."

Ivy looked at Vinca. "Did he learn it?"

Vinca shrugged, a smile playing on her raspberry lips. "I don't know, but I miss his services. You think maybe you can heal him?"

"I don't know." Ivy looked at Seal, wondering if she had enough forgiveness in her heart to call him her friend again. "Do you want it healed?"

"Yes," he said, not meeting her eyes. "Please."

"I found the *Canticles Al Farasakh*, if you think that'll help," Vinca said. "I mean, maybe you have to undo the dragon's magic or something."

"Sometimes the easy way works best," Ivy said, shifting to unicorn form. *But it's good to know the book didn't get sucked into the second dimension . . . although if it had been, maybe Blaze would have been able to find his way back.*

"He'll find his way back," Vinca said. "I know it."

He hasn't yet, Ivy said, letting the Heart's power imbue her root chakra. She recognized lust as it filled her, but somehow it didn't touch her core. Easily she wove the lust, and her healing power coalesced in her horn. The green loops swirled around her spiral, and she let them fall over Seal.

"But you haven't found Tchili's horn yet either," Vinca said.

Ivy had to agree, but she didn't think that was the point. She had everything she'd ever wanted—Uroboros was forever vanished, her horn was restored, her forest was safe. No other unicorn would suffer what Tchili had suffered, and Ivy held out hope she'd be able to restore her cousin.

But her heart ached for Blaze.

"Wow!" Vinca said, fluttering just above the healing swirls. "You're good."

Tell me when to stop, Ivy said as Seal's cock began to shrink.

"Stop now!" Seal cried. His cock hung down to his knees.

"You've got to be kidding me," Vinca said. "Who're you going to fuck with that? Godzilla?" She looked at Ivy and said, "Keep going."

"No!" Seal cried as Ivy continued to shrink.

"There," Vinca said. "That looks about right." Seal looked proportionate to Ivy too.

You sure he learned his lesson? Ivy asked.

"No, but I'm not waiting any longer." Vinca turned toward Ivy and winked. "You can always change it back, right?"

Ivy smiled but shook her head. *Is that size okay with you?* she asked Seal. *Seriously?*

Sullenly he nodded. "Thank you," he said and fluttered away.

Not very gracious, is he? Ivy noted.

"Well, he's a little embarrassed, I suppose."

Hugely embarrassed, perhaps?

Hey, I'm the one who's supposed to make the jokes.

Ivy shifted back into human form, appreciating the ability to do so. She realized she could have lived without her horn, but she wouldn't have liked it. "I'm glad you've forgiven him."

"Have you forgiven yourself?"

Ivy would have loved to play the innocent, but she'd known Vinca for too long. "If only I'd listened to him."

"What are you talking about?"

"Maybe Blaze didn't need my help to send Uroboros to the second dimension. He might still be here if I hadn't interfered."

Vinca landed on her shoulder and stroked her cheek. "But

you're the Guardian of the Forest. You can't—you couldn't—leave its safety to chance. You must protect it. You gave up your horn to protect it."

"And my heart."

Vinca sighed. "And your heart."

"I need to find another warrior virgin, Vinca."

"You mean, so you can hunt down Tchili's horn?"

"Yes," Ivy said. "And I don't want to. I don't want a different warrior virgin. I want Blaze."

"But Tchili's waiting."

Ivy nodded. "I know."

"You want my wand? You never know what wacky thing it'll do for you."

"I don't think it can bring back Blaze."

Vinca paused for a moment. "Probably not." Then she fluttered off Ivy's shoulder and said, "You'll try again tonight, won't you? To find a warrior virgin and hunt down Tchili's horn?"

"Yes."

"Then I'll leave you to it." Vinca gave her a kiss on the nose. "And I'll let you know how well Seal's resized cock works."

Lying back in her bed, Ivy remembered the first time she'd tried to hunt down Tchili's horn. It was the night she'd met Blaze, though she hadn't known it. An inexplicable sense of hope had filled her that night.

And, strangely, she had it now.

It wasn't that she would enjoy the tour of inappropriate virgins, and it wasn't that she thought she'd find Blaze. But she found she didn't have to dredge up her melody. Instead, her unicorn song filled her heart almost unbidden.

Ivy drifted into the ether, floating on a trill of heart-wrenching notes. As before, the song reached out to all the virgin dreamers.

She let the song build, luxuriating in its beauty, filling her—

unexpectedly—with joy. With a hope-filled soul, Ivy loosed the song in the ether, letting it float over the pulsing, jeweled souls, awakening the innocent, unburying their magic.

Now. Now she could sift through the ether, looking and seeking.

But then a tigereye glow grabbed her attention. She didn't simply see the tigereye and wonder; the honey-brown soul blasted its glow right into her eyes, into her heart.

She knew. It was Blaze.

Ivy paused for a moment, disbelieving. How could he be here? He was in the second dimension. But something about its beauty gnawed at that ache in her heart, and she recognized Blaze.

The ether was dimensionless.

Pulling power from the Heart of the World, Ivy wrapped her song around Blaze's. His melody burst into her heart, a perfect counterpoint to her unicorn rhapsody. His song completed her own.

Blaze! she cried. *Where are you?*

The tigereye glow grabbed her and sang to her, filling her with images of Tchili's horn, just as she'd done to Blaze all those weeks ago. The curve of Tchili's horn, the emerald and ruby color of it, the citrus scent of it . . . these details filled her mind.

As before, their combined power was so perfect the wait was no more than a heartbeat. All that longing and the beauty of the melody called to Tchili's horn. And, as before, the horn's cells sang back.

Ivy's excitement at finding Blaze threatened to ruin her focus, but his strength steadied her.

Together they followed the wisp of magic singing from Tchili's horn. From the ether, Ivy slid her soul into her human body, and then she followed the rope of power toward the horn's location. Was Blaze doing the same?

Breathless, her booted feet hit the ground with precision. Where was Blaze? He had to be here!

But where was she? Ivy looked around. She wasn't in Central Park; she was in a sprawling apartment. Was that a Cézanne on the wall? It matched the angular leather couch and the chrome light fixture.

"Blaze?" she said. But her voice bounced off the walls. Ivy knew she was alone.

Fighting a growing anxiety, she concentrated on the horn's song. It would lead her where she needed to be, if only she could find it again.

And there it was. The song pulsated through her, and she breathed a sigh of relief. She inhaled a little deeper when the tiger-eye soul throbbed with pure strength. Across the dimensions, she and Blaze were back in synch, and together they invited the cells of the lost unicorn horn to sing with them.

The horn sang. Last time she'd heard it, its melody had been muffled, but Blaze's melody was stronger now. Now the horn sang from inside this expensive-looking apartment. Were the dimensions united here?

"Blaze?" she said again.

And then she saw Tchili's horn. A red sphere surrounded it as it lay on a cherry table. Two other unicorn horns glowed in similar bubbles, sending revulsion through Ivy. Brownroot had done this to other unicorns, and she hadn't been able to help them. Were they someplace on the other side of the globe? Had they lived? She and the wizard—her wizard—would find them and restore them.

If he wasn't permanently stuck in the second dimension, the ether their only way to communicate.

"Blaze?" she asked a third time.

Just then, a warm hand slid over her stomach, and a deep voice, reverberating with melodic strength, whispered in her ear so only she could hear.

"I'm here."

His words might have stopped Ivy in her tracks, but it was his scent that froze her, tantalizing her, making her knees weak with desire. She'd willingly follow him to the ends of the earth.

He was hers.

"Are you a ghost?" She turned toward him. "Or are you real?"

"I'm very real, my love," he said, taking her hand and kissing her palm like a knight from an ancient tale. Then he gathered her in his arms and kissed her lips. He kissed her again. And again. As his tongue slid over hers, passion flooded her sorrow and washed it away.

"And the second dimension?"

"Quickly relegated Uroboros to her place. She won't bother anyone again."

"You escaped on my song, didn't you?"

Slowly Blaze nodded.

Ivy looked at him, joy filling her heart so words failed. His dark hair hung in his face so the ruin of his eye barely showed.

His good eye reflected only love.

Ivy? he asked, touching her mind as gently as a floating feather. *Are you okay?*

Better than that, she answered. Then, drawing on the Heart's power, she shifted into unicorn form. She turned toward Blaze and lowered her head.

We can reattach Tchili's horn, he said.

Yes, she breathed, *and the others. But not in this heartbeat.*

Swirling rings of gold began to loop around her horn, growing stronger and fatter with each of her heartbeats, but still she pulled more power from the Heart.

Then what are you doing?

Let me help you, she offered. *Let me heal your eye.*

But I see so much better this way, he said, pushing that shock of hair from his face. *My blindness led me to you, has let me see through your eyes.*

And you've loaned me your magic. She sent the healing coils toward him, offering but not insisting.

Blaze accepted.

As gently as a hummingbird touches a trumpet vine, Ivy touched Blaze's ruined eye with her horn. She wasn't sure what would happen. The wound had healed with her use of residual magic, and old wounds were more difficult to cure.

But as soon as the golden loops swirled into the socket, she knew her magic was strong enough, that it could heal him and make him whole.

The empty socket swelled, and the flesh uncrinkled. The skin of his eyelid and the fragile flesh below his eye normalized in color. His lashes reappeared, thick and black and beautiful.

When he opened his eyes and looked at her, Ivy found she couldn't breathe. She hadn't restored Blaze to his original form. She had changed him.

In his new eye, a golden moon graced the tigereye iris as before. But in the black of his new pupil lay something alien, something new—a golden mark in contrast to the black, and it formed an extraordinarily clear figure eight—but the figure eight lay on its side. She'd seen that symbol in mathematics texts and in philosophy.

Under her own command, Ivy used the power of the Heart to shift back to human form. She needed to see this change through human eyes. Hooves gave way to hands, and the gray tones of animal visions gave way to the vivid hues of human sight.

But when she looked through the eyes of a woman, the flaw in his eye remained.

The gaze looking back at Ivy held infinity.

Turn the page for a preview of
Delilah Devlin's devilish story,
"The Demon Lord's Cloak,"
in DAMNED, DELICIOUS, AND DANGEROUS!

On sale now!

Prologue

"We'll all be dead by morning." Martin's voice quavered as he emptied another glass of Frau Sophie's precious peach schnapps.

"Who'd have guessed it'd be nigh onto impossible to find a virgin in this valley?" his companion said.

"Pah! Even my own daughter," Martin moaned. "What's the world coming to, Edgard? Young women giving themselves like barmaids . . ."

Edgard's shoulders slumped. "I tell you it was the last May Day celebration. The bürgermeister should never have let Sophie provide the drink."

"We should have locked every last one of the unmarried maidens in a cellar. Well, no use grousing." Martin set down his glass. "We have a problem. Now's the time for clear thinking."

"There's no solution. The village will disappear, swallowed by Hell itself when we fail to provide *his* bride." Edgard's reddened eyes widened. "Couldn't we mount a raid on Fulkenstein down the valley . . . take a girl or two . . ."

"There's no time left. We only had the new moon to give

that devil his due. It ends tomorrow night. We'd never be back in time."

Edgard shook his head, sighing. "We've failed. Daemonberg will be no more. Best get the women packing tonight so we can flee come morning. A thousand years of prosperity and health— gone for the lack of a single maidenhead."

"We're doomed, I tell you." Martin lifted the schnapps bottle and tilted it over his glass. He gave it a shake, and then slammed it down on the table. Turning toward the bar, he shouted, "Sophie, *liebchen*, bring us another bottle, will you?"

As he turned back to his friend, he saw a woman step through the doorway of the inn. Her beauty arrested him: far prettier than any of the strapping blond women of the village, this one was slender and delicate, with deep reddish hair that glinted like fire in the torchlight, reminding him of the bay he'd bid on and lost at an auction in early spring.

He elbowed Edgard beside him. "Look there."

Both men turned to stare at the young woman.

"Where's her escort?" Edgard whispered.

"She looks wary. I'd wager she's on her own."

They shared a charged glance, shoulders straightening.

"What do you suppose the chances are she's a virgin?" Edgard asked softly.

"She's beyond fair. What man would care whether he was her first just so long as he's her last? Besides, what other options have we?"

Sophie slammed another bottle in the center of the table and gave them a scathing glance. "If you go home to your wives legless with drink, I'll not take the blame."

"We'll have just one more glass," Martin assured her, reaching around to pat her rump. "For the road. We've business to attend."

Sophie rolled her eyes and turned, her ample hips rolling as she walked across the room to greet the young woman, who waved her away.

"If they only knew the solemn duty we perform," Martin whispered. "They'd call us heroes."

Only, Martin and Edgard could never tell a soul. That, too, was part of their sacred oath, handed down from father to son.

Edgard poured them both another drink, then lifted his glass. "To another hundred years of peace and wealth."

Martin lifted his glass with one hand and crossed himself with the other. "To the fair maiden with the red hair—God rest her soul."

1

Voletta felt faint with alarm; her stomach was in knots. *I can't have lost it. Someone must know where it is!*

But what were the chances anyone here would just give it back to her? She didn't have any gold to offer as a reward for its return. She'd already had to steal the voluminous cloak she wore so she wouldn't walk naked into their midst.

She stepped farther into the entryway.

"Hullo, Miss," an elderly gentleman said as he approached, his avid gaze sliding over her hair.

She clutched the edges of the cloak, only too aware its thick folds hid her nudity. "Good evening, sir."

"You're a stranger here."

Her nose twitched at the sour smell of liquor and unwashed skin that emanated from him. Not many men believed in the value of a thorough cleansing.

If only she hadn't been so fastidious herself, she might never have paused beside the gurgling brook, then noted the thick green curtain of foliage that rendered the glade an irresistible temptation.

"Miss, are you looking for someone?" he asked, his gaze looking beyond her shoulder furtively.

She took a deep breath. How to explain? "I lost something."

"Yes?" he said quickly. "Perhaps we can help you find it. Why don't you come have a seat? Can I take your cloak?"

"No! I'm chilled. And I won't be staying long. I've just come to make an inquiry."

"Come along, now," he cajoled. "You must join my friend, Edgard, and myself. I am Martin, by the way. I promise we are as harmless as we are hospitable. We might even be able to help."

The old fellow seemed a friendly sort, although she didn't feel quite comfortable with the way his gaze kept searching her face.

"Come, come. You seem overset. Have a wee drink with us—just to warm you up. Then we'll help you find whatever you've lost."

Unused to talking to men, to anyone for any length, really, she tried to demur. "I shouldn't. I must keep looking."

A frown drew his thick peppered brows together, then quickly faded as he smiled once again. "What is it you've lost?"

She nibbled her bottom lip, then blurted, "My fur. I've lost my fox fur."

"A fox fur, you say?" His glance slid away, and his gnarled fingers scratched his head. "Was it part of a garment?"

"No . . . not yet. It was . . . a gift. I need it back."

"Come along. Edgard purchases furs. Although one fur is hardly distinguishable from another."

"Oh, mine was unique," she murmured.

She let him lead her to a table at the rear of the establishment. Another man stood, younger than his companion, with a large, round belly and ruddy cheeks. He drew up a chair and indicated that she should sit.

"No," Voletta said, holding out a hand. "I really should be on my way."

"But your fur . . ." the elderly man began.

Each passing moment deepened her unease. "I'm sure I just missed it in the darkness. I'll retrace my steps."

"A fur, did you say?" the fat man said, giving a pointed glare at his companion. "Where did you leave it?"

"Beside a brook. I put it down for only a moment."

"Today?"

"Yes, just before dark."

His gaze sharpened. "A fine fur, was it? Unblemished by any trap's teeth?"

"Of course!" she said, feeling hope at the man's brightening expression.

"And red as your hair, miss?"

"Yes, as a matter of fact, it is."

"I saw just such a fur. The bürgermeister brought it to me. My wife is even now sewing it onto a fine cloak."

"Sewing it?" she asked, pressing her hand to her belly.

"Yes, as part of the dowry for a nobleman's bride."

Voletta reached for the man's arm. "I must have it back."

The heavy man dropped his gaze to her hand, then reached up slowly to pat it. "And you shall. We will go to my shop in a moment. Would you have a drink with us first?"

Relief made her lightheaded, and she nodded. "But quickly, please."

"Of course. Don't fret yourself."

Voletta accepted the beaker the older man handed her and took only a sip, then set her glass on the table. "Sir, I apologize for rushing you, but could we please go retrieve my fur?"

"Of course." He stared expectantly. "How are you feeling?"

Voletta shook her head. "Fine, can we go now?" Only she didn't feel fine. Her head swam. The men before her seemed to teeter and stretch. "How odd," she said, her voice sounding to her own ears as though it rose from the bottom of a deep well.

"Best get her out of here, Edgard, before she topples."

"Come, miss. You wanted to see my shop?"

She tugged at the collar of her cloak. "S'warm."

"Catch her!"

"Seems a shame. A beautiful girl like her."

The voice, Edgard's, she remembered, came from right beside her.

"Just get the trunk off the cart," Martin whispered harshly.

Voletta tried to lift her head, but the movement made her nauseous. She pried open her eyelids and found herself looking down at a rutted track. Graying daylight stabbed like tiny daggers at the backs of her eyes.

The air around her was damp and cold. Her skin prickled— she was naked! A fog had rolled in, droplets catching on her breasts and cheeks. The bastards had taken her cloak!

She forced up her head and stared after the men riding atop a cart rolling down a long, steep trail. Then she noticed other things: her hands were tied behind her; a rope was wound around her waist to keep her upright against a pole.

She pulled at the ropes around her wrists, to no avail. Should she call out? Naked, she felt terribly vulnerable . . . *human*.

Then she heard a sound . . . soft, measured footfalls.

In front of her a shadowy form appeared beyond a dark iron gate at the end of the trail. The outline of the figure shimmered, then solidified before her widening gaze. She blinked. Maybe the apparition had just been a floating tendril of fog that had given her that impression.

The fog cleared for a moment to reveal the imposing figure of a man.

Voletta's breath caught. The man stood still, only feet away, his hard-edged face devoid of emotion, his lips drawn into a thin line.

He was tall, his shoulders broad, his hair and eyes black as midnight. The cotte and chausses he wore were equally dark, unrelieved by any embroidery or a bright cuff. He lifted his hands, pushed open the gate, and stepped through it.

"Please," she whispered, "untie me."

"I shall," he replied, his voice deep and ragged, as though rusty from disuse.

He stepped behind her, and his fingers glanced against her wrists. The ropes fell away.

Voletta turned, ready to flee down the rough trail, but his hand snagged her wrist. Alarmed, she gazed back.

"You don't understand," he said slowly. "I know you are frightened, but you must come with me. You are mine, now."

She tugged her hand, hard, but his fingers wrapped tighter around her wrist, and he started to walk back through the gate.

Digging her heels into the ground, she said, "You must release me. Those men kidnapped me. I'm not supposed to be here. I can't belong to you."

Silence greeted her outcry, and he forged onward, forcing her to walk behind him or fall to her knees.

"I'm expected. My family will be looking for me," she lied, shortening her steps only to stumble when he walked faster. He was strong; his fingers banded her wrist like steel. She tried to pry them away, but his grip bit into her flesh, and she gasped.

"You only harm yourself," he said, his voice as devoid of softness as his clothing and his face.

"I beg your pardon, but you are the one dragging me, sir," she bit out.

He shot a glance over his shoulder. His eyes peered at her, curiosity easing his dour expression. "Don't you fear me?"

"Of course not," she said automatically, but then realized it was true. She didn't fear him, *exactly*, but she was wary, and growing increasingly so the further into his demesne they went.

The man grunted and turned away, tugging her behind him.

They continued along, lush grass giving way to slick cobblestones. Above her stretched a tall, imposing keep made of large gray stones. Two menacing towers stood watch at the ends of a long wall. A portcullis, its gate raised, loomed like a great, toothed maw.

Voletta shivered, and her alarm caused her heart to thud loudly in her chest the closer they approached. Despite her creeping trepidation, details began to niggle. No heads appeared above the crenellated curtain wall. No gatekeeper greeted them inside the portcullis. In fact, no one appeared to be inside the bailey as they entered.

And yet, everything was perfectly attended. The cobblestones were clear of falling leaves; the grass beyond the cobblestone was perfectly manicured; the iron chain that lifted the portcullis gleamed with oil. As she stared behind her, the gear that lowered the gate began to move and creak, and yet no one stood beside it to work the mechanism.

Again the fog licked in front of her, and, in the mist, she saw the outline of a ghostly figure leaning over the lever he turned.

Cold, afraid now, Voletta quivered, her knees shaking so badly she stumbled behind him and landed on her knees at last.

The dark man halted, his back to her, his hand still clasping her wrist. A sigh escaped him, and he turned. Bending over her, he pushed away her outstretched hands and lifted her into his arms.

Voletta had been close to a man a time or two—had felt the hardness of their muscular bodies pressed to hers, had breathed their hot breath and inhaled the musky scent of them. They'd been pleasant to touch, delicious to kiss.

They'd also been easy to evade when their caresses grew too intimate, too unnerving.

With this one, however, she sensed strength beyond the tensile muscles that held her easily to his chest. His square jaw and straight lips spoke of an inner will that would brook no arguments.

He held her naked, completely vulnerable to his will. That

she wasn't squirming, fighting tooth and nail for her freedom, shocked her—and deepened the shivers that pricked her nipples into tight buds.

She had to find the cloak with her special fur, and quickly. This man tempted her to linger and discover just what belonging to him entailed. Voletta guessed his possession would be a carnal form of enslavement. For what woman wouldn't be drawn by his rugged form and fierce, enigmatic gaze?

However, she'd managed to escape manly lures for a very long time. No matter the fascinating package, she'd just as soon flee before she saw him fully unwrapped!

She'd heard the men talking. Her fox's fur had been sewn onto a cloak for a nobleman. This nobleman, she had no doubt. It must rest in the trunk they'd dropped on the trail outside the gate.

"You've left the trunk behind," she said, in a small voice, not wanting to let him see how much it meant, and certainly not wanting to draw his gaze downward. The thought of him staring closely at her body heated her skin.

"The trunk does not concern you," he murmured, sounding not the least winded by carrying her so far.

"But it contains things that belong to me."

"I will provide all that you need."

Her legs squeezed together. He hadn't purred, hadn't injected a hint of heat into his voice, but his low, growling words still scraped her nerves raw. "That's so arrogant! What if there is something that means the world to me inside that trunk?"

He halted on the steps leading into the keep and stared into her eyes. "From this day, I will be your world, your only companion, your only lover."

A shudder racked her body. He'd said it so intently, as though making her a promise.

A sudden fullness choked her throat. She read steely determination in his eyes, yet at the same time, she detected a hint of vulnerability beneath that hard gaze. The yearning she sensed pulled her, and she drew back. This man could make her question her need to escape.

Voletta knew in that moment he would never willingly let her go—and part of her, the weak and feminine dimension of her being, was grateful he intended to remove the choice.